Praise for Kathr[yn]
AMERICA'S BRAV[EST]

"From first page[...]
Ms. Shay captures reader attention…"
—Pamela Cohen, *Romantic Times Magazine*

"All the characters are so real,
as are the descriptions of the fire fighting.
The way these devoted individuals deal with their
lives and loves makes for fascinating reading."
—Tanzey Cutter, *Old Bookbarn Gazette*

"WOW! Shay is an immensely talented author
who has succeeded in recreating the world of
urban firefighters with impressive fidelity.
She has also created memorable characters
and given them a compelling story."
—Jean Mason, *The Romance Reader*

"Ms. Shay pays homage to the country's
brave firefighters in an entertaining trilogy that will leave
fans appreciating the efforts of professionals and the
author who depicts them accordingly."
—Harriet Klausner, *Amazon Reviews*

"I'm very sorry to see this trilogy end.
I thoroughly enjoyed each book in it and I'll definitely
be looking for more books by Kathryn Shay. The care she
took in researching the world of a firefighter is evident,
and she created a family on these pages
about whom you'll want to read more."
—Andrea Pool, *All About Romance*

America's Bravest by Kathryn Shay

HARLEQUIN SUPERROMANCE

Dear Reader,

The AMERICA'S BRAVEST series continues this month with Reed and Delaney's story, thanks in great part to all of you. I received over five hundred fan letters on the trilogy, most of them asking for a continuation of the series. Many of the letters were from firefighters themselves, the wives of firefighters and EMT personnel. I read with great satisfaction that people thought the books were accurate, that they enjoyed a new kind of setting, and it was particularly nice to hear people say they never knew firefighters were such heroes.

They are! And the story of these particular firefighters continues with *The Fire Within*. In *Code of Honor*, we left Reed and Delaney with a passionate and unexpected kiss at midnight on New Year's Eve. This story begins on that special night and follows them into the spring. I think you'll be surprised at how they interact. Delaney is her usual feisty self, but once she falls in love, nothing can stop her from getting what she wants. Reed tries to halt their involvement because of his past. But with the redeeming power of love, they find each other and a bond that is, indeed, unbreakable.

On the pages of this book, you'll get a chance to visit with the Cordaros, the Templetons, the O'Roarkes and the Scarlattas and see what's happened to them. You'll meet other old friends whose stories you've asked for, too. But if you haven't read any of the other books, you can start with *The Fire Within*, as it's a self-contained storyline.

I hope you enjoy this book. Please write and let me know what you think. I answer all reader mail. Send letters to Kathryn Shay, P.O. Box 24288, Rochester, New York, 14624-0288 or e-mail me at kshay@aol.com Also visit my Web site at http://home.eznet.net/~kshay/ and the Superauthors Web site at http://www.superauthors.com

Kathryn Shay

The Fire Within

Kathryn Shay

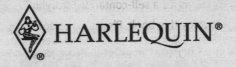

HARLEQUIN®

TORONTO • NEW YORK • LONDON
AMSTERDAM • PARIS • SYDNEY • HAMBURG
STOCKHOLM • ATHENS • TOKYO • MILAN • MADRID
PRAGUE • WARSAW • BUDAPEST • AUCKLAND

ISBN 0-373-71018-6

THE FIRE WITHIN

Visit us at www.eHarlequin.com

Printed in U.S.A.

The men and women
of the Rockford Fire Department

Ben Cordaro: Rockford Fire Department (RFD) Battalion Chief; father of Francey Templeton; married to Diana Cordaro.

Sam Leone: RFD firefighter; married to Theresa Leone; two children—Marcy and TJ.

Tommy Leone: RFD firefighter; brother of Sam Leone; ex-husband of Jeanine Leone.

Reed Macauley: RFD psychologist.

Beth Winters O'Roarke: RFD Academy EMS instructor; married to Dylan O'Roarke.

Dylan O'Roarke: RFD Lieutenant; married to Beth Winters O'Roarke.

Joey Santori: RFD firefighter; formerly engaged to Francey Templeton.

Eric Scanlon: RFD captain at the Academy.

Chelsea Whitmore Scarlatta: RFD firefighter; wife of Jake Scarlatta; half sister of Delaney Shaw.

Jake Scarlatta: RFD Captain; husband of Chelsea.

Delaney Shaw: private psychologist specializing in adolescent behavior—freelancing with RFD; half sister of firefighter Chelsea Scarlatta.

Chase Talbot: Rockford Fire Chief.

Francey Cordaro Templeton: RFD firefighter; married to businessman Alex Templeton; daughter of Ben and Diana Cordaro.

To my sister Patty. From the tea parties and games of Monopoly when we were little, to the hours of listening and wise words since we've grown up, thanks for your unflagging love and support.

ACKNOWLEDGMENT

There are many people to thank for their help and contributions to my AMERICA'S BRAVEST trilogy.

The first group is the Gates Fire Department, particularly their chief and officers, who invited me to the firehouses and shared their experiences with me. Thanks, too, go to the many Gates line firefighters who let me wear their gear, taught me how to hold a hose, put out a fire with an extinguisher and observe several of their drills, including live burns.

Next, I had the privilege of working with the 542-person Rochester, New York, Fire Department. I extend my appreciation to several fire stations for allowing me to visit. With meals, tours of their firehouses and the recounting of many of their experiences, the men and women at Engine 16, Engine 17, Quint/Midi 5 and Quint/Midi 9 gave me a feel for the professional life of a city firefighter. Specifically, my deep gratitude goes to Firefighter Lisa Beth White for sharing her insights into the life of a female in this predominantly male department.

The Rochester Fire Academy personnel could not have been more welcoming. Battalion Chief Russ Valone, in charge of training, allowed me access to classes, training sessions, practicals and permitted me to observe recruits simulating life in a firehouse and putting out fires. Special appreciation goes to the 1997 Fall Recruit Class and their trainers.

I want to express my gratitude and affection to the Quint/Midi 8 firefighters. They were all gracious in letting me ride along on the rigs, wear old gear and eat several meals with them. These guys spent many afternoons and evenings sharing their experiences, answering my questions, giving advice on my story lines and suggesting possible improvements. From that group, Firefighter and Paramedic Joe Giorgione was the best "consultant" an author could ask for.

Any "real feel" these books have is due to all these brave men and women who told me their stories. Any errors are completely mine.

PROLOGUE

New Year's Eve

REED MACAULEY SWORE ripely as Dr. Delaney Shaw exited her sister's living room, leaving behind the millennium's New Year's Eve party, which was in full swing. He followed her through the kitchen and upstairs to the third-floor guest room. In the moonlight, he could just make out her silhouette. She was staring out the window, her back to him, her shoulders hunched and her arms circled around her waist; she seemed small and slight—and afraid. He had a flash of another woman, a long time ago, reacting with fear to him. Because of that past, Reed had stayed away from this lovely woman for a long time. But tonight, he'd blown it big time.

"I'm sorry," he said from the doorway. "Are you okay?"

She didn't answer right away. Then she said, "Of course. It was just a New Year's kiss." Her voice was hoarse.

Stepping into the room, he switched on a light and crossed to her. Without warning, he drew her around. She shook back her cascading hair and clamped her elbows with her hands.

Reed leaned back and stuck his fists in his pockets. He didn't want her to see that his hands were shaking. "Then why did you run away?"

She bit her lip and surveyed the room as if searching for an answer in the slanted oak ceiling, dark beige walls and thick taupe carpet. "I, um, didn't expect to feel this way about you."

He had to smile. Sometimes she was as ingenuous as the kids she worked with. Very different from his first impression of her when they'd met more than eighteen months ago at a psychology seminar at Rockford University, where she'd gone head-to-head with him on every issue they'd discussed. He was the staff shrink for the Rockford Fire Department and she had her own private practice in a swank downtown office. They'd argued about theory, clinical practice and treatment.

But several months later, they'd worked together when Delaney—a specialist in adolescent behavior— was called in to help with a firefighter's teenage son. It was then that Reed had developed a healthy respect for her ability and intelligence, and felt an attraction that kept him awake many nights.

He'd managed to hide his feelings, but tonight, he'd lost control and kissed her at twelve; even now, he could feel himself losing his grip. Which was a reaction that usually sent him running in the opposite direction.

"Reed, you're staring at me."

He didn't say anything. Instead, he grasped her arms, ran his hands up and down her biceps. Tugged her close.

"This isn't a good idea," she whispered against his sweater.

"I know." His lips grazed her hair and she drew back. "One more kiss," he said, and smiled down at her; passion flared in her face.

Good. There was a firestorm brewing inside his chest and pride demanded *some* reaction from her. What he was doing wasn't smart, hell, it wasn't even sane. He knew all too well that, for a man with his past, getting involved with her—with any woman—would have repercussions, but at that moment, he couldn't make himself care.

"Reed," she whispered raggedly.

"Say it's all right. To kiss you. One more time." Her blue eyes glowed like sapphires. "Then I'll leave." He would, he promised himself.

The struggle inside her was clear. Finally, she raised her arms and entwined them around his neck. The soft velvet of her sleeves tickled his skin. She smelled like jasmine, and he basked in the scent.

He lowered his head and covered her mouth with his. He took what she offered, sinking into her. She tasted so sweet that something inside him stirred. Contact with this woman awakened a need in him that had been dormant for a long time. Eight years, to be exact. That was how long it had been since he'd allowed himself to get involved with anyone who could elicit this response in him. His hands roamed her back, caressing every pulsating hollow he could reach. The kiss became hungry, then carnal.

When she pressed herself against him, when her velvet-clad legs rubbed against his tan Dockers, the rein on his emotions snapped. Not gently, his hands slid down her body, clasped her bottom and locked her to him.

He thrust forward. She thrust back.

And that was all it took....

HOURS LATER, REED LET himself relax into the pillows and adjusted the sleeping beauty in his arms. Her long black hair curled around his fingers and she burrowed into his chest. He allowed himself to hold her like any normal man would do. He was in that twilight between sleep and waking, remembering the gut-wrenching ecstasy of making love to her, when he began to sweat.

The nausea came.

Then he couldn't draw a breath.

Half asleep, he shook himself to ward off the all-too-familiar symptoms. His body jolted with an adrenaline rush.

Delaney murmured something against his chest.

The murmur was obliterated by a shout—a loud one....

"Get out of the way, Macauley," Marx called from behind him.

Reed saw the flash.

There was an ear-deafening explosion—like rapid rounds of gunfire—and suddenly he was on the ground.

He heard the screams of his men and tried to stand but couldn't—

"Reed!"

He groped for his leg; it hurt like a bitch. He had to get to them....

"Reed!"

More noise. Loud, unfamiliar noise.

"No...no....no..."

Something slapped him hard across his face. He grabbed whatever it was.

"Ooh...Reed, you're hurting me. Stop, please."

The sweet voice, the plea, dragged him back to reality.

He was sitting up; Delaney knelt next to him. He'd manacled her wrists, squeezing as hard as he could. When she came into focus, he let go. Gulping, he touched her hair and her shoulder, trying to assure himself she was real. In the sliver of moonlight, he could see that her eyes were wide and frightened.

"Reed?" she finally said. "What happened?"

He shook his head.

"Please. Tell me."

He'd never told anybody about the flashbacks or the incident that precipitated them. Even in therapy he'd never been able to articulate what had happened. As a result, the psychologists could only offer coping strategies.

To preclude the attacks, he'd deliberately avoided relationships or circumstances that might bring them on. But somehow Delaney had slipped through the barriers he'd erected.

He lay back against the pillows and took deep breaths. The images began to fade. Unclenching his sweaty hands—every inch of him was covered with perspiration—he willed each muscle in his body to relax. "I don't talk about it."

"Why?"

"I just don't." He threw back the covers and got out of bed. "I have to go."

Suddenly chilled, Delaney dragged the dark brown sheet to her chest, sat back on her heels and watched the man she'd just made incredible love with pull away.

The impassive mask—the one she'd spent a year trying to remove—was back in place. It had slipped earlier tonight. Fallen away completely once they were in bed. For the first time, she'd met the real Reed Macauley.

And known immediately that he was a man she could love. The awareness had been coming for months, and they'd both fought it by denying their attraction to each other and using their very real differences to distance each other.

He dressed silently. She switched on a small table lamp. He wasn't tall, maybe five ten, and his broad chest was covered with a sprinkling of dark hair. At forty-one he kept himself in great shape. Before he pulled on his tan pants, she saw the scar that ran around his thigh to the back of his left leg. She winced. Whatever had happened to him must have hurt like hell.

He glanced over his shoulder. "Put some clothes on, will you?"

Quickly, she pulled on her blue-and-black-checked boxers and a black T-shirt she'd planned to sleep in. Then she rose and approached him. He was fully clothed, and turned toward her, the bulky off-white cable-knit sweater making him appear larger. His gaze focused on her shirt.

"Blasphemous." He cradled her cheek with a callused palm. "How like you."

Delaney collected T-shirts related to her profession and wore them to bed and sometimes to dance class. This one read I Used to Be Schizophrenic, but We're Better Now.

"Tell me what happened," she said, leaning into him. She felt dwarfed, though she was five seven.

His arms came around her and he held her close. Kissed her hair. She wanted nothing more than to crawl under those covers with him.

"I can't, honey."

"Don't leave."

"I have to." Drawing back, he studied her face and curled his hand around her neck. "I'm not good at this."

The imp surfaced. "You could have fooled me. I thought you were great."

"I mean the emotional part."

"We could work on that." She cleared her throat. Lovingly, she traced his cheekbones. "Together."

"No, not after..." He looked at her wrists, saw red marks beginning to form where he'd gripped her. Tenderly, he kissed the damage he'd done.

"I want you in my life, Reed."

"No! You should have some normal guy without a lot of baggage."

She inched closer. "I'm good at dealing with baggage. That's what I do."

"Nobody can help me. I've tried that route. People only get hurt when they get close to me."

"Please, Reed, I..."

He pushed her away before she could say any more. His face was ashen and his eyes bleak. ''No, Laney. *No.*''

Pride battled desire. Delaney had learned from her mother—if only by negative example—*never* to beg. But something told her to follow her heart now. ''This was the best night of my life, Reed.''

''Mine, too.'' The words were wrenched from him. ''I'll never forget it.'' He found his shoes and grabbed his coat. ''But it was a moment of weakness that I won't repeat.'' He faced her before he left, locked his hand around her neck again and kissed her hard. When he drew back, he whispered, ''Happy New Year, love.'' And then he was gone.

Her legs wobbling, Delaney sank onto the bed. Absently she picked up a pillow and hugged it to her. It smelled like him.

She stared at the door. She felt abandoned as she had during her childhood when her mother had accompanied her father from town to town on his singing gigs. Delaney and her half sister, Chelsea, had been left alone for days on end. She'd learned to cope then. But tonight for the first time in her entire adult life, Dr. Delaney Shaw didn't know what to do.

CHAPTER ONE

Five months later

BATTALION CHIEF BEN CORDARO smiled at Delaney as he settled his big frame into one of her dark blue leather chairs. Looking much younger than his fifty-some years, Ben said, "I'm here officially from the Rockford Fire Department. We'd like you to be part of our Family Assistance Network, or FAN, as we call it."

From behind her desk, Delaney stared at the man who her sister's husband thought walked on water. And who was probably Reed Macauley's best friend. If Reed allowed *anyone* close. Battling back the tiny pinpricks of pain that came from the thought, Delaney smiled at Ben. "What exactly is FAN?"

"A nationwide movement to help firefighters and their families cope with the stresses of their daily lives. The chief finally got the mayor to okay our involvement in it." He looked exasperated. "Mayor Jordan took some convincing. She didn't think our firefighters needed this kind of support."

Hmm, Delaney knew of *one* firefighter who could use help. Big time. "Help as in support groups after a traumatic incident?"

"Not just that. FAN needs to be proactive." Ben's black eyes flashed with high emotion. "Wives, husbands and kids of firefighters have a tough time coping with the lifestyles of rescue workers whose schedules are a nightmare and whose lives are at risk every day." He glanced out the window where the birds chirped their announcement of summer.

Delaney could relate to this. She worried constantly about Chelsea.

"I have a special interest in FAN because of my situation, I guess. Because of Diana and my daughter, of course," Ben continued.

Delaney knew that Ben and his wife had divorced years ago over her inability to deal with the danger of his job. They had recently reunited.

Ben's son-in-law, Alex Templeton, had also had difficulty in handling the danger his wife faced on the job. Reed had helped them last year, and they were both doing better now; as a matter of fact, Francey Cordaro Templeton was expecting their first child in September.

"We need you, Delaney, because Reed Macauley can only do so much," Ben added.

At the mention of his name, Delaney's heartbeat sped up. "I assume Reed will be integral in this Family Assistance Network, right?"

"Uh-huh." Knowing eyes bored through her. "Except he doesn't have your expertise in working with kids."

No, but he had other areas of expertise, some of which she'd bet would surprise Battalion Chief Cordaro. Reed's hands had been magic on her body that one night months ago.

"Is that what you want—my input on how to set up programs for kids?" Maybe she could manage that, if she avoided Reed.

"No, we want you to head up the adolescent division and run the kids' programs."

"Head it up?"

"Work with us in the trenches out at the academy." He glanced around at her chic office with its glass and chrome and soothing colors. "As much as your private practice will allow."

Delaney pretended to study the bank of open windows facing her. She let the warm breeze settle her. "There are several problems. The first is that I have a full load of patients here."

"You've got five partners. Chelsea said they covered for you when you went to Illinois for three months. The training you took there was on the special psychological needs of the children of rescue personnel, wasn't it?"

"Yes, the program was called Rescue the Kids."

Again a grin from Ben. "Well, there's another reason we want you—that training will be invaluable. Then there's the miracle you worked on Derek DeLuca."

"My favorite rookie," she said, thinking of the dark-haired boy with hollow places in his soul from fatherly neglect. Something Delaney knew all about.

"Derek's makin' a great career for himself. Thanks to you." From his shirt pocket, Ben drew out some photos of the young man Chelsea's husband regarded as a son. "I thought you might like to see these."

She took the pictures and shuffled through them. Derek in his uniform, at his first station, funny firehouse shots. She came across one of him and Reed—which brought tears to her eyes. The sight of the man's tender smile brought back too many memories.

After their passionate New Year's Eve night together, she'd waited a week to seek him out. The visit hadn't gone well....

She'd been ushered into his office by one of the lieutenants at the academy who kept flirting with her. Reed's private space was so different from hers. Slate-blue paint, well-worn utility carpeting, firefighter memorabilia displayed on the walls. She'd been studying his bookcase when he came in. He wasn't happy to see her.

''What do you want?'' he'd asked tightly.

She'd circled around. ''Well, hello to you, too.''

He strode over to her, devouring her with his eyes. Standing before her, he seemed to struggle internally. ''Honey, don't do this to me,'' he finally said, as if the sight of her softened him. ''Why are you here?''

''To see if you've changed your mind.'' She moved closer to him and slid her hands up his chest. He smelled just like he had that night they'd made love. ''To see if I can change your mind.'' She tossed back her hair. ''There's something between us, Reed. I'm not giving up on it.''

His face was a study in torment. *Damn it,* she'd thought. *Why is this so hard for him?* He was about to speak when the phone rang.

As he took the call, she turned back to his books. The spines of basic psychology tomes written by Freud, Jung and modern academics faced her. Some firefighter manuals. Some on the Oklahoma City bombing and its aftermath.

And nestled right next to the books on the terrorist attack were five others all on the same topic: *Posttraumatic Stress Disorder and the Vietnam Veteran; Vietnam Wives, Women and Children Surviving Life with Victims of PTSD; A Trauma Survivor's Handbook; The Crime Victim's Book.* And the eye-opener, *Posttraumatic Stress and the Rescue Worker.*

Suddenly, the answer to his puzzling behavior on New Year's Eve struck her. Reed's sweaty disorientation. The flashback-like symptoms. His oblique statements about his inability to maintain close relationships—typical of people suffering from PTSD.

When he hung up, she picked up *Posttraumatic Stress and the Rescue Worker.* "This is it, isn't it? You had a PTSD attack on New Year's Eve."

He eyed the book as if it was a snake waiting to strike. In some ways, the syndrome *was* a viper, coming out of nowhere, and it could be just as deadly.

"Yes."

"What happened to you?"

"An incident. When I was a firefighter."

"What was it?"

"I lost…I lost men…I…" He raked a hand through his hair. "I don't want to go into it."

Her heart hurt for him. "Oh, Reed, I'm sorry. Did you get help afterward?"

"I tried. But since I've been in Rockford, the attacks have gotten worse."

"Why?"

He shook his head. "You don't need to know any

more than that. It's enough to keep us apart. Life with a PTSD sufferer can be hell, and I won't subject you to it.''

''Isn't that my choice to make?''

''No, it's mine.'' When she started to protest, he got angry. ''Stop it! You can't bulldoze me on this one. I won't change my mind.'' Then he'd turned and exited his office; he didn't come back.

She'd tried on four other occasions to see him, called several times, and finally threw in the towel. His rejection brought back too many unpleasant memories.

''Delaney?''

She peered up at Ben from the photos she held. ''These are great. Thanks for letting me see them.'' Handing back the pictures and sinking down into her chair, she looked directly at the chief. ''Ben, I'll cut to the quick. Reed Macauley won't want me working in this program.''

Ben watched her for a minute. ''I talked to him about it. He said this was your decision.''

Delaney remembered how Reed had avoided gatherings at Chelsea's house when he knew Delaney would be there. He also declined to play baseball with the academy's guys when they were up against Quint/ Midi Twelve, since Delaney had joined that team with her sister. Hell, it had hurt so much the few times she'd bumped into him, she'd eventually decided to go to the course in Chicago so she'd be out of town for a while and not run into him at all.

The time away had helped. She'd accepted his decision even if it meant losing the one man she thought she could love.

"He doesn't want me there, Ben, take my word for it. And, frankly, I don't want to work with him."

Ben's eyes narrowed thoughtfully. "I see."

"Look, I care about Reed, but working at the academy with him would hurt us both. I'm sorry, I can't say more without betraying a confidence." She didn't know why she was telling him this much; maybe because he was a great father. And Delaney's life had been irrevocably marred by the absence of a father.

"All right. I'll respect your decision. But it's a damn shame that we won't have your expertise in this program."

"Reed can handle kids."

"He's got too much on his plate already. Over the last five months he's…I don't know…gotten more weary, sadder."

Her heart turned over in her chest and thumped hard against her ribs. "I'm sorry to hear that. I wish I could help."

She'd tried to do just that. She'd sent him a note, with the name of a specialist it had taken her weeks to locate in New York City. He treated PTSD in rescue workers. In her usual frank style, Delaney had told Reed that if he wouldn't let her help him, maybe this guy could. She also said this would be the last time she'd contact him, and wished him good luck. It was her final attempt at communication before she left for Illinois. He hadn't responded.

Ben stood. He reached in his pocket and drew out his card. "If you change your mind, call me. I—" His hand went to his hip. "Oh, hell, that's the department pager." He glanced at the clock—it was almost six. "I have a date with my wife tonight...." His face tightened as he read the pager. "Damn."

Delaney stood. "What is it?"

"A fire. A bad one. The message says to call Reed right away."

"Reed?"

"On his cell phone."

Delaney picked up her phone and dialed Reed's cell number, handing the receiver immediately to Ben.

"Reed, it's Ben, what's going on?" He waited a minute, then glanced worriedly at Delaney.

Fire. A bad one. Chelsea was on duty tonight.

Delaney's breath stopped in her throat. She heard Ben say, "I'm on my way."

Giving her back the phone, he faced her squarely. "An industrial complex caught fire—all ten buildings are endangered. Chelsea's at the blaze, but she's fine as of now." Chief Cordaro understood family fear and knew how important it was to relay all available information.

Delaney watched him. "But?"

"There's a problem—two firefighters were caught in a dust explosion. They're on their way to the hospital."

She gripped the desk. "Who are they?" Please don't let it be Jake, her brother-in-law.

"Brothers. The Leones, from Engine Seventeen."

"Will they be okay?"

"Reed doesn't know."

Ben headed for the door.

After a split second, Delaney grabbed her purse and keys. "I'm coming with you, Ben."

He faced her. "Good, you can help Reed."

With a sledgehammer of fear pounding in her head, Delaney followed Chief Cordaro to his car.

SMOKE AND HUGE MULTICOLORED flames poured from the windows and roofs of several buildings of the industrial complex. As Delaney exited the car with Ben, she cursed yet again the day her sister had decided to become a firefighter. Chelsea was somewhere in that mess.

On the drive to the site, Delaney had heard the details crackling out over Chief Cordaro's radio: The fire had started at Conner Technologies. The blaze had spread to two other buildings, and there was a very real danger that the whole complex would go up in flames. Three alarms had been called already—meaning three different sets of trucks had been dispatched, six companies in all. She heard terms Chelsea routinely spouted—a hydrant had been made and an eight-hundred-foot hose was dumping water on the Red Devil. Ladder trucks were positioned on the west side of the building, while one company went east to check for fire spread.

The acrid smell of smoke assaulted Delaney as she hurried behind Ben, cursing the white strappy sandals she wore with her simple white skirt and sleeveless blue top.

"Chief Talbot's in charge of Incident Command," Ben told Delaney as they neared a car where papers were spread out on the hood and men talked on radios. Tall and fit, and also looking young for his near-fifty-year age, Talbot spoke into one radio. A second white-shirted officer was on another.

"Cordaro," Talbot said, nodding.

They'd gotten closer to the buildings, and Delaney was encompassed by the heat of the blaze—a big smothering blanket, stealing the breath out of her. It was…menacing.

"Talbot." Ben stuck his hands in his pockets. "Can I help?"

The chief glanced worriedly at the complex. "Maybe. This one's a bitch. Fire started in the Con-Tech site and two other buildings are fully involved. It's still spreadin'. Scarlatta's team is breachin' the steel door of the fourth building now."

Scarlatta's team. Her sister was on Jake's team.

Ben squeezed Delaney's shoulder.

"Maybe you should suit up and go over there," Talbot continued. "I'd like to go in myself. I've got a bad feeling about this one."

Delaney knew that gut instinct was never taken lightly in firefighting. In fact, Jake's premonition had once saved Chelsea's life.

Someone materialized with turnout gear for Ben. He stuffed his legs into heavy pants and bunker boots, donned the dark blue jacket of the RFD and pulled on headgear; without a word, he jogged to the east side of the complex.

Delaney stood in back of Talbot, out of the way. Worried as she was, she knew enough not to intrude. Instead she observed the dramatic details of the scene before her: a sky clouded with thick, heavy smoke, the loud slap of water as it hit the building, and sirens in the distance, signaling more help on the way.

"Benson?" Talbot asked. "What's the news from the ambulance?"

"They're at the hospital. It doesn't look good, sir."

"For both?"

"Sam's regained consciousness. Tommy…he's not responding."

Chief Talbot cursed, and Delaney's blood chilled. People died in fires. Where was her sister? She shivered despite the heat.

"Delaney."

The soft sound of her name blocked out the sirens, the radio static, the shouts of men and women fighting against impossible odds. "Reed?"

For a moment, he just stood before her, his white officer's shirt in stark relief against his dark hair and eyes. Finally, he grasped her arm. "Come with me. Down here." He drew her close.

"Where is she?"

"Inside the Optical Design building." He took her hand and clasped it in his. His eyes were weary and he wore his glasses. "Honey, they're trained firefighters. They can do their job."

"Two people are already critically injured."

"Yes, the Leone brothers." Reed nodded to Incident Command. "Did you hear anything over there?"

She gave him the grim report. His lips compressed and his jaw muscles tightened. When they reached the second building, he let her go. Wrapping her arms around her waist, Delaney glared at the gaping hole in a side of the building. Had her sister cut through it? Chelsea was so strong, so brave. Delaney was bombarded by a prophetic childhood image of the two of them. Chelsea had been twelve, Delaney six. They were dressed for Halloween—Chelsea as a firefighter, Delaney, a ballerina. They'd grown up in the same household, but their interests—and the careers they'd eventually chosen—were very different. However, as sisters and friends they couldn't have been closer.

In silence, she and Reed watched the action. They were about thirty feet away from the building when she heard a rumble inside.

"Oh, my God, what was that?"

Reed's arm went around her, pulled her close again. Unconsciously she turned her face into his broad shoulder. "I don't know exactly," he told her, kissing her hair. "Something inside probably gave way."

Seconds passed, seeming like hours. Delaney prayed. Reed kept her at his side. Gray smoke began to curl out of the hole in the door, like a lazy cat stepping outside for a stroll. Delaney knew the color of the smoke was determined by what was burning and was an indication of how serious the fire was. The darker the smoke, the worse the conditions.

More time passed.

Suddenly, figures emerged though the gray curtain. One firefighter carried another slung over his shoulders. Behind the two, partially obscured from view, a third firefighter staggered from the building, dragging somebody else out.

Delaney prayed hard.

Paramedics rushed to the group and surrounded them; Reed and Delaney followed.

Gingerly, both firefighters set their charges on the ground. Both whipped off their masks and helmets—

one was Ben, and the other Chelsea. Her face grimy, a wicked-looking burn on her neck, she didn't take her eyes off the firefighters on the ground.

Delaney went weak with relief. When her knees started to buckle, Reed supported her with his arm. "Easy, Laney," he whispered.

Drawing in a breath, she straightened. She needed to help here, not to be taken care of. *But, oh, God, thank you for watching over my sister.*

From behind the paramedics, Delaney stared down at the men who'd been brought out. She recognized them as the other members of Chelsea's group. Both were coughing and one was holding his shoulder. But they were alive.

Delaney couldn't help herself. She circled around the medical personnel and threw herself at her sister. About the same height, Chelsea was more muscular and stronger, but tonight she felt fragile and slight in Delaney's grasp. Chelsea hugged her. "You're gonna get that pretty skirt all dirty, kiddo."

With a watery grin, Delaney drew back. "I'll send you the cleaning bill."

Giving Delaney one more hug, Chelsea looked past her sister's shoulder. Delaney felt her freeze. "Where are they?" she asked Ben. "Jake and Dylan?" Chelsea's husband and their good friend. "I thought they followed us out."

Surprised, Ben turned, too. No one was behind them.

A flurry of activity at Incident Command, then a crew of men hustled past them. Grabbing his helmet and mask, Ben raced to the building with Chelsea right behind. Reed and Delaney followed.

At the door a grim-faced firefighter spoke Ben, "Scarlatta and O'Roarke didn't get out. They radioed that a common wall between ConTech and Optical Design fell and beams are blocking their path." Delaney noticed the men carried axes and picks. Ben donned his helmet and fastened his mask; Chelsea started for her equipment. *Oh, no.*

Ben grasped Chelsea's arm. "You're not coming in, Whitmore." To avoid confusion, Chelsea went by her maiden name at the station.

"Like hell."

Gently Ben said, "Your neck and hands are burned. And your husband's inside. You're too close to this, Chels."

"No closer than you. Jake and Dylan are like sons to you."

Ben glanced over her shoulder. "Reed, I won't argue with her. Keep her back."

But it was Delaney who tugged on her arm. "Come on, Chels. You're hurt. You'll only hamper Jake's rescue."

Chelsea looked to Reed, who nodded his agreement. Her face was ravaged and frightened, like it used to get when they'd been left alone for days at a time as kids.

Finally she stepped back.

It was the longest ten minutes of Delaney's life. Reed kept an arm around Chelsea and intermittently reached out to touch Delaney. All traces of strain between them disappeared.

Finally, silhouettes materialized once again in the doorway. Delaney felt her sister straighten and grip her hand so tightly it hurt. Someone was being carried by two men. Two others followed them out and took off their face masks and helmets.

For a minute, Chelsea deflated like the balloons they used to blow up as kids and then let go. When she recovered, she ran toward the building and threw herself at her husband, who'd come out next to Ben. Jake grasped her, whispered something in her ear and bent his head—as if to savor her, and life.

Delaney's eyes misted, and she turned away from the sight. Briefly, Reed drew her against his shoulder again, then walked with her over to the group.

They all stared down at the man who'd just been carried out. Covered with dirt, Dylan O'Roarke, husband of one of Chelsea's best friends and a paramedic for the RFD, stirred. Ben removed his helmet and mask and knelt down. "Where the hell's the stretcher?" he barked.

"It's coming." Reed squeezed Ben's shoulder. He let go of Delaney and knelt down, too. "Is he all right?"

"Some burns, and his leg is twisted bad."

Jake said, "He pushed me out of the way and dived on top of me when the wall beams fell. Damn hero." Delaney knew that O'Roarke had been called on the carpet many times for his risk-taking.

On the ground, Dylan opened his eyes, which watered badly. He coughed, sputtered, then managed to say, "You ungrateful wretch." Then he turned serious. "Everybody make it okay?"

Ben took Dylan's hand. The tender gesture made Delaney's throat catch. "Yes. Your whole crew did."

Dylan sighed. ''Beth's gonna kick my ass for this one. She was already mad that I subbed at Quint Five tonight.'' Dylan's wife, who trained paramedics at the academy, had almost forgone a relationship with him because of his daredevil attitude.

''You deserve it, buddy.'' Jake had knelt, too, and was smiling weakly.

''I saved your hide, Scarlatta. Show some sympathy.''

The paramedics arrived, and everybody stood back. Delaney saw Talbot, who'd approached the group, motion Reed to the side. The chief's features were grim. Stoically Reed listened, but Delaney could tell he wasn't hearing good news by the way he shook his head and jammed a hand through his hair. Everyone else sensed something, too.

Reed came back and said to Ben, ''I'm going to the hospital.''

''What happened?'' Ben asked.

''Tom Leone just died.''

A hush came over all of them.

Chelsea turned into Jake's chest. Dylan swore, and Ben straightened. ''We'll see you there,'' Ben said.

Delaney faced Reed. His complexion was chalk white. Worried about Chelsea, she hadn't noticed how he'd hardened himself, turned into himself. She noticed his reaction now, though. ''What can I do?''

''Come to the hospital with Ben. I'm going to need your help.'' He swallowed hard. ''You have no idea what the repercussions of this death will be.''

CHAPTER TWO

SAM LEONE KNEW HIS BROTHER, Tommy, was dead when Reed Macauley walked into his cubical in the ER. He'd suspected all the way to the hospital in the ambulance, as the kid had moaned and coughed in an unconscious state, that his baby brother wasn't going to make it. Smoke-eaters had a sense about these things. The psychologist's glum face confirmed his premonition.

"I'm sorry," Reed said, not mincing words. "Tommy's dead. He didn't make it through the surgery."

Sam tried to draw in a breath, but smoke still lingered in his lungs and he coughed violently. Tears sprang to his eyes. From the smoke. He couldn't break down now.

Reed clasped his arm, avoiding his bandaged hand. "I'm so sorry, Sammy," he repeated.

"Hey." Sam tried for bravado. "We know every day when we leave the house…"

But he hadn't believed, not really, that something would ever happen to Tommy. Both he and his brother had thought they were invincible.

"We gotta tell Ma and Pa," he said finally. Could his parents, in their late sixties, handle this? He glanced down at his bandaged legs and arms. "Shit. I can't go nowhere like this."

"I'll head over there now. Is Tony any stronger? His heart?"

Damn. His father was not fully recovered from his bypass surgery. What would this news do to him? And their mother. "It'll be Ma that goes nuts." Sam gave a stupid grin. "Tommy was always her favorite."

His brother's devilish eyes swam before him. *She likes me best!*

That's because you're a sissy and you need your mommy.

You're just jealous.

But he hadn't been. Neither of them had ever been jealous of the other. Except maybe when Theresa, Sam's wife, had the kids. Tommy had always wanted a family, but his marriage hadn't worked out. Instead, he'd become a second dad to Sam's children. "Oh, God, my kids. And Terry. They love…loved him."

Thoughts of his family strengthened Sam's resolve. He tried to get up, but the action tugged at the tubes in his arm and groin. He moaned.

"Sam, stay still. You can't go anywhere."

"Will you get Terry and the kids? But, jeez, they see you, they'll think it's me that's dead."

"Chief Cordaro and Chief Talbot already went to your house. They told your wife you were all right as soon as she opened the door. Just a split second of terror, Sammy. Talbot's great at this kind of stuff. And Theresa's tough. She handled it."

"Where is she?"

"Out in the waiting room with Marcy and T.J."
Thomas Joseph.

You're namin' your kid after me? Tommy's eyes had
teared. *I don't know what to say.*

Just hope he doesn't grow up as ugly as you.

It was a joke between them. Whereas Sam was an
ordinary-looking Italian with dark hair and eyes and a
wiry build, Tommy was...had been...tall, blond and
blue-eyed. The women loved him.

So did everybody else. He was a favorite at the firehouse, with just the right balance of firefighter tough-
ness and brotherly affection. Terry always said Sam
should be more like Tommy. But it was hard for Sam
to show his emotions. He kept everything inside, unless
Tom dragged it out of him.

Which was why he didn't know what to do with the
tears that streamed from his eyes. His brother was dead.
Dead.

Reed sat down on the edge of the bed. He kept his
hand on Sam's arm. "Let it come, Sam. Before you
deal with your family. It'll help."

The psychologist was wrong. Nothing would help.
Still, he couldn't stop the flood. He sobbed like a baby.

REED HAD WRITTEN *Death in the Line of Duty*—a guide
for personnel dealing with the loss of a firefighter—so
he knew the drill. Still, he needed to make sure the
woman in the car with him understood procedure, too.
How ironic, he and Delaney working together again.

Talbot had offered to go with him to the Leones',
but it was the psychologist's job to notify the family,

and Reed's gut instinct had told him a woman should accompany him to inform the elderly parents that their son was dead. Theresa Leone was a wreck, so she'd be no help. Delaney had sat with her and the kids in the waiting room, talking soothingly to them. She'd finally gotten Theresa calmed down, and had even coaxed the kids to talk to her. The woman was an excellent psychologist. And dedicated. Despite what was between them, she'd come willingly. The thought pushed at the walls of his heart.

A heart that he had forced himself to harden tonight. Later, he'd deal with all that had happened. He smiled grimly. Whether he wanted to or not.

"You need to know some things," he said in the dim confines of the fire department Jeep. *Always go in a fire department vehicle.*

She squeezed his arm. He allowed her touch because he couldn't help himself. "All right, what do I need to know?"

"We don't make the death notification on the doorstep. We ask to be admitted to the house."

She nodded.

"We suggest the family members sit down, then inform them slowly and clearly. We don't use euphemisms like *passed away*. We give as much information as possible."

Again the silent understanding. Her grip became a soothing stroke, back and forth on his bare forearm.

"I'll answer all questions honestly, being sure to use Tommy's first name." His voice cracked.

"Pull over, Reed."

"Huh?"

"Pull over to the side of the road for a second. You're upset."

He stared ahead at the pavement. "I can't afford to be upset." Being upset was being out of control. "I have to do this."

"Five more minutes won't matter. If you're composed, telling the family will go better."

Drawing in a heavy breath, he swerved to the side of the tree-lined city street where the Leones lived and shut off the engine. "We ask what we can do," he continued as if reciting from his manual. "Offer to make phone calls."

"Have you done this before? Notifications?"

No, he hadn't. He'd been a young lieutenant fighting for his own life when the families of his men had been notified. Little had he known that the "life" he'd be left with would be constantly shaken by nightmares and all-too-vivid memories.

Viciously, he shook off the thought and glanced over at Delaney. She looked so strong and competent. She'd toughened up as soon as she'd found out Chelsea and Jake were all right.

A smile breached his lips.

"What is it?" Delaney leaned over, brushed something off his shoulder and gently touched his cheek. He got a whiff of her flowery shampoo. That scent had stayed with him for weeks after New Year's Eve.

"I was thinking about the hospital waiting room. Jake, all grimy, holding Timmy O'Roarke, sound asleep on his chest."

Delaney smiled. At fourteen months old, Beth and Dylan's son was a terror, but he quieted with Jake for some reason. "The kid wouldn't let anybody else hold him when Beth went to be with Dylan while they set his leg."

"Just Jake. How funny." Reed's voice was bemused.

"A psychological phenomenon worthy of studying."

Reed raised his arm and rested it on the back of her seat. His fingers played with her hair. "Thanks for coming. For doing this. Theresa's concerned about Tommy's mother."

"I'll take care of Rosie Leone." She leaned into his hand a minute. "I'm here, Reed, for you, and anyone else who needs me during this crisis."

He wouldn't depend on her. He couldn't. Years ago, another woman, his wife, Patrice, had tried to help him, to be there for him, and he'd almost destroyed her. Drawing away, he started the car and drove down the street. "The kids'll need you. You were great with them."

"Thanks, I love working with kids."

"I wish you could…"

"What?"

"Nothing. We're here." They pulled up to a tidy gray-sided house. The yard was surrounded by a white picket fence and flower beds lined the walk. So normal. So sedate. The couple inside had no idea their world was going to come crashing down on them in a few minutes. Hell, did anybody, right before it happened?

Silently Reed and Delaney exited the car, met on the sidewalk. Before they made their way up the stone steps, Reed grabbed Delaney's hand.

And though it scared the hell out of him, he couldn't change the fact that he needed her.

AFTER SEVERAL KNOCKS and the ringing of the bell, Tony Leone pulled open his front door. A big man with snowy white hair, he wore a terry-cloth robe and a wary expression on his face. Delaney's heart ached for what was about to happen to him.

"What's going on?" the older man asked. Reed had told Delaney he'd met Sam's father briefly a few years ago at a social event, but clearly the older man didn't recognize him.

"Mr. Leone. I'm Reed Macauley, the Rockford Fire Department psychologist. And this is Delaney Shaw, an associate. May we come in?"

"Tony, who is it this hour of the morning, trying to wake the dead?" Rosie Leone's voice came from inside, tinged with concern.

Sammy's father stilled. A retired firefighter—the damn profession ran in the blood—Tony sensed what was coming. Silently he stepped aside and allowed them in. Reed closed the door. Tony crossed to his wife, a robust woman in a pink chenille housecoat and a hair net around her head and circled his arm around her. "Sit down, Mama." He led the woman to the couch. Standing beside her, a hand on her shoulder, he faced Reed bravely. "It's about my boys, isn't it?"

Reed moved in close to them. Delaney followed suit. He grasped Tony on the shoulder.

"I'm sorry," Reed said. "Tommy was killed in a fire tonight. Sammy's okay."

It was hard watching the older man try to be brave. His eyes moistened, an his entire body went taut. Simultaneously, Rosie crumpled. Delaney knelt in front of the woman and took her hand. "Oh, Mother of God, not my baby," Rosie said.

"I'm sorry, Mrs. Leone," Delaney whispered, sliding an arm around her.

"How..." Tony cleared his throat. "How'd it happen?"

"There was a three-alarm fire at an industrial complex. Tommy was inside when a wall collapsed. Sammy was with him, but he was on the other side of the room. The doctors say Tommy didn't feel much pain." Reed's recitation was accompanied by Rosie's soft weeping. "He died in the hospital a few hours ago."

Tony shook his head. "I see. Anybody else hurt?"

"Some injuries. Sammy suffered from smoke inhalation. But no one else was killed." Reed smiled sadly. "Would you like to sit down?"

Tony nodded and sank onto the couch next to his wife. She let go of Delaney and turned into her husband's arms. "Oh, Anthony. Our boy. Our baby..."

Again, Tony was stoic as he encompassed Rosie in his arms. "I know, Mama, our baby."

Delaney stood, battling back the emotion. She glanced at Reed. His face was drawn and a muscle tensed in his jaw. He looked over at her, then pulled her close. Slid his arm around her waist. She leaned into him, as much for him as for herself. His grip was tight, desperate. For now at least, he needed her.

And she'd be there for him.

IT WAS 4:00 A.M. WHEN REED strode through the hospital glass doors into the cool June morning. He'd waited until everybody had gone home, except Theresa and Beth, who were with their husbands. Typical of the firefighter family, the whole crew had pitched in. Even Chief Talbot had stayed until everybody left. Ben and Diana took the elder Leones home and planned to stay with them for a while. Francey, Ben's daughter, and her husband, Alex, had shown up and shepherded Joe Santori's grandparents—he was the other firefighter who'd been injured—back to the senior citizens' complex, Dutch Towers. Chelsea and Jake, of course, were in charge of Timmy O'Roarke. And Delaney had offered to go with the Leone kids to their own house, but the children had opted to be with their grandparents and the Cordaros.

Everyone had been seen to, and Reed was ready to crash. He prayed to God he could sleep, that no attacks came tonight. Though he tried not to think about her, he wondered who'd taken Delaney home. He could still see her holding a sobbing Rosie Leone in her slender arms, whispering soothingly to the older woman, and finally disappearing into the bedroom with Rosie so she could get ready to go to the hospital. Reed didn't know what he would have done if Delaney hadn't accompanied him.

Tony Leone had reacted just as Reed had expected. A former firefighter himself, he'd accepted the news of his son's death with stoicism. Reed recognized the tactic, wanted to warn the old man he should let his emotions out, but figured he would give in to them eventually. Instead, Reed had sat with Tony and listened to stories about Tommy until the women were ready to go.

Now, searching for the keys in his pocket, Reed reached his car.

"Hi."

His head snapped up. "Delaney? What are you doing here?"

"I need a ride home. I rode to the fire with Ben."

His eyes narrowed on her. Best to get back to distancing her now. He'd already spent too much time with her tonight, and knew he'd pay for it later. "There were plenty of people to take you home earlier."

She said unabashedly, "I wanted to be with you. I'm worried about you."

"I'm fine." He wondered what to do. He couldn't very well leave her stranded at Rockford Memorial Hospital at 4:00 a.m.

"You're not fine." She shivered, and for the first time tonight he noticed the sleeveless blouse and the thin summer skirt she wore. For a woman who looked impeccable every time he saw her, she was pretty mussed, her clothes streaked with dirt from hugging

Chelsea, her hair a mess from the breeze. That mane was longer now, more than halfway down her back.

I love this, he'd said, fisting his hand in the thick strands as she straddled him. *I've been dying to touch it for months.* He'd turned into a different man that one night with her. The man he used to be. He'd weakened, showed more vulnerability than he had to any other person in his entire life, even his ex-wife. He had to get a grip now.

But he noted the fatigue smudging the skin beneath her eyes and the weary droop of her shoulders. She'd had a hell of a night, too. "Come on, I'll give you a lift."

He opened the door for her and watched her skirt hike up as she climbed in. He wondered briefly if she had on one of those thongs like she'd worn New Year's Eve. *Hey, what's this?* he'd asked, snapping the band of the lacy why-bother underwear.

You like?

Hmm. I like.

Man, where was his mind going? And even his body, he thought, feeling a tightening in his groin as he circled the car. He was dead tired, emotionally drained, and forty-one years old, but just a glimpse of her thigh could turn him on.

Neither spoke until they were on their way. Dawn had not yet broken, and headlights of a few oncoming cars illuminated the interior of the vehicle. "Thanks for what you did tonight," he finally said. He wanted to reach over and hold her hand. Instead, he gripped the steering wheel.

"You're welcome. I'm so sorry for Rosie and Tony. And, of course, the kids."

"Your area of expertise." The stark, disbelieving faces of the two Leone children flashed before him. "What made you choose to specialize in adolescents?"

"I remember what it was like to be a teenager and to need help."

He wanted to know more about that but refused to let himself probe. It would bring them closer together. "I really appreciated your being here tonight."

She waited a long time before she said, "I'd do anything for you, Reed."

He remembered the visits, the calls, and finally the doctor she'd found. "I know."

"But you don't want me to. Still." It wasn't a question, just a confirmation of what he'd told her in a thousand different ways. And for the first time in a very long time, he felt angry that he was so different from other men. Unable to have the kinds of connection normal people had.

You can, Reed. You just won't let yourself.

Unknown to the woman beside him, Reed had gone to see Bill Connally, the New York psychologist she'd located. *Yeah? And why the hell wouldn't I let myself, Dr. Freud?*

Survivor guilt would be my guess, though you won't tell me the details. Maybe a basic savior complex you couldn't adhere to.

Reed had stormed out then. But had gone back. Because of Delaney Shaw.

It was the most intense episode I've had in years. It's her fault.

What do you mean?

I connected with her. On more than a physical level. See, if I let myself feel anything too intensely, the episodes are worse. It's emotional overload. All the literature confirms it.

All the literature says you can deal with PTSD, Reed. You'll probably never get rid of it, but you can manage this if you want to.

I know that. I had it under control, but it's back. Because of her.

She can help you.

No! I won't do that to her.

It should be her choice.

You don't know what I did to my wife. He remembered the bruises on Delaney's wrist. Worse, the hurt in those eyes when he shut down....

"Reed, did you ever go see the doctor whose name I sent you?"

Damn, talk about connection. She could read his friggin' thoughts.

"Yes. It didn't help."

"I can help."

"That's not an option."

"So you said." He exited the expressway and headed toward her house in the quiet suburb of Gates. "How do you know where I live? You've never been here."

Like a lovesick teenager, he'd driven by a hundred times since he'd cut her out of his life. It was almost as stupid as the other covert connection he'd kept with her. "I just know." He was too tired to lie.

In minutes, he pulled into the driveway. He stared at the Frank Lloyd Wright-style house. One-story, it sprawled invitingly over a heavily wooded acre of land. He frowned. "Your car? It's probably at the office."

She nodded. "That's okay, I can catch a ride later in the morning."

Something made him probe, although he wasn't sure he was ready for the answer. "Is there a guy in your life now? It's been six months since we…"

"Actually, it's been five months, two weeks and three days." Her eyes flashed blue fire; he could see it spark in the glow from the garage lights. "Yeah, there's a guy in my life."

He knew it. "I saw you a couple of times with someone."

"I saw you, too. Who is she?"

"A woman I've known for a long time. She understands my need to stay…"

"Removed? Distanced?"

"Yes."

"And she doesn't bring on your waking nightmares like I apparently do?"

Ellen Marshall didn't bring on anything for him, of course, like each of the women he'd dated over the years, all the semirelationships he allowed himself to have. She agreed to his terms, had become a friend, too. Which was why he could continue to see her. Only the beauty beside him had slipped past the iron bars of his defenses and incited a whole host of emotions he preferred to keep locked away. "I already told you I won't talk about this."

Clearly piqued, she reached for the door handle. Then stopped and faced him. "Just to set the record straight, when I said there's a guy, I meant you. I've been with other men, sure, but no one's come close to what I had with you."

I've been with other men. The thought leveled him. He bit the inside of his mouth to keep from telling her that.

He stared at her. She stared back. Studied his face.

"Oh, hell!" she said, obviously reading his distress. "I meant I *dated* other guys. I haven't slept with anyone else," she added hoarsely. "I couldn't."

"I didn't ask." But, God, he'd wanted to know.

"Reed, I don't understand all this. You're obviously upset by the thought that I'd sleep with someone else. Why won't you let me help you?"

He didn't want to say any more, but her distress got to him. "I can't be with you, Laney. Be close to you, or anyone. PTSD is an insidious condition. I know what it does to the people I get close to, and I refuse to subject you to that."

"Then why did you take me to bed New Year's Eve?" She shook back her hair. "You came after me, you know."

"I'm sorry I did that. I lost my head. I *always* do with you. But it's not good for either of us. Trust me on this."

She sighed deeply. "All right." She reached for the door again, but *he* stopped her this time. "Wait a minute. We might as well clear up something else now. I know you were with Ben tonight when he got my page. About the Family Assistance Network.''

She stiffened. ''Yes, I was.''

''What did you tell him?''

''That I couldn't be a part of the network because you wouldn't want me to.''

''I don't.''

''I know.''

His hand fisted and he banged it on the steering wheel, making her jump. ''Damn it. I feel selfish depriving the team of your services.''

She leaned back into the seat as if she knew where this was going. ''And, selfishly, I don't want that proximity to you, either. I went to the Rescue the Kids program to get away from you.''

He'd suspected as much.

He felt compelled to say, ''I won't change my mind about us, Delaney.'' He couldn't.

''Yeah, Doc, I got that message loud and clear.'' She leaned over then and kissed him. A smart-mouthed kiss, full of sass. ''But your stubbornness doesn't change how I feel about you. Remember that when you go home at night and wonder where I am. Who I'm with. I won't be celibate forever. Know that it could have been you.'' She threw open the car door and her skirt rode way up again—as she'd probably intended it to do. She caught him looking. ''Thanks for the ride.'' She jumped out and headed for her house.

Thanks for the ride. Hell, she had him on an emotional roller coaster he wasn't sure he could survive.

And he cursed a blue streak on the way home about it.

Later, when everything came back in his dreams, he was still cursing...her, the fire department and life itself.

WHEREAS HER SISTER CHOSE to work out her frustrations with hundred-pound weights and a treadmill, Delaney cleansed her body and soul with dance. Chelsea and dance had been the only constants in her life growing up, and she hadn't forsaken them as an adult. She and Chelsea were as close as ever, and she still took a ballet class twice a week.

On the night after the fire, she'd come to The Weight Room, the gym her sister owned, and headed to a back room that housed a wood floor, a huge mirror and a barre. Chelsea's staff ran aerobic classes here, one of which had just ended.

"Mind if I use the room now?" she asked the gym manager, Spike Lammon.

"Hey, for my favorite girl? Of course I don't mind." Spike gave her an Olympic-caliber smile. Men had always been good for Delaney's ego.

I won't change my mind about us, Delaney.

Well, some men.

"Need any help?"

"No, thanks. Gotta work out my frustrations alone."

He gave her a friendly squeeze on the shoulder. "Ready to take me up on my offer yet?"

"Hmm." He'd been begging for a date. "Maybe. I'll let you know."

When Spike left, Delaney flicked the soothing sounds of Debussy on the CD, shucked off her jeans, donned her ballet shoes and poised herself in front of the mirror. Dressed in a black leotard and tights, she lifted her chin and squared her shoulders.

She'd dance her heart out and not think about Reed Macauley tonight. *First position.* Heels touching, feet pointing out. Arms extended, hands curled…

He'd held her hand twice last night, once at the fire, once when they went to the Leones'. They'd linked fingers as they'd made love New Year's Eve, too. The connection had been intimate. Sweet. Who would have guessed there'd be that bud of acute tenderness between them just waiting to blossom?

Demi plié. A graceful bend at the knees.

He'd kissed the back of her knees that night six months ago…. Ordering herself to close her eyes, get lost in the music and the discipline of ballet, she took a *croisé* position and *chasséd* into an *attitude*, left leg raised.

You have no right having legs this long, he'd said, sliding his hands down the full length of one.

I'll wrap them around you anytime you want, Doc.

He'd laughed, deep and from the belly. She'd been startled at the masculine rumble she'd never heard before.

Disgusted with her inability to banish Reed Macauley from her mind, Delaney went into an *arabesque ouverte*—balanced on the right foot, left foot at a perfect 90-degree angle to her body, arms extended.

A good dancer, she could have been better. An instructor had once told her she was his best pupil—and that she could be a star. Moving from town to town during her adolescence had precluded that dream and dashed a myriad others.

She stumbled at the thought of her mother's bohemian lifestyle with the two different men she'd married. "Damn."

"Don't think I've ever heard a ballerina swear before." Delaney pivoted to find her sister in the doorway.

"What are you doing here?" Delaney asked. To assure herself that Chelsea was all right after the fire, Delaney had gone over to the Scarlattas' house and tucked her sister in for a nap about three o'clock this afternoon.

"We took the baby back to Beth, and I wanted to stop in here and make sure everything's running smoothly." She ambled into the room, dressed in navy fire department sweats, her blond hair loose around her shoulders. Shoulders that slumped—unusual for Delaney's in-the-clouds sister these days. Since her marriage to Jake, Chelsea had never seemed happier.

Walking to the CD player, Delaney switched it off and dropped to the floor. Cross-legged, she patted the space next to her. "Sit."

Chelsea eased down onto the floor.

"You okay?" Delaney asked.

"I'm so sad, Laney."

Delaney grasped Chelsea's uninjured hand. "It's hard when someone dies."

"Yeah. I didn't know Tom Leone well, but I worked with Sammy a lot. I feel so bad for that family."

I could help them. Especially the kids.

Her sister's brows narrowed and her lips trembled. "It could have been Jake." Stopping, she took a deep breath. "He was trapped in that fire." She bit her lip. "You know, I never worried about him before."

"He's probably had this same conversation with Ben or Dylan. My guess is he'll worry about you, too, for a while, anyway."

"God, firefighting's a tough business. I'm so glad they're starting FAN at the academy. We all need it."

"I'd like to be a part of the program." Damn, that just slipped out.

"Really? I'll bet they'd jump at the chance to get you."

"They already tried. I turned them down."

Thoughtfully, Chelsea perused her sister's face. "Does this have anything to do with Reed?"

Delaney nodded. For the first time ever Delaney had kept something from her sister. In the past, she'd confessed everything, even the night she'd stayed out till dawn with Eddie Tabor and *become a woman*. But what happened between her and Reed was too private, too painful to share. "I don't really want to work with him."

"He's a great guy, Laney." She watched her closely. "You just don't like Reed because you can't wrap him around your little finger, like every other male you come in contact with."

You could wrap me around your little finger if I let you, lady.

"No, it isn't that." Delaney was uncomfortably aware of the yearning in her voice.

"What is it?"

Suddenly Delaney longed to share her troubles with her sister. And because her feelings for Reed had been unexpectedly rekindled by this incident, she needed to talk about them. She was also very worried about him, wondering what effect Tom Leone's death had had on him. "Something's—"

"There you are."

Two hundred pounds of handsome male flesh poked his head in the door. Jake frowned when he took in their position. "Is this private?" he asked. "I can wait out here."

Delaney stood. "No, it's okay. Your wife should be in bed, after last night."

Jake's gray eyes danced. "Bed sounds good to me."

The smile Chelsea gave her husband made Delaney's stomach pitch. As did the way Jake cradled his wife to him after they said their goodbyes and left. What was between them was so good, so right.

And for the first time, Delaney wanted that kind of love in her life, too. Unfortunately, the only man she'd consider pursuing something permanent with had rejected her outright. And it hurt. A lot.

She stood and crossed to the CD. Switching Debussy back on, she approached the mirror and stared at the lonely woman before her.

First position...

SEATED ON HIS LIVING ROOM couch, Reed stared at the box he'd taken to calling Pandora's box because he'd once made that association with Delaney. *You know, any contact with you is like opening Pandora's box. All hell breaks loose.*

She'd bristled at the insult, of course. He'd chuckled at her reaction and walked away.

Shaking his head, he smiled down at the deep, twelve-inch-square box. It was covered with peach-and-white silk, and suited her perfectly—so soft, so feminine, so…pretty. He'd discovered the treasure in one of the antique shops he frequented and immediately knew it was meant for Delaney.

Slowly, he removed the cover to add the newest *present.* Damn, he was losing his mind. Yet there was something cathartic about what he was doing. Whenever he bought another gift to stow secretly away in here, his need for her lessened. Collecting these items seemed to have precluded a few of the attacks. Maybe it allowed him to release his feelings for Delaney slowly. He was in control. Just the opposite of how things were when he was with her. Bill Connally, the psychologist Reed had seen a few times, would have a field day with this little ritual.

Like a kid poring over memorabilia of his first love, Reed studied each item. One was a T-shirt he'd come across in New York, so outrageous she'd love it. You're Just Jealous Because the Voices Are Talking To *Me*. He fingered the cotton; it was soft, but not as soft as her skin. He'd told her she felt like Chinese silk. And she'd melted at his touch and at his words.

Replacing the shirt, he drew out a small scroll he'd

ordered over the Net. Scripted on it was one of the funniest mockeries of psychology he'd ever seen; he'd wanted to share the joke with her so badly, he ached with it.

The phone rings....
Click...
Recording: Hello, welcome to the psychiatric hotline.
If you are obsessive-compulsive, please press 1 repeatedly.
If you are co-dependent, please ask for someone to press 2.
If you are paranoid-delusional, we know who you are and what you want. Just stay on the line until we can trace the call.
If you are schizophrenic, listen carefully and a little voice will tell you which number to press.
If you are manic-depressive, it doesn't matter which number you press. No one will answer.

Delaney would laugh at the sentiments.

There were a few other items—a sleek carving of her unusual first name, a rare first edition of Freud's autobiography. But the one that had come from a mail order catalog today was the best. Attached to a chain, a delicate gold charm read, in pretty script, *Firefighter's Lady*.

Something she would never be, at least not *his* lady, anyway. He scowled as he buffed the gold of the charm with his sleeve. Some smoke-eater might snag her, though. He'd caught the guys at the academy eyeing her. Several of the young lieutenants tripped over themselves every time she'd visited him. Reed couldn't bear the thought of her with another man. When she told him in the Jeep two nights ago that she hadn't slept with anyone else since the New Year, his heart had trip-hammered in his chest with absolute joy.

But he was crazy to rejoice in that admission.

He had to let her go, even in his mind.

He should throw out the box and its contents, stop this macabre rite. Even if it did make him feel closer to her. *Because* it did.

Vowing to get rid of all the gifts—soon—he stood.

Gently, he fitted the cover back on the box and then replaced it in the window seat.

CHAPTER THREE

THE FUNERAL PROCESSION began at the closest fire-house, Engine Six, which was about three blocks from St. Mary's Church, where the Leone family worshiped. Delaney was grateful that the distance wasn't any longer, given that Theresa Leone and the kids had been barely able to function since that fatal fire six days ago. Sam, however, had been stoic and solicitous, meeting everybody's needs but his own. Reed worried most about him.

And Delaney worried about Reed, who'd gotten more and more haggard as the days progressed. As department liaison, he was the one assisting the family with the funeral arrangements. He simply had too much to do. On top of all that, there was the stress of Tommy's death—the first death in the line of duty in the RFD in years. Delaney knew that these kind of high-stress conditions could trigger PTSD episodes.

The mournful wail of bagpipes preceded the procession. Weepy notes echoed through the streets. Then the mournful parade came into view. The bagpipers led the way, each musician in authentic Scottish garb, complete with kilts and plaids.

From her position on the church's left-side stairs, under inappropriately bright skies, she watched

Tommy's station house truck come first—Engine Seventeen, bearing the casket on its flatbed. Stripped of hose, draped with black bunting, with huge sprays of flowers atop the casket, the engine moved slowly down the street. On either side marched firefighters outfitted in full dress uniform.

The truck passed her. Seeing Tom's turnout coat, boots and helmet fastened to the back of the engine caught her behind the knees. She fought down the emotion that had clogged her throat for days as she'd helped out with this official firefighter funeral in an attempt to lessen some of the burden on Reed.

Behind the truck walked the family, except for Tommy's mother, Rosie, who'd waited at the curb in front of the church with a relative. In fire department dress blues, a brimmed hat and white gloves, Sam stood tall next to his father, who, though he was retired, also wore his uniform. Tony Leone's face was as neutral as his son's. Theresa flanked Sam's other side, crying softly, holding her husband's hand. Marcy, their daughter, openly sobbed and clung to her mother's hand on the right, and to T.J.'s hand on the left. The boy held his head high like his father. Another woman Delaney didn't know walked next to T.J. A soft, gentle breeze flowed over them, mocking the profoundly sad moment.

Next in the somber procession was the impressive sight of hundreds of firefighters, parading stiffly in double file down Main Street, which had been cordoned off by the police. Delaney guessed that probably the only RFD personnel absent were those on duty.

It was tougher for Delaney to remain composed when Reed came closer. He marched behind the family with Ben Cordaro, Chief Talbot and three battalion chiefs she didn't know. In the intervening days, Reed had told her that Talbot's son had died in the past year in a wildfire out west. The chief's face was grim and blank, shielded by his dress hat. Reed, too, was in full dress uniform; she noticed that his hands were fisted in his white gloves and his hat shaded his eyes. But she knew what she'd see underneath the brim. Pure exhaustion. And a bleakness that broke her heart. He'd been too overwrought to fight her during the hellish week....

"Sit down," she'd ordered him three days after the fire when she'd visited him at the academy. The flags on the building flew at half-mast. Reed wore a badge band—a strip of black cloth placed over the midpoint of the badge on his shoulder. All RFD personnel would wear the mourning bands for thirty days. After he was seated, she took a chair opposite him and told him firmly, "Make a list of what I can do to help."

Looking as if he might balk, he watched her with hooded eyes. Then he drew out a file, donned his glasses and studied the contents. Finally, he said, "You can arrange for the flowers. Find out which florist the department uses from Ben's secretary. Go over to the place, though, would you, and make sure you like what you see? We need a Maltese cross arrangement, a badge, a helmet, maybe..." His voice had cracked during the recitation; clearly emotion was getting to him.

She'd whipped out a notebook. "I'll find out the

standard arrangements for this kind of thing. What else?''

"Take care of the disposition of the flowers afterward.''

"Done.''

He stared out the window.

She said, "How about after the burial? What happens?''

"I've got to set up some kind of reception. There'll be hundreds of people at the funeral. It should be simple, near the cemetery, and quick. The family wants to go back to the house with their close friends after an hour or so.''

Her heart aching at his stricken expression, Delaney reached across the desk and covered his hand. "Let me take care of that, too.''

Briefly he'd squeezed her hand; surprisingly, he'd agreed to let her arrange the reception.

The procession halted dramatically in front of the church. A small group of firefighters next to the truck broke away. The pallbearers. Delaney recognized Joe Santori, his shoulder in a sling, as one of them. Jake was another. Reed had told her the final two men were members of Engine Seventeen—Tommy and Sammy Leone's crew.

With the aid of the funeral parlor personnel, the firefighters eased the casket off the truck and onto a platform. Slowly they wheeled Tommy inside. Delaney could barely watch this part. One of Tom's group was openly crying. After the family entered the church, the rest of the department personnel filed in, followed by those remaining friends and acquaintances who weren't already in the pews.

Delaney took a deep breath and stepped inside the church. As she looked out over the assembled group, she thought that she'd never before really understood the meaning of the term *America's Bravest*.

THE HONOR GUARD GUNS went off in a big burst, startling Reed. He prayed the sound didn't trigger anything else now. His nerves were shot, and he was edgy. The past week had been a nightmare. From his position behind the family at the cemetery, he surveyed the scene: colleagues, family and friends positioned around the grave, bagpipers on the hill, the crossed aerial ladders at the entrance, forming an arch under which they'd ridden, the mahogany casket with a spray of flowers, and Tommy's helmet perched on top.

The sight of the helmet got to him. He began to sweat when he thought of Marx, the big burly German who'd been his best friend, and how after his buddy's funeral—which Reed had missed because he was lying hurt and immobile in the hospital—the brass had brought the headgear to him. Spots swam before his eyes. Adrenaline rushed through him. *Please, God, not now*. He'd already had one PTSD episode since Tommy died. The prayer steadied him and he was able to concentrate on the present.

Chief Talbot approached the microphone. He concealed his own private agony well. ''The alarm code 716 signals the return of a truck to the firehouse. We will ring out the code now, to welcome home firefighter Thomas Joseph Leone one last time.''

A fire department bell clanged. Reed breathed deeply, steeling himself against the sound that would surely affect even the hardest of hearts. Wrenching sobs from the gathering accompanied the chimes.

Ben Cordaro broke away from the officers. The funeral director pulled the flag off the casket, and the pallbearers folded it. One firefighter handed it to Ben. He approached the Leones. Standing in front of Tommy's parents, Ben held out the flag. ''On behalf of the Rockford Fire Department, I am honored to present you with this flag, a symbol of the country and the people your son served.'' When Tony took the flag, Ben stepped back and saluted sharply.

Another officer came up to T.J. and handed him the helmet. Reed had to avert his eyes, and his vision blurred for a second.

The bagpipes, about seventy-five feet away, began to play a song. Reed knew he'd heard it somewhere but couldn't place it. God, he was so tired, things were slipping his mind these days. The honor guard saluted, ''Taps'' rang out over the sprawling cemetery, and then it was over.

But Reed, being all too familiar with death, knew that this was just the beginning.

SAM DUCKED OUT OF THE TENT set up in the park adjacent to the cemetery and strode to the building that held the bathrooms. Circling around to the south side, where he couldn't be seen, he found the peace and quiet he was after. Sighing heavily, he drew out a cigarette and lit it.

Those cancer sticks'll kill you, buddy.

Instead, the Red Devil had gotten Tommy. Sam ran his hand through his hair. How *was* he going to make it without that kid in his life?

"It was a nice funeral, wasn't it?"

Damn. Company. He turned to the speaker, whose voice he'd recognized as Reed Macauley's. "Yeah." Sam took a long drag on the Marlboro. "Real nice. Thanks for all you did."

"I'm glad to help."

Glancing sheepishly at his cigarette, Sam said, "I didn't want the kids to see me smoke."

"Good idea." Reed leaned a shoulder against the wall. They'd all removed their jackets—long sleeves were hot in June, but formalities had been extended to show respect to Tommy; the epaulets on Reed's white captain's shirt sparkled in the sun.

Sam indicated the tent beyond. "This was a good idea. Informal, not claustrophobic. You do all this, too?"

The shrink's smile was...tender. "I had help with this part." Then Reed got that *I'm serious* look on his face. "Sammy, *you* need help. Let me be there for you."

"You've done a lot already."

"You know what I mean."

The concrete block in his throat gagged him. "I can't talk about it, Reed. I can't let it out."

"It'll come out another way."

''Nah. I'm fine. I've dealt with death before.'' Just not Tommy's.

''Not your brother's.''

Another long draw on the smoke, then he ground it out with his fancy shoe. ''My mother, Terry and the kids need me.''

''You won't do them any good if you bottle everything up inside. It'll pop when you least expect it.''

Weary, Sam closed his eyes. ''Maybe.''

Reed straightened. ''Look, I won't press you now. This is a tough day and getting through it is about all you have to do. But I'd like you and Theresa and the kids to come see me this week.''

''Why?''

''To talk. To see how you're doing.''

''This part of that FAN stuff you sent around?''

Hey, look at this, Tommy had said. *They're startin' some groups to help firefighters and their families deal with the stress of our jobs.*

Sam had made a crude remark.

It's a good idea, Sammy. Wish they'd had it when Jeanine and I split.

Jeanine, the bitch who'd had the nerve to come to the funeral after she'd broken Tommy's heart. Even in his grief, the sight of her made Sam's fists clench.

''Yes, it's part of the FAN stuff.'' Reed's voice was gruff.

''I don't need it. I can handle everything myself.''

''The typical firefighter attitude.'' Reed stared across the wide expanse of green grass and maple trees. ''You can't, you know. But in any case, think of your family.

We can help them, even if you're a hopeless case, Leone.''

The razzing felt better than the sympathy. ''Okay, Doc, I'll think about it.'' He lit another cigarette. ''I'll be in when I finish this.''

Reed recognized the dismissal. ''Okay.'' He clapped Sam on the shoulder with a strong, brotherly hand. ''Don't try to do this alone, buddy. We're here to help.''

''Sure, I know.''

He'd lied. After Reed left, he turned his face to the building. Nobody could help. He *was* alone now, in a way he hadn't been since he was three and Tommy came bursting into the world all smiling and happy. Resting his forehead against the wall of the shed, feeling the cool metal against his skin, he let the thought that had been rattling around in his brain surface.

Why couldn't it have been him, and not his baby brother?

DELANEY NOTICED the two Leone teenagers leave the tent and bob out toward the woods. Uh-oh. This didn't look good. Discreetly, she slipped out the side and followed them.

She'd worn sensible shoes today so her progress across the grass was fast. Catching up to the kids, she stood behind a tree at the edge of a clearing and watched them plunk down on the rungs of a jungle gym. The late-afternoon sun cast crisscross shadows on them. Marcy's blond head was bent in toward T.J.'s dark one, the contrast startling. Maybe Delaney had overreacted. Maybe the kids just needed to be alone, to talk. Marcy spoke to her brother, then reached in her purse and drew something out.

"You're an asshole," she heard T.J. say.

"Yeah, well, you don't have to do it."

Frowning, Delaney watched as Marcy lit a cigarette—no, a joint—and took a long drag. With a sideways glance, she handed it to her brother, who scowled but accepted the weed and drew in a puff.

Without hesitation, Delaney pushed away from the tree and into plain sight. The two young teenagers froze.

Delaney approached them. When they were face-to-face, she crossed her arms over her chest and said, "Put it out, guys."

Soulful brown eyes stared at her guiltily, and a little gratefully, then T.J. crushed the joint into the sandbox below the jungle gym.

"You gonna tell?" Marcy asked belligerently. Her eyes, though—as blue as her uncle's—were full of pain. And the quaver in her voice told Delaney she wasn't nearly as brave as she was pretending to be.

"I have to think about what I'm going to do." She nodded to the jungle gym. "Can I sit?"

The kids exchanged worried looks. They reminded her of herself and Chelsea as kids, the two of them against the world.

"Yeah." Again, Marcy took the lead.

Perching on a rung not too close, Delaney stared at the playground equipment—a huge set of swings, a sliding board, which used to be her favorite, and a low spinning platform. "It was hard today, wasn't it?"

As if on cue, both of the kids hunched over.

Put their heads down.

"I can help," Delaney said softly.

Marcy looked up with tears in her eyes. T.J. cleared his throat and kept staring down.

Marcy nodded, then Delaney scooted over and slid her arm around the girl's back. Marcy turned her face into Delaney's shoulder. Delaney soothed her hair down. "It's all right to feel bad."

Choking sobs from Marcy. T.J. got up and walked to the slide, his back to them. She saw him wipe his eyes. Minutes passed in the warm afternoon so heavy with hurt.

Finally Marcy straightened.

Delaney pulled a tissue from her pocket and handed it to her. "You okay?"

"Better." The girl wiped her eyes.

"T.J.?"

He held up his head. Boys were often harder to reach. "I'm fine."

"Come over here a minute, will you?"

A hesitation, then T.J. scuffled over and reseated himself. Closer to Marcy, so their shoulders brushed.

"It's not unusual to turn to chemicals in times of stress or real sadness," she began softly, less critically than she would have given different circumstances.

Marcy scraped the toe of her sandal in the dirt below.

T.J. wouldn't look at her.

"I need to know a few things. And I want you to level with me."

"Okay," Marcy squeaked out.

"Do you smoke dope regularly?"

Marcy shook her head. "I did it a couple of times. And this is T.J.'s first time."

"Second." Kids were so honest sometimes. "I had a few puffs right after Uncle Tommy..." He didn't finish. Instead he averted his head again.

"You can't keep it up, guys." Delaney hoped her voice held the right balance of understanding and disapproval "It's addictive."

"We learned in health class it wasn't." Marcy's voice held little conviction.

"Not physically, maybe, but psychologically." Reaching out, she soothed Marcy's arm. She noticed T.J. leaned into his sister now. "You've got to get your emotions out another way."

After a long silence, Marcy asked, "How?"

"Talk about what you're feeling. Let yourself cry." She smiled sadly. "Throw things when you get mad about Tommy dying."

"Dad would love that." This from the son.

"Your dad won't mind." Delaney hoped not. "Neither will your mom." She waited. "Can you discuss how you feel with them?"

"Dad doesn't ever talk about his feelings," T.J. said. "And Mom's a basket case over Uncle Tommy."

Drawing in a deep breath, Delaney thought for a minute. "Maybe you can talk to Dr. Macauley from the fire department."

Marcy lifted her face; her gaze was full of womanly wisdom. "You're a psychologist, aren't you?"

"Yes, I am."

"Maybe we could talk to you."

From the corner of her eye, Delaney saw Reed had approached and was listening by the tree. "Do you think that you *could* talk to me?"

T.J. shrugged. Marcy nodded.

"All right. I'll discuss this with Dr. Macauley." She stood and motioned him over. "There he is now."

Reed saw the gesture and came toward them. "Hi, guys." God, he looked exhausted. Delaney had the deep urge to comfort him.

Standing, the kids nodded sheepishly.

"Feeling bad?" he asked.

They looked away.

"Want to talk about it?"

"Not now." Marcy threw Delaney a meaningful look. Then she grabbed T.J.'s hand. "Come on, squirt, let's go find Ma. She'll bust a gut if she thinks we bolted." She glanced at Delaney. "Walk back with us?"

Delaney smiled. "Sure." She nodded to Reed.

The Leones got a few steps ahead as he held her back. Warm brown eyes met hers. "Thanks" was all he said.

She squeezed his arm. "You're welcome," and took off with the kids, one at each side of her.

REED HAD COME TO LIKE Pumper's, the firefighter hangout in the city, even though he limited his visits

here. Long and narrow, it had a cool, dim atmosphere
that was a welcome respite after the hot glare of grief
all day. As he made his way through the front bar area,
he passed the firefighter memorabilia—laminated
newspaper articles, recruit class pictures and commen-
dations—that covered every available inch of wall
space.

"Hey, Doc," the owner, Jimmy McKenna, called
out from behind the bar. A former firefighter, the wiry
little man knew almost all RFD personnel by name.

Reed nodded to him. "Hi, Jimmy."

"They're in the back room." McKenna's eyes narrowed on Reed. "There's food back there. You look
like you could use some."

"Thanks." Reed tried to remember when his last
meal had been. Bagpipes sounded in his head, and the
image of Tommy's mother and sister-in-law and niece
sobbing over the mahogany casket killed all desire to
eat. He could make a million on a new diet—the Firehouse Death Weight Loss Program.

What was he doing here? he asked himself as he
headed to the back room.

Avoiding the nightmares for just a little while.

Ben had suggested that anyone who wanted should
come to Pumper's today after the services and reception. Firefighters took care of one another. Reed agreed
with the psychology of bonding during a crisis, though
he wanted nothing more than to collapse by himself at
home. Well, almost nothing more, he admitted, thinking of Delaney in the pretty navy blue sleeveless dress
with ruffles down the front. But this gathering *would*

help everyone. Sometimes, all you had were your friends and colleagues.

Until they were taken away, too.

Shaking his head to clear that pessimistic thought, he stepped through the doorway to the back room. The place was packed. A small U-shaped bar had been installed, and several firefighters were seated at it. Including Ben. Reed crossed to them.

Joe Santori, his arm in a sling, his face drawn from the stress of a buddy's death, was in the middle of a story; several rookies had gathered around him. Joey had once been engaged to Francey Templeton, and though he was tense whenever she was around, he was otherwise laid back and a lot of fun. Like now. "No, seriously, see we get there, and there's no answer at the door. A neighbor had seen fire flickering through the blinds of the downstairs bedroom and called in the alarm. So we jimmy the door and storm in, going straight to the back of the house."

"What'd you find?" Trevor Tully asked. A recent academy graduate, he was hanging on Joey's every word.

"Get this." Joe strung out the suspense. "In the midst of a shitload of candles, a couple in their sixties were doin' it to beat the band. Man, I hope I got that much energy and enthusiasm for the big nasty when I get up there." Joe glanced up. "Hey, Macauley, you still good in the sack at your advanced age?"

This was the best night of my life, Reed.

"I've already forgot things you'll never even know, Santori."

The group laughed, including Joey.

At the sound of Reed's voice, Ben swiveled around on his stool. "There you are. We thought you weren't coming. Talbot came and waited a while to talk to you, but he just left."

"Today must have been hard for him."

"It was. Where were you?"

"I had some loose ends to tie up with the funeral director, and the family wanted me to stop over at the house." He checked his watch. "Wow, it's seven already?"

"Buy you a beer?" Jake asked.

If Jake was here, so was Chelsea. Maybe Delaney had come with them. "Yeah, a draft sounds good."

Seeing a space at the bar, he went to lean against it and accepted the drink from the bartender. Nonchalantly he turned to scan the crowd. A table of women in the corner. Chelsea. Beth O'Roarke. A couple of female rookie firefighters. Diana, Ben's wife.

But Delaney wasn't here. Thank God.

Liar. What would he have done without her today? This last week? She'd been around constantly, pitching in, insisting he let her handle some of the chores. And today—

"You okay?" Ben had come up to him.

"Fine."

"You look like hell."

"Thanks, buddy." Reed took a healthy swig of his beer. The ice-cold liquid felt good on his throat. "This was a tough one."

"Uh-huh." Ben's gaze strayed to the far side of the room. "We owe Delaney, Reed."

His heart jump-starting, Reed tracked Ben's gaze. So she *was* here. Still dressed in the soft-looking navy dress, her hair wild around her face and down her back, she sat surrounded by five lieutenants, which was why he hadn't seen her initially. Even from here, he could see the guys vying for her attention.

"Cordaro, come here a minute. Tell these rookies about Cuffs."

Ben rolled his eyes. "They're in a mood tonight."

"Stress relief. You'll hear every funny story, every save, every prank that happened within the last five years before the night's over."

Ben turned and said, "All right, you guys. One more story. Cuffs was a buddy of mine on the line when I was a lieutenant. He had an…adventurous sex life, to put it mildly. We didn't believe half his bragging until one night, when he was off duty, our group got a call from his current girlfriend to come over to her house right away. And bring metal cutters."

"Metal cutters?" Tully asked, his eyes round.

"Mmm-hmm." Ben smiled at Reed over the rim of his glass. "Seems he and his lady friend were into a little bondage. She handcuffed him to the bed and then found out the key didn't work. I had to cut the cuffs off."

"And you told everybody?"

Ben's grin was young and devilish. "Are you kidding? It spread through the whole department like wildfire. Everybody called him Cuffs till the day he retired.''

Reed chuckled and began to relax. He'd been right to come here and be with his buddies. For the next thirty minutes he half listened to the banter. It seemed that Jake had taken over Dylan's firefighter trivia game. Originally, the game had been a contest in Dylan's station house to see who could answer questions about firefighting. Proceeds went to charity and house equipment. When Dylan did his stint at the academy, he'd introduced the game over there. Now all the fire stations wanted in on the action, and Dylan had turned it over to Captain Scarlatta to orchestrate.

Amid the discussion, Reed heard Delaney laugh out loud. His gaze swung to her. A smoke-eater was showing her some trick balancing knives. She looked heartbreakingly young and innocent. One of those guys was going to scoop her up quick, Reed knew, the thought piercing his soul.

''You keep looking at her that way, and the whole department's going to guess your feelings.'' Reed glanced over into the knowing eyes of Beth O'Roarke. One of his favorite people. Also one of the few friends with whom he'd let down his guard. Which, of course, he'd also paid for.

He tossed her an I-don't-know-what-you-mean look.

''It's written all over your face, Macauley.'' She and Dylan had apparently gone home and changed into jeans and T-shirts. ''Want to talk about it?''

''What do you think?''

She edged onto a stool beside him and sipped a glass

of wine she'd brought with her. "Jeez, Reed, you're a tougher nut to crack than I was." For years, Beth, an instructor at the fire academy, had refused to share her feelings or let anybody know the demons that haunted her. Only Dylan had managed to break through to her.

"Now, that's impossible." He grinned. "Tell me how that baby boy of yours is doing these days."

"Changing the subject won't work on me, Doc." She paused. "Let me just say one thing and I'll drop it."

"No lectures tonight, Beth, please," he said seriously. "I'm too whipped."

"All right. But remember how you told me once that letting Dylan into my life was worth the risk?"

"Yes."

"It was."

Reed turned his back on Delaney. "I don't know how that applies to me."

Sighing, Beth pivoted, too. "Fine. I'll drop it. Let me tell you something else. This you'll like hearing."

"What?"

"Dylan and I want to help in FAN."

"Really, how?"

"One of the components is physical fitness, isn't it?"

"Yes. Preferably activities for families to do together."

"I thought maybe I could plan some things for that." She nodded to a six-month-pregnant Francey Templeton, who was sitting with her husband and Dylan on the other side of the room. Alex Templeton clearly wasn't happy. "Francey said she'd help and I'm sure we can rope Chelsea into working with us. And Dylan can do research work on the Net along with other administrative stuff now that he's off work for six weeks."

"We never got to talk about how you handled his injury, Beth."

Her hazel eyes flickered with fear for a minute. "It was hard, but I got through it. And thank God it was just a broken leg. I'm doing better with all of it." Her gaze strayed to Francey. "Better than Alex, I think."

Reed sighed. "He asked if we're going to have another spouses' session this summer."

"I know. I'll be at it if you do."

"You all face your fears bravely, you know that?"

Standing, she hugged him. "We had a good teacher to help us. I just wish he could help himself as much."

"You don't give up, do you, kiddo?"

"Nope. Not with you. Let's get together this week to talk about the physical fitness thing."

"You're on."

Fifteen minutes later, Reed sat alone at the end of the bar, nursing his second beer. The other guys had wandered off to see their wives, some people had left, and he was thinking about going home when someone slid a plate of food in front of him.

"You need to eat, Macauley." Delaney's soft voice curled over him.

He glanced at her. Even after a day of grief and sorrow, she looked remarkably refreshed and...young. He couldn't wrest his gaze from her.

"What, do I have sauce on my face?" she asked.

"I was just thinking about all you did today. And this week. Have I thanked you enough for it?"

She nodded to the meal. "You can thank me by eating."

He picked up his fork and, without enthusiasm, speared into the pasta and meatballs. The food was spicy and hot and surprisingly good. "You want something to drink?" he asked her.

"A cola." She nodded to his beer. "You should switch, too. You're liable to keel over if you keep drinking alcohol."

"Takin' care of me, are you, babe?"

"Somebody's got to. You look like hell." When he didn't say anything, she reached out to touch his arm. "Are you all right? I'm worried about you. That you'll—"

"I'm fine." His tone was dismissive, so she removed her hand.

He ordered soft drinks and ate half the food on his plate, then turned to her. She'd sat quietly next to him scanning the crowd as he ate. "I saw what you did for the Leone kids today, Delaney."

Though she smiled at him, her eyes were troubled. "How long were you there?"

"Long enough to hear them ask to talk to you, not me."

"I like them."

"They know it."

"You missed the part about the joint?"

Reed sputtered his cola all over his shirt. *"What?"*

"The Leone kids were smoking a joint. I made them put it out, and after we left you, I insisted they hand over their stash."

"Damn, this isn't good."

She crossed her legs and treated him to a beautiful expanse of skin. "Actually, it's pretty common to experiment, especially in times like this. Be bad because a bad thing happened to you."

"Did you tell Theresa or Sam?"

"No. I wanted to talk to you first. I'm not sure how much more they can take."

Reed hesitated. "I'll tell the Leones this week. I'm worried about Marcy and T.J."

"So am I. They need help, too."

He faced her fully. He hadn't planned on getting into this tonight, but the opportunity was here. Ever since he'd seen her with the kids today, he'd known he had to do this. "I think you should accept the fire department's invitation to work in FAN."

She bit her lower lip. "You know that's not a good idea for either of us."

"I know, honey. I'm sorry. But Tommy's death is having a ripple effect on the department. Do you have any idea how many calls we received from firefighters and their families just this week about FAN?"

"Everybody's running scared."

"I can't handle it all." God he hated to admit that, but it was true.

"Then hire somebody else in the field to work with you."

"Actually, I'm looking into that. But it's tough to get a good psychologist fast. And we need help now."

She was quiet.

Reaching out, Reed grasped her hand. It felt small in his. "The Leone kids need you; so do the other children of the firefighters. I think we have to put our own feelings aside here."

She linked her fingers with his. "Are you saying *you* need me, Reed?"

"Yeah, I need you." Both personally and professionally, though he couldn't give in to the first. The reminder made him let her hand go. "But don't mistake this for anything other than what it is. I haven't changed my mind about a relationship between us."

He saw her stiffen.

"I'm sorry," he said.

"Yeah. Me, too."

"So, what do you think?"

After a moment, the Delaney Shaw he'd first met surfaced. Her ability to make decisions. Her willingness to jump in with both feet. Her selflessness in helping others. "All right, I'll do it."

"Good." He waited a minute before he added, "I want you to promise me something."

She stood and smoothed down her skirt. "I have a feeling I'm not going to like this."

He held her gaze, wanting to touch her almost more than he wanted to be free of the past.

"All right, what?" She sounded like an impatient little girl.

"That you won't try to…" Jeez, how did he put this delicately?

She scowled at him. "That I won't try to *what*, Reed?" When he still floundered, she suggested, "Seduce you?"

He swallowed hard, the words conjuring memories of their night together.

"Yes," he said as sternly as he could.

He expected anger, maybe even a pout. At the very least, he expected the sass she always came back with.

But instead, her eyes darkened with hurt, her lips trembled slightly, her throat worked convulsively. It was worse than any reaction he'd anticipated.

"Don't worry," she finally said, "I won't come on to you again, Reed. I'm not a glutton for punishment." She held his gaze, her eyes moist. "I've given up on us."

He wanted to say "good" or "finally" or even "it's for the best." But he couldn't get the words out. And as he watched her walk away, he had the grim feeling that he'd just lost the most precious gift a man could be given.

CHAPTER FOUR

"THANKS FOR COMIN', LADIES and gentlemen. Before I turn this over to Reed, I wanted to thank you all personally for givin' this program a shot." In his southern drawl, Fire Chief Chase Talbot addressed the thirty or so smoke-eaters assembled in the academy classroom, the smile on his face warm and affectionate. As Delaney watched him, she noticed his easy manner.

Almost self-effacingly, he concluded his comments and introduced Reed. "Here's Reed Macauley, the brains behind the idea."

"All right, all you clowns, listen up," Reed said, joking when the guys razzed him about Talbot's comment. A pleasant June breeze blew in from the window and ruffled his dark hair. The sun highlighted a sprinkling of gray at his temples.

Delaney had never seen him as "one of the guys" before. He fit right in, easing a hip onto the front desk, squarely facing his audience. She'd spent the greater part of the week since Tommy's funeral with Reed and other RFD personnel, organizing the implementation of FAN. In an effort to get it off the ground quickly, she and Reed had worked countless hours. Together. In such close proximity that she could smell his aftershave. It had been hell.

And paradise.

Today, he drew the crowd in with that unique I'm-your-friend charm. "The Family Assistance Network will function both proactively and reactively," Reed began, flashing the two words on the screen from a computer. "Who knows the difference?"

Mumbles around the group. Finally, Eric Scanlon raised his hand. Blond and beautiful at nearly fifty, he'd asked Delaney out after bumping into her several times at the academy. She'd said yes.

"*Reactive* means responding to a situation, as in taking steps *after* something happens." Eric's voice was a deep bass, his whole demeanor confident. "*Proactive* means taking action *before* something goes wrong, preventing it if possible, preparing for it, if not."

"Way to go, professor." This from Joe Santori, who sat in the back.

"Screw you, Santori," Scanlon said, winking at Delaney. "Pardon my French, Dr. Shaw."

Reed stiffened at the byplay but continued.

"Good definitions, Captain Scanlon." Reed called up another screen, which explained his first point. "Reactively, the RFD already has several things in place. I'm available to meet individually with anybody who needs to talk after a traumatic event. If it's far-reaching, like Tommy's death, we'll have more extensive sessions, or we'll set up programs if necessary."

Mention of the Leone family quieted the crowd. The joking stopped and faces sobered. Reed exploited the moment. "We're having in-house counseling for Tommy's group at Seventeen's tomorrow. On-duty personnel will be taken out of service for the morning.''

"They want that?'' a big guy in the back asked. It was a logical question, as firefighters normally played things close to the vest.

"They know they're hurting, Duke. They don't know what to do about it. I offered to come over and shoot the breeze with them about it.''

And do a lot more, Delaney knew, if he could get inside their heads a bit. Reed jammed his hands in his back pockets, the action stretching the white captain's shirt across his chest. "Tommy's group needs to talk. Nobody can keep all emotions inside and expect to heal.''

Hypocrite, Delaney thought. Dr. Reed Macauley was very good at getting others to open up to him. Apparently, he'd never heard the saying *Physician heal thyself.*

"It isn't mandatory,'' Reed clarified.

"That means they wouldn't have no choice, Santori.'' This from a young officer down front.

"Stuff it,'' Joey called out congenially.

"But I'm hoping they'll all participate. Just like you guys. By the way—'' Reed's gaze darted guiltily to Delaney "—the traumatic incident doesn't have to have happened recently. I know some of you smoke-eaters have gone through rough things in the past. I'm available to sort that out, too.''

Sheesh, he couldn't describe his own situation better.

"Proactively, we have several things in mind.'' Reed fiddled with the computer. She watched his hands dance lightly over the keys, remembering what they had felt like on her body. Damn, she wasn't going to do this. He told them about his office hours for anyone wanting to talk, and he mentioned some support groups for partners. "Wives, husbands and mates have trouble with our lifestyle, ladies and gentlemen. We have to acknowledge that."

There was a rumbling in the group, which the leaders had expected. Firefighters didn't like to admit to weakness. Up on the screen, Reed flashed a six-part test. "See if I'm right. Mentally check off the situations that apply to you."

The group read the screen, growing more and more silent as reality set in. The list starkly capsulized the life of a firefighter.

Delaney scanned it.

Are any of these stress-causers in your life?

1. You cannot leave your job to pick up a sick child, coach soccer games or fill in for a sick spouse at home.
2. Your schedule is erratic, four days on, four days off, three nights on, three nights off. You often suffer from sleep problems.
3. You seek out high-risk activities like flying, riding motorcycles and sky-diving.
4. Your spouse is often forced to play both mother and father, do all the basic child-rearing duties like attending school functions and car pooling.
5. In some ways you are closer to your group than your significant other. You certainly share more of your job with them.

6. Firefighting is both physically and emotionally draining. Humping hoses and climbing out on roofs, as well as staring death in the face, depletes you by the time you get home.

Silence.

Reed nodded to the side. On cue, two non-RFD people rose and came to the front. "If you don't believe me, I'll let you hear it from the horse's mouth."

Diana Cordaro stepped forward, looking stunning in a lilac pantsuit and with chunky amethysts at her ears and neck. Her blond hair framed her face in soft curls. "I'm Diana Cordaro, Ben's wife." She smiled at the back of the room where Ben sat with Francey. A quick glimpse at the chief's stony face told Delaney this was not easy for him to witness.

Diana continued, "It's no secret what went on in my life. I left my family years ago because I couldn't handle the firefighter's lifestyle. It was the worst mistake of my life, and I have nightmares remembering it. If I'd had counseling, if I'd had a group like Reed's set up, I might not have missed out on so much of my children's or Ben's lives. I can't tell you what that regret feels like in here." She rested a delicate hand, gleaming with a gold wedding band, over her heart. "Encourage your wives and husbands, girlfriends and boyfriends to at least try these sessions." She bit her lip, and Delaney could feel the testosterone rise in the room. Firefighters were a protective lot. "Don't let what happened to Ben and me happen to you."

Before anyone could react, Alex Templeton stepped

up to Diana. Immediately Joe Santori stood and left the room.

Alex, looking very confident, smiled at Diana and slid an arm around her. "Looks more like my sister than my mother-in-law, doesn't she?"

The laughter broke some of the tension. Alex knew how to work a group. "I'm Alex Templeton, for those of you I don't know. And Diana here saved my life."

"Thought your wife did that, Templeton." This from one of Francey's group.

Smiling easily, Alex said, "Francesca did rescue me, physically." Diana eased to the background and Alex settled his hip against the desk. "But Diana helped me emotionally. I was a basket case. You guys, and ladies, have no idea what it's like to think about somebody you love walking into a burning building." He tugged down the sleeves of his lightweight Armani suit and adjusted his cuff links. His eyes were sad. "I can't handle it on my own. I've been part of the RFD's significant others support group for a year. It's starting up again this summer, and I'll be there. All of you should encourage your spouses to attend and to take part in the family-oriented activities FAN will provide." He smiled to the back of the room at Francey. "It's worth it to be married to you heroes, but it isn't easy."

"Thanks, Alex." Reed turned to Delaney after Alex took his seat.

From the table where she sat, she rose and joined him.

"As many of you know, this is Dr. Delaney Shaw. She's a noted child and adolescent psychologist in town, and she's setting up individual counseling and group sessions for your children.''

"Can I come with my kids?" a rookie asked. "Please."

Choruses of "Me, too" and "I wanna be in Delaney's group" echoed around.

"How come we get your ugly puss, Macauley, and the kids get *her*?" Duke asked.

Though Reed laughed along with the others, she saw something dark and dangerous in his eyes. "Calm down, you animals. You can't be trusted in the same room with her."

After more razzing Reed introduced Beth O'Roarke, who outlined a physical fitness program that would be offered for three groups at a time. Delaney had suggested she help out in the kids' classes and use the opportunity to get to know them better.

Then Dylan O'Roarke hobbled to the front. On crutches, he took grief from his co-workers.

"Hey, gimp, how ya doin'?"

"It's what you get for bein' a freakin' hero."

Dylan smiled boyishly and his Tom Cruise eyes twinkled. "You wouldn't gloat so much if you knew the TLC I was gettin' from my wife, guys."

A chuckle. Delaney saw Beth, off to the side, roll her eyes.

"I'm in charge of the fun," Dylan told the crowd.

"Now, why aren't we surprised?" Reed joked.

Dylan ignored the jibe. Soberly, he said, "The family that plays together, stays together. I've got a whole laundry list of ideas, but I want your input." He flicked a list of activities on the screen. Bantering back and forth with the audience, he encouraged them subtly to give their input.

After Dylan finished, Reed wound up the session with a plea. "Remember, we all need one another in the crazy world of firefighting we live in."

He put up a quote on the screen. "This is a line from F. Scott Fitzgerald. I think he meant it for all you smoke-eaters out there. *Show me a hero and I'll write you a tragedy.*"

When people started to file out, and Reed faced the desk again, Delaney caught his eye. "Someday, Doc, you should practice what you preach," she said.

And then she turned to find the handsome Eric Scanlon behind her.

REED STALKED TO HIS OFFICE. Once inside, he breathed deeply, went to the window and yanked it open. He sucked in air like a rookie on his first air pack. It didn't help. This wasn't a PTSD attack, either. It was pure male jealousy, something he'd never felt before. He could still see Scanlon's hand close around Delaney's arm. Still see her smile up at the guy.

Still hear her make plans to see him tomorrow night.

In the privacy of his own space, Reed swore vilely. He hadn't expected this emotional sucker punch.

Think about something else. How you're going to help Joey Santori. He left the meeting when—

A brief knock on his open door.

As he pivoted, Delaney stepped into his office. Chic and sophisticated in a short white skirt and matching jacket, she wore her hair tied back in some kind of knot; gold glistened at her ears, throat and wrists and she wore high heels, making her legs look incredible. No wonder all the guys drooled over her.

"It went pretty well, don't you think?" she asked, closing the door.

Feeling claustrophobic, he turned back to the window. "For the first session, yeah."

"Some of those guys have real problems, Reed. I could see it in their faces."

"I know."

"I hope we can help them."

"Just stick to the kids, Delaney. I'll work with the guys." His voice held more edge than he intended.

"What's that supposed to mean?"

He faced her. She'd perched her cute little fanny on the end of his desk. "I just don't think it's a good idea for you to get involved with..." He drew in a breath, knowing he shouldn't go there. "Never mind."

For a minute, she didn't respond. Then she said, "You're a little like the dog in the manger, Reed. You don't want me, but you don't want anybody else to have me."

He gave her a scathing look. Her comparison infuriated him. "Scanlon's old enough to be your father." Nastily, he added, "Or is that why you're going out with him?" He winced as soon as the comment left his mouth. It was an unconscionable betrayal of trust. Once, when he'd talked to her without fighting, she'd told him about her mother's two marriages to restless men who were rarely home. One was Chelsea's father. One was hers.

Temper lit her eyes. They gleamed like the blue flame of fire. "That was a low blow. And very unkind of you, especially since I took this job because you asked me.'' She straightened. ''I'll be leaving.''

He reacted without censoring his response and bolted across the room as she reached the door and got it part way open. Pushing it shut before he could stop himself, he moved in close. Her back was to him. The scent of her hair, lemony and sweet at the same time, teased his nostrils. They flared, and his body hardened. ''I hate your seeing him.''

''He's a nice guy.''

''I don't care if he's Cal Ripken Jr. The thought of you with another man makes me crazy.'' He swore, more vehemently than he should in her presence. ''Damn it, Delaney, I can't control my reactions when you're around.''

She leaned her forehead against the cold wood. His hands came up and squeezed her shoulders. ''That's the whole problem, isn't it?'' she whispered. ''I make you lose control.''

''Yes.'' He drew her against him. Kissed her hair. ''I'm sorry.''

''I know you are.'' She straightened. ''But it doesn't help, Reed.''

His hand came out to cover hers on the knob. ''Will seeing other men help?''

''I've got to get on with my life,'' she said raggedly.

The words chilled him like water seeping into a No-mex hood in the winter.

Her delicate shoulders were rigid. ''I'm not trying to make you jealous, Reed. But let's not forget that *you* pushed me away. You still refuse to—'' She broke off, clearly having said more than she intended to. ''Look,

I'll be careful not to flaunt my dates. But I won't become a nun just because my social life bothers you.'' She tossed back her head. "Now, let me go, and I'll try to keep my love life from you.''

Oh, that helped. But what could he say? Stepping back, he fisted his hands on his hips. "Go ahead, go.''

She did, without a backward glance.

REED ARRIVED at the Broad and Allen Street firehouse at eight-thirty on Saturday morning. He'd given Tommy's group—the three guys who rode the pumper with Tommy and the firefighter who was replacing him—time to do chores, have coffee and shoot the breeze in an effort to prepare themselves for today. Duke had been right yesterday. These guys were wary of a counseling session, and probably only agreed to let him come down because things were so bad around the firehouse.

He didn't blame them. Wrenching emotions wasn't pleasant. After all, Reed had been avoiding it for eight years.

It's how you lost Delaney.

Don't think about that, he ordered himself as he pulled open the bay door, the unique smells of the garage assaulting him. Gasoline. Burned rubber. The acrid hint of smoke. Sometimes he missed being on the line. Sometimes he longed for the adrenaline rush, the spiked tension that accompanied running into a burning building.

But mostly, the smells tended to trigger memories in him and he had to make a conscious effort not to react. Summoning up that stamina now, he headed for the living quarters. Like most stations, the house sprawled in a one-story layout of kitchen, exercise room and TV room to the right, bunk room and showers to the left.

"Hi, guys," he said as he entered the kitchen.

Three men were seated around a large picnic-style table, one reading the newspaper, one studying a form, another leafing through a manual. Sam Leone was nowhere in sight. No surprise there.

Reed received a few lukewarm hellos. He dropped the doughnuts he'd bought on the table. "Thought you might like some of these."

Carl Roncone gave him a half smile. "Bribes are always welcome."

Returning the grin, Reed joked. "Hey, I need all the help I can get. I know this is tough for you guys."

"Maybe we shouldn't be doin' it, then." This from Jim McCann, the lieutenant on the shift.

After drawing a cup of coffee and taking out a cherry Danish that he didn't want, Reed sat down next to Jim. "You know you gotta get some of this grief out if you want to function, Jimmy." He glanced around. "Where's Sammy?"

"In the bunk room." Jimmy nodded to the back of the firehouse. "He won't do this."

Reed shrugged. "I'm not surprised." Sammy and his family had *not* come in to see him this week. Since Saturday's session had been planned, Reed decided to wait until afterward to try to convince the grieving man he needed help. "Doesn't mean we shouldn't talk, though."

Absolute silence around the table.

"If it's any consolation," Reed said, "I know exactly what you're feeling right now."

"Yeah?" Carl asked sincerely. "You ever lost anybody in your group?"

Reed felt the familiar chill take over his body. It invaded him like an alien virus every time he talked or even thought about what had happened that evening so long ago. "Yeah. I have. And I know how lousy it feels. I also know that if I'd been able to talk about it, get it out, I wouldn't be where I am today." It was the most he'd ever said about his past to anybody in the department. But if his screwed-up life could help these guys...

"I hear ya," Carl said, his tone soft.

"Me, too," Jimmy put in.

From the far side of the table, the third member of the group, the new member, the one who had replaced Tommy, looked on silently.

"What about you, John?" Reed asked.

John Wanikya's chiseled face didn't change a bit. He held himself still, and straight. "I can see the need here. But maybe I shouldn't be involved. I didn't know Tom Leone very well."

"You have to deal with his crew and there'll be a lot of fallout. I'm hoping you'll take part in this session."

"I'll try," John said.

Reed nodded to the doughnuts. "Eat first."

Everybody took doughnuts. They chowed down, sipped coffee and chatted. Jimmy picked up a paper from the table. "Hey, Doc, you can maybe buy our cooperation by helping us with Scarlatta's trivia game questions.'' He smiled. ''They're all psychological and we don't never win.''

Thank you, Jake. Everybody was doing their part for FAN, Reed thought. ''Okay, shoot.''

Jimmy squinted at the paper. ''After the Oklahoma City bombing, the divorce rate among smoke-eaters rose by what?''

''Three hundred percent.'' Reed had studied the cases documented since the tragedy.

''Emergency responders in the bombing have experienced how many suicides?''

''Six.''

''No shit?'' Carl said.

''Firefighters suffer from how many more divorces than the general population?''

Again Reed knew the answer. One and a half as many.

''Last one. A study done in 1997 shows what as the leading cause of death among firefighters?''

Without hesitation, Reed said, ''Heart attacks, usually caused by emotional stress and physical overexertion.''

When they were done with the game, Reed reached into a briefcase he'd set on the floor and pulled out some papers. He passed them around.

''I'd like you to take a few minutes to fill these out. Your responses will give you a chance to think about what you're feeling.'' He smiled. ''Jake's questions should make you understand the need here even better.''

''How come we ain't hearin' the calls?'' Jimmy nodded to the PA system in the ceiling, which broadcast all the city fire alarms. Its ubiquitous staticky background noise was obviously missing.

"Since your engine has been taken out of service for the morning, I asked to have it turned off," Reed said easily. "Didn't want you jumping out of your seats every time you heard a call."

The three men attended to the paper he'd handed out. When it was obvious they were done, Reed said, "All right, we'll go around the room. Feel free to elaborate on any point. Jimmy, will you start?"

The lieutenant, who'd been a teacher, answered the first question, How do you feel right now? "Right now I feel like a jerk."

"Care to explain?"

"I hate these things." He rapped his knuckles on the paper. "We had a principal once who was into this touchy-feely crap and it drove me nuts to have to participate."

"Then I appreciate all the more your cooperation."

Jimmy blushed. "Okay, okay. Right now I feel like somebody ripped out a piece of me."

"In a sense," Reed said, "somebody did. Carl?"

"I feel sad...I miss Tommy."

"We all feel sad, Carl. And sometimes it seems impossible to deal with that sadness." He gave the man a sympathetic smile. "John?"

"I feel resented," he confessed in a strained voice. "Like I felt all my life." As the only Native American in the entire fire department, John Wanikya had warmed up to the others considerably during his stint in the academy, mainly due to Dylan O'Roarke's dogged attention.

"You aren't, man." This from Jimmy. "It's just that you're sleepin' in Tommy's bed, ridin' his position on the truck."

"Doesn't feel any better to me than to you," John said. "But I can see how you'd resent it."

"We resent Tommy being gone. Not you."

They talked for a long time. Each question revealed more and more of the men's emotions. Their pain was a tangible force in the room.

As he'd admitted earlier, Reed knew exactly how they felt.

SAM FELT AS IF HE WAS gonna bust right out of his skin as he made the twenty-minute drive from the station to his house. Rummaging on the dash for his shades—the goddamn summer sun almost blinded him—he found them and stuck them on his head. He lit another butt. His lungs burned from smoking. So what? Maybe it would kill him.

He'd rather be dead than listening to that bull with Macauley, so he'd holed up in the bunk room till he heard Macauley leave. Nobody knew how he felt. Nobody could possibly know. Tommy was part of him. Sam had buried a part of his soul with his little brother.

Briefly he thought about going to a bar and getting smashed. Then he remembered Terry, crying as he turned his back on her again last night. *Please, Sammy,* she'd begged through her tears. *Talk to me. Touch me. Don't shut me out.*

Wanting to bawl like a baby, he'd feigned sleep. He had a good marriage, he loved his wife, adored his kids, but hell, he couldn't share this with them. What was inside him was too big, too black to let out. If he did, he wasn't sure he could control what he'd do. And control was important.

A jazzy red Eclipse was parked in his driveway. He wondered if that lady shrink was here—what was her name, the one the kids kept talking about? They said she had a sports car.

Maybe he *wouldn't* go inside.

Nah, it'd be just like Macauley to call, and then Terry'd be worried if he didn't come home. The shrink had come to the bunk room before he left, tried to talk to him, but Sammy had clammed up. God, he felt closed in. Suffocated. By Macauley. By his crew, who'd played Benedict Arnold and spilled their guts to the psychiatrist today. By his family who kept looking at him as if he should fix things, should fix himself.

Pulling in next to the Mitsubishi, Sam got out of his car and strode into the house through the garage side door. What he found in the kitchen made him see red.

His wife was there, in a cozy little chat with his ex-sister-in-law, the one who had dumped Tommy. *She wants a divorce, Sammy. I can't believe it. She says she hates her life...I found a letter from another guy. She's been cheatin' on me...Jeanine moved out today, buddy. I wanna die.*

Sam slammed the door. ''What the hell is she doin' here?'' he roared at his wife.

Both women jumped. Terry glanced at the clock. ''What are you doing home? I thought—''

He cut her off. ''Macauley cut us loose early.'' He stalked over to the table and braced his hands on it.

Towering over Jeanine, he spat out, "Get out of here, you bitch."

Jeanine's perfect face paled. Her baby blues, which Tommy always said could make him crawl on his hands and knees, filled with tears.

"I said *get out.*"

"Sammy, please." Terry grabbed his hand.

Ruthlessly he shook his wife off.

Jeanine stood. Stepped back as if she were facing a rabid dog. "It's all right, Terry. I'll leave."

Drawing away, Sam said, "Don't ever come back here again." He straightened to his almost five-ten height. "You won't like the consequences if you do."

Tears ran from Jeanine's eyes, Terry started to cry, and Sam felt like a bully. Jeanine gathered her purse and rushed out the door.

The only sounds in the house were the clock ticking from the living room and the soft weeping of his wife. The wife he'd sworn to love and protect. The wife who only wanted the best for him. The wife he was destroying.

It was too much. Losing Tommy. Everybody battering at him to talk about his feelings. And hurting the girl he'd loved since he was sixteen. The pressure cooker inside him was about to burst.

To avoid the explosion, to control it, he turned and strode to the basement door. He had a workshop down there. He'd go pound some nails, maybe put some time in on the storage chest he was making Marcy for her birthday. Whipping open the door, he had enough sense to lock it with the inside latch he and Tommy had put on to keep the kids out when they were finishing up Christmas presents.

Sammy took the stairs quickly. The storm swirled menacingly inside him. He needed to...

When he saw it, he stopped still. He hadn't been down here in a while. The last time had been with his brother. He'd forgotten what Tommy had been working on. Crossing to the table, he gently fingered the hand-carved jewelry box Tommy had been working on for his mother. It was made of light oak, and Tommy had struggled to get all the compartments just right inside. They'd been joking before he died about how Ma would cry when she saw it.

He picked up the box. Smelled its cut-wood scent. Pictured Tommy's grin when he'd said, *Ma's gonna love it, Sammy boy.*

The pressure cooker erupted. Sam lifted his arm and hurled the box across the room. It struck a clock on the wall. Sounds of shattering glass split the silence.

And then Sammy took the rest of the basement apart.

"DR. SHAW?"

Delaney heard the quivering voice on her cell phone. It was a miracle she'd even answered—her phone had been in her bag, which she'd just now retrieved after her dance class.

"Yes, who is this?"

"It's Marcy." Tears. Sobs, really. "Marcy Le—"

"Hi, honey. What's the matter?"

"You said to call. You gave me your cell phone number if I needed you."

Delaney's heartbeat escalated. "What do you need, Marcy?"

"It's Daddy. He's gone wild."

Slipping a short black skirt over her leotard, Delaney slid into shoes as she talked. "Wild?" She headed for the door.

"He's locked himself in the basement. Mom's hysterical, knocking on the door, trying to get him to come up. I found her screaming and crying when I came home from my job."

"Give me your address."

Between sobs, the girl relayed the information.

"I'm on my way, Marcy. Hang in there."

"T.J. He'll be home soon from baseball practice. I don't want him to see them like this."

Delaney hurried out of Dance Dimensions to her car. "I'll be there as soon as I can. Just hang on, Marcy. You don't have to deal with this by yourself."

"Okay."

With a few more words of advice, Delaney clicked off. And immediately punched in Reed's cell phone number.

Please, please let him answer.

"Macauley."

Thank God. "Reed, it's Delaney. I just got a panicky call from Marcy Leone. I'm en route to her house now. Sam's locked himself in the basement and, to quote Marcy, is going wild. Theresa's hysterical and Marcy's crying."

"I'll get right over there, too. I'll take the fire department Jeep. Use the siren."

She felt relief swamp her.

"We'll handle this, Laney."

"I know we will."

She felt better until she arrived at the Leones'. She flew through the open front door and found two sobbing women pounding on the door to the basement.

And from below, the sound of glass shattering, the thunk of furniture and the growl of pain reverberated up the steps.

CHAPTER FIVE

"SAMMY," REED YELLED through the door. "Open up."

No answer.

This was Reed's third attempt to reach Leone, who had barricaded himself in the basement. Time to play dirty. "Your wife and daughter are crying up here. Only you can make that stop." He waited. "Open the door, man. For them."

Still no answer. Reed leaned against the wall and closed his eyes. When he'd arrived at the Leone household, Delaney—she really was a gift from the gods—had led Marcy and Terry into the living room to talk, and Reed had concentrated on Sam. It had gotten quiet downstairs within minutes. Apparently, Sam's rage had been spent. Though it was upsetting to everybody else, Reed was glad the lid had blown. Sam had been suppressing his feelings for too long.

Reed tried one more time. "Let me come down, buddy."

It took some time, but finally Reed heard the click of the inside lock, then noise on the steps; he whipped open the door and went downstairs.

The basement rivaled the aftermath of a tornado. Almost no spot had gone untouched—furniture upended, lamps broken, a workshop table torn apart. The rug was so littered, you could hardly see it. Sammy stood in the midst of the carnage and tracked Reed's gaze; the distraught man let out a disgusted sigh. Throwing up his hands, he turned a stool upright and sank down onto it; from his shirt pocket, he pulled out a pack of cigarettes.

Pretending to survey the mess, Reed mentally listed his options. He swore softly when the solution hit him. He took a deep breath, righted another stool and sat across from Sammy. He nodded at the wreckage. "I did this once, too."

Shock covered the emotionally battered features of the man before him. Sammy was only thirty-four, but his face was that of a man at least a decade older. "You?"

"Yep."

"When?"

"When I lost somebody close to me."

"Don't bullshit me, Macauley."

"I wouldn't do that. When I was a firefighter. Before I left the Fire Department of New York...on my group...a long time ago." Reed felt panic nip at his insides. He nodded to the pack of cigarettes. "Can I have one of those?"

Sam scrutinized him. "You smoke?"

"No, not anymore."

They shared an understanding male chuckle.

"Who died?" Sammy asked after Reed lit up and took a few puffs. God, it tasted awful.

He'd only tell as much as necessary. "Another firefighter. He was like my brother, but we weren't related by blood.''

Eyes clouded, mouth tight, Sammy watched him. Reed could only guess at the raggedness of his own face as he stared back.

Sammy finally said, ''I'm sorry, man.''

''You gotta talk about it, Sam. Gotta get it out.''

''Did you?''

This was going to be tricky. He didn't want to lie.

He said, ''I made mistakes then that I try to get others not to make, Sammy. I made a mess of some things.'' He glanced upstairs. ''I was married. Nobody in Rockford knows that.''

Sam's eyebrows lifted.

''I drove her away. Behaved like a jerk.'' His grin was self-effacing. ''Like you.''

''Any kids?''

''No.'' He had to take in air to continue. ''Sammy, I let loss bring about more loss in my life. You've got a chance to stop it now. But you can't do it on your own, trust me.''

Finishing his cigarette, crushing it out in an ashtray, Sam buried his face in his hands. ''What the hell am I gonna do?''

''Just talk to me, buddy.'' Reed stubbed out the vile-tasting butt and reached over to squeeze Sam's shoulder. ''That'll be a start.''

WHEN REED CAME UP the basement stairs behind Sam, Delaney noticed he had the same grayish cast to his skin as the night he'd made love with her and he'd had the PTSD attack. Usually his white captain's shirt flat-tered his dark complexion. Today it didn't. Delaney saw that his hands were also unsteady. Whatever it was he'd done for Sam down there in the past three hours, it had cost Reed plenty.

He threw her a meaningful look. *Keep it low-key,* it told her.

"Hi, guys," she said cheerfully.

Reed said, "Hi." He nodded to where she stood at the sink, washing up a few dishes. "Doing maid duty?"

"Yeah. Some. I bet Marcy I could beat her at pinball." She rolled her eyes. "The little hustler won. This is my payment."

"Pinball?"

"I took the kids for dinner and a game or two."

"Where's Terry?" Sam asked with a note of panic in his voice.

"Upstairs taking a bath." She smiled kindly at him. "Her sister came over for a while, so the kids and I blew this pop stand."

"Where are they now?" he asked.

"In one of their rooms, watching a rerun of *Buffy the Vampire Slayer*."

Sam looked to Reed, helplessly.

Reed looked to Delaney. She said, "I'd start with Terry. The kids are okay." She gave Sam another understanding smile. "But you should talk to them tonight."

He ducked his head shyly. "Thanks."

In answer, she touched his arm as he passed her by.

When they were alone, Reed stepped closer. Curling his hand around her neck, he squeezed gently.

"Thanks." Something about him seemed a little desperate, as if he needed contact. And he was shaky.

She leaned into him, rested her forehead on his chest. "I'm in for the duration, Doc. You don't have to keep thanking me."

"All the same, I appreciate your dropping everything." He scanned her maroon leotard, skirt and T-shirt that read, I Haven't Lost My Mind; It's Backed Up On a Disk Somewhere. "Where were you?"

"Dance class."

He traced his finger along the scooped neck of the shirt.

She stayed right where she was. "Did Sam talk?"

"Yep. He agreed to come in Monday."

"Good. Have him bring the kids. I already told them we'd get together next week. They can see me at the same time."

"Maybe we can meet with the whole family first. Get that ball rolling."

"Sounds good."

"I'll set it up." Visibly summoning strength, he stepped back. She knew that he was trying to distance himself. She said, "I made coffee. Want some?"

He crossed to the Leones' window and stared out over the setting sun. "No." He sighed. "Everything seems so normal. Pretty yard. Nice house. Damn, life is tough."

Leaning against the Formica table, she studied him. "You ever want all this, Reed? The nice house, the two kids, the *normal?*"

"Actually, I had it." It seemed to slip out, without

his meaning to say it. "Except for the kids. We were trying to have them."

Delaney felt as if somebody had tilted her world upside down. The fact that she didn't know any of this threw her. It hurt. "You've been married?"

He nodded. "For eight years. We divorced when I was about your age."

"Why?"

"A hundred reasons."

She came closer, grasped his arm. "Talk to me, Reed."

He shook his head. "Nothing to say, really. As Jake's trivia game pointed out this week, firefighters have a seventy-five percent divorce rate."

"Did you divorce because of the PTSD?"

He straightened. "Yes. I've been telling you, it ruins lives. The condition is hardest on the family."

"You told Sam about this, didn't you."

"Some. I did what I had to do."

"You can tell me all of it, Reed," she repeated.

"You just don't understand." It came out harsh, angry.

Refusing to be intimidated, she smoothed his bare arm, reveling in how his muscles bunched under her hand. They were alone, but in the house of clients. Professional behavior needed to prevail. So she just slid her hand down, linked their fingers, brought them to her mouth and kissed his.

The tiny, tender gesture seemed to soften him. He sighed deeply. "You're so strong," he said. She didn't know what that meant. He raised his eyes to the ceiling. "All right, maybe I can try—"

A ringing interrupted him. Startled her. Her gaze, and his, dropped to her bag on the table. She sighed. "I have to answer that. It might be an emergency."

He didn't let go of her hand, just held on, so she awkwardly fished inside, got her phone and clicked it on. "Delaney Shaw."

A sexy male baritone answered, "Ah, the elusive doctor."

"Eric." Oh, my God, she'd forgotten. She had a date with Eric Scanlon tonight.

"You remember me, but not our date. I'm wounded."

"I'm sorry. I forgot about tonight. Where are you?"

"Right at this moment, I'm at your house. On the porch."

"Oh, Lord."

She felt Reed stiffen. His hand clenched hers.

"No harm done. It's a lovely night. I thought we'd go up to the canal for dinner and eat outside. Then maybe go dancing at my country club."

She locked her gaze with Reed's. After a long, intense stare, she asked, "Can you hold on a second, Eric?"

"Sure."

She clicked the privacy button and held Reed's gaze.

"You have a date with Scanlon tonight." He said it tonelessly. Resignedly.

"Yes." When he offered no more, she tried to remain silent. But even knowing she'd resolved not to do this, knowing she'd supposedly given up on them, she said, anyway, "Tell me not to go."

"*What?*"

"Tell me not to go to dinner on the canal. Tell me not to go dancing at his club."

Reed's mouth formed a thin, angry slash in his face.

"Tell me you won't let me go out with another man."

Warm brown eyes flared lethally hot. "Damn you, Delaney." He let go of her hand. Gave her his back. "Go to Scanlon. Sleep with him. Put us both out of our misery."

It was as if he'd slapped her. She recoiled. But she fought back the tears that threatened. Her childhood-learned reaction to rejection surfaced. *Toughen up, Delaney.* She spoke briefly to Eric, telling him she'd be right home, clicked off the phone, then picked up her bag.

Without facing Reed again, she said, "I'll tell the kids goodbye." Saying no more, she headed into the living room, leaving him staring out of the normal house at the normal yard on the stupidly normal Saturday night.

I LOST SOMEBODY...GO TO BED with Scanlon...he wasn't related by blood...put us both out of our misery.

Feeling bereft and so angry he could spit nails, Reed was ready to tear his own basement apart when he pulled into his driveway an hour later. For that reason, he sat in his car and stared at his Victorian house with its peaked roof, gabled corners and attic that he'd yet to refurbish. He'd spent years therapeutically restoring his home in the long hours he chose to be alone.

Alone. He pounded the steering wheel, shooting pain

up his arm. Talking to Sammy and arguing with Delaney meshed in his brain, leaving him cold.

And nauseated.

Shit! No! He wouldn't let this happen again. He wouldn't. All he had to do was get control. Stop letting his feelings surface like this, then the attacks could be kept at bay. If he could just push everybody out of his life, he could get back to normal. Or what had become normal for him.

Flinging open the Blazer's door, he hopped out. Dizziness hit him. Made him grip the car handle. He took deep breaths, hoping to steady himself. Straightening, he stumbled up the sidewalk to the front door. He managed to unlock it, cursing his shaky fingers.

When he turned on the overhead foyer light, it flickered and snapped. Then the world exploded and Reed was thrust back into another time and place...

"Macauley," Marx shouted, "get back here with us...get out of the way."

Reed stood where he was, in front of his men, staring at a short guy, wiry as hell with frenzied eyes. Later he'd found out the man's name was Jack Cummings.

"Look, you're a smoke-eater, aren't you...? Come on, buddy, we can..."

The sound exploded first in his ears and he fell to the ground. More sounds and pain shooting through his leg. Reed grasped for his knee, and his hand came away wet and sticky. Then the world faded away....

"REED!" SOMEONE WAS shaking him. He didn't move.

"Call 911."

"Honey, I'm a paramedic and you have a master's

degree in anatomy and physiology. Let's take a look at him first.''

The voices were familiar. But he couldn't place them. He moved, and pain splintered from his head to every nerve ending in his body. "Reed. Wake up. It's Dylan and Beth.''

Dylan and Beth? They didn't belong here. They were part of…he moaned when he tried to lift his head.

"Here, use this on his temple. He's bleeding.''

"Yes, ma'am.''

Reed felt a cold compress on his head. It hurt like hell. He tried to bat it away but couldn't raise his arm.

"I think we should go to the hospital, Dylan.''

"No.'' Reed forced himself to speak. To move, despite the jackhammer beating in his brain. "No hospital.'' Turning his head to the side, he managed to open his eyes. "I'm all right.''

The O'Roarkes were both kneeling over him, their faces shadowed with worry. "Reed?'' Beth's hand brushed back his hair.

"I'm okay.'' He was staring up at the antique lamp he'd hung himself.

"What happened?'' Dylan asked.

"I must have fallen.''

"Fallen?'' Beth's tone was incredulous.

"You been drinkin' this early on a Saturday night, old man?''

Reed ignored Dylan's question. "What time is it?''

"About eight.''

He'd left the Leones at seven. The last thing he remembered was feeling as if somebody had driven a stake through his heart on the way home.

Sammy...telling him a few details...the words he'd had with Delaney. Then, when he'd walked in the house, he'd been ambushed by another PTSD attack.

He struggled to sit up.

"Hold on a second, buddy." Dylan pressed the cloth onto his forehead, slid an arm around his neck and assisted him.

Reed managed to sit up, though his stomach roiled with the movement.

"You should go to Emergency, Reed." Beth's delicate features were frowning.

He shook his head, which forced him to close his eyes. "I just have a bump."

"You got a goose egg the size of a plum." Dylan took his pulse, checked his eyes. "But you look okay. I'd worry about a concussion. Any nausea?"

"No," he lied, and tried to stand. That made the pain intensify, his stomach lurch and the dizziness return. Still, helped by Beth and Dylan, he managed to get to the couch.

Once seated, he asked, "What are you doing here?"

"We got lucky and managed to con Sandy and Connie—" two former recruits who were crazy about Timmy O'Roarke "—into baby-sitting. We came over to drag you to the movies with us." Beth exchanged a quick look with Dylan. "When we pulled in, your front door was wide open and the lights were on. We found you kissing that fancy hardwood floor you put in."

He scrambled for an explanation. "I must have slipped on something."

Beth frowned down at her lightweight summer sundress, scanned's Dylan's shorts and T-shirt. It was mild and perfectly dry outside.

"Look, I appreciate your concern, but I'm fine." He smiled. "Not up to a movie, though. You guys go ahead."

"I don't think we should leave you alone." Beth's eyes were clouded. She didn't take injuries to those she cared about lightly.

Dylan said, "Reed, we're here for you. We know you've been under a strain with Tommy's death and the deluge of calls from firefighters and their families afterward. How about if we stick around, get a pizza and have a few beers?" He waited a heartbeat. "And talk."

Oh, sure. Talking was what had brought this all on. "Not tonight, Dyl. But thanks."

Beth said, "Dylan, wait for me in the car."

"Huh?"

"I want to talk to Reed alone, hotshot."

"Jeez, Lizzy, subtlety isn't your strong point." He stood. "Listen to her, Reed. She's been there."

When Dylan left, Beth sat close to him on the couch. "Talk to me."

"Beth I…" God, his head was pounding.

"Is it Delaney Shaw? Don't deny it, I know it is."

Weak from the attack, from the confrontation with Delaney, from everything else in his life, he said, "Yeah, it's Delaney Shaw."

"I think she's perfect for you."

Reed laughed, though it hurt. "Given your wedded bliss with Boy Wonder, you would."

"Let her in, Reed."

He almost had tonight, and look what happened. "No can do, Beth."

"Why?"

"I can't talk about it."

"Remember when I couldn't talk about Tim and Janey." Beth's husband and child had died twenty years ago in a freak accident. "You got me to talk about it. *That* got me to Dylan."

"This is different."

"And pigs fly." He stared at her. She watched him with that assessing, I'm-gonna-fix-a-problem stare. Finally she said, "All right, just promise me you'll think about opening up to somebody."

"I promise I'll think about it."

Glancing around the room, she said, "I don't like leaving you here alone, especially with that bump."

"I've got medical training, Beth. I'll be fine."

"Physician, heal thyself." Standing, Beth leaned over and kissed his cheek. "You deserve what Dylan and I have, Reed."

I can't risk it. I can't risk her. I have to remember what I do to people. Have done to those I love. But he just smiled. And promised to call their cell phone if he needed them. From the couch, he watched Beth leave.

He was glad she was gone.

He was lonely as hell.

Lying back on the pillows, he wondered what Delaney was doing. Was dinner on the canal good? Did she go dancing at the country club? Later, would she take Reed's advice and sleep with Scanlon?

Damn, now his heart hurt worse than his head.

DELANEY WAS STARING out the window at the back of the academy, where a few of the staff sipped coffee before beginning their day. Over the weekend, Reed had left a message on her service to meet him at his office at nine; they'd talk about strategy and be ready for the Leone family when the four of them arrived at ten.

It was after nine, and he still wasn't at work. Ben had seen her waiting in the hall and let her into the office. He seemed as concerned as she that Dr. Macauley was late.

Maybe he had a wild weekend.

Because the thought turned her stomach, she pushed it away. *Her* weekend—well, her Saturday night—had been surprisingly enjoyable. Eric Scanlon had proved to be an entertaining dinner companion and an awesome dancer. They'd danced at his country club after a terrific dinner at Alladin's. For several hours, she didn't think about Reed, didn't wonder how he was spending his Saturday night.

"Well, this must be my lucky day."

She pivoted to find Eric behind her, handsome and tanned and very male. "Hello, Captain Scanlon," she said flirtatiously. "I was just thinking about you."

"I like hearing that." His smile was pure Robert Redford. "I was looking for Reed, but you're a lot prettier."

"I certainly hope so." She laughed. So did he. One thing she'd learned during their evening together was how easy he was to be with.

"I had a terrific time Saturday," he said honestly.

"I did, too." Surrounded by Reed's things, she could still say it and mean it. That was good.

Eric crossed to her and stood by the window, too. "Given any thought to my invitation to sail this weekend?"

The handsome captain had asked her to go up to Toronto on his boat, a big cabin cruiser. She'd hesitated, wondering if the invitation meant a physical commitment she wasn't ready to make. The thought of another man touching her intimately was unpleasant, though she'd responded nicely enough to his goodnight kiss.

"I'm not sure I can get away for the whole weekend."

He reached out and tucked a strand of hair behind her ear. The gesture felt personal. "I—"

"Am I interrupting something?"

Letting his hand drop to her shoulder and stay there long enough for Reed to see it from the doorway, Eric turned. "You've got lousy timing, Macauley. I was just about to get Dr. Shaw here to agree to a jaunt to Toronto on the *Lovely Lady* this weekend."

"Ah, well, be careful of this one, Dr. Shaw." Reed's tone seemed teasing, but she wondered if Eric caught the underlying tension in it. "That cruiser's a regular love boat."

Reed came into the room and faced them fully. When she got a good look at him, Delaney's mouth dropped open. Over his right temple was a gauze pad that didn't quite cover a purplish bump. "Reed, what happened to you?"

His hand went to his injury. "Ran into a door in the dark, I'm afraid."

Something about his tone...

He glanced at the clock. "Sorry to steal her away from you, Scanlon, but we have to talk before our appointment at ten."

Eric said, "No problem. I came to give you these recruit profiles for the September class." He set down a folder on Reed's desk and turned back to Delaney. "Stop by and see me before you leave? I'll buy you coffee."

She caught the slight stiffening in Reed's jaw. She said, "Sure."

When Eric left, Reed closed the door. Leaning against it, in a deceptively casual pose, he said silkily, "Toronto on his boat? It looks like you took my advice." Then crudely, he added, "Is the captain as good in bed as he says he is?"

REED CURSED THE WORDS as soon as they were out of his mouth. He didn't need this. After almost capitulating Saturday, and then the attack, he'd resolved that he'd made the right decision with this woman. "Never mind, I don't want to know."

She walked over to him, looking like a fresh spring flower in a green linen suit, white blouse and sassy yellow scarf. Her black hair cascaded around her shoulders and down her back. Up close, she seemed rested, too. Happy. Reaching out, she ran a finger around his bandage. "What really happened?"

"Nothing you need to concern yourself with."

"Was it another flashback?"

His shoulders sagged. "Yes."

"Reed, you—"

"Leave it alone, Delaney." He shook his head. "We have work to do before the Leones arrive." He drew away and took a seat behind his desk, giving her no choice but to sit across from him, far away, in a chair.

"Fine." Her tone was resigned. She sat down and dug a pen out of her briefcase. Crossing her legs, she looked up at him, pen poised above the paper. There was pain in her eyes but she was all professional now.

Her emotion was hard to ignore, but he tried. "I think we should get straight to the point with Sam and his family. Say we know they're all hurting, they need to talk to us, to one another, and get everything out."

"I wonder how Sam will react. Saturday, the kids indicated they were too afraid to tell him how they really feel."

"Has he done something to them? Hit them?"

"No, nothing physical. But he's got a terrible temper, one that he's been fairly successful at keeping in check. Since his brother's death, he loses it easily. The kids don't have a clue how to act when he gets that mad, let alone burden him with their own grief."

"Men hide behind anger."

She glanced meaningfully at his bandage. "Or they evade reality." When he didn't comment, she asked, "Should we mention that the kids are afraid?"

"Maybe." He rubbed his eyes. He'd had a constant headache all weekend, had taken painkillers for it, which had led to his oversleeping this morning.

"I'm here to help, Reed," she said gently.

He'd expected recriminations from his earlier out-of-line remark, from his blatant rejection and obscene advice Saturday. "Are you always this generous to people who hurt you?"

She gave him a half smile. "No. Just you."

The unconditional nature of the response kicked him in the gut. But she looked so innocent sitting there with the sun shining in behind her. She was so lovely and young. He couldn't drag her into his nightmares. Destroy her with them. Remembering what he'd done to his wife, then witnessing what Sammy was doing to Theresa, confirmed in Reed's mind that he'd had made the right decision.

"Reed?"

"Let's go with our instinct. Tread lightly, but see where everything takes us."

"All right." She peered at him intently. "Are you okay?"

"I'm fine, Delaney. Just fine."

"THANKS FOR COMING IN, everybody," Reed said easily, never belying the fact that he was in pain. From the pinched lines around his mouth and eyes, Delaney could tell he had a headache. He nodded to her. "Dr. Shaw and I think it's a good idea if we started with each of you talking about how you're coping with daily life, now that the reality of Tommy's death has settled in."

Dressed in jeans and an RFD T-shirt, Sam sat stiffly, his face a stone mask, his eyes bloodshot. Theresa, also dressed casually, was more composed than the last time Delaney had seen her. The kids looked scared to death.

Surprising them all, Sam spoke up. "I've been a

bastard to live with. Makin' everybody's daily life hell.''

Reed settled back into his chair. "Why is that, Sam?"

"It...I...hurt...inside. I can't stand it." He started to rise, but Theresa grasped his arm.

"It's okay to hurt, Sammy."

Hesitating, he gripped her hand. "I can't dump this on you. It's my pain."

Reed's gaze snapped to Delaney's briefly, then he looked away.

"Don't you think I can feel your pain, too?" Theresa said. "It's worse because you don't share it."

"Daddy, we loved Uncle Tommy, too," Marcy put in. Her blond hair was pulled back in a ponytail, making her look very young. "We're also very sad."

Sam's fatherly instincts came to the surface. "I know you are, princess."

Delaney asked, "Marcy, what do you need from your father now?"

"To talk to us. To be with us."

Bingo! The psychologist in her breathed a sigh of relief. "T.J.?"

Staring at his sneakers, he fiddled with the tie on his sleeveless sweatshirt. "I want Dad back the way he was before..." The fourteen-year-old's voice cracked.

Reed waited, but T.J. couldn't go on. "Well, we're all in agreement here. Let's hash some of this out right now." He glanced at the clock. "Just for about a half hour. Then we'll split up. Dr. Shaw can take you—" he nodded to Marcy and T.J. "—for a while." He looked at the couple. "I'll meet with you two."

Everybody nodded, though Sam white-knuckled the chair.

Delaney sighed and sat back to watch Reed Macauley work his magic.

SAM FORCED HIMSELF to listen. To participate. But every word Terry said, every suggestion Macauley made, scraped his already-raw nerves. He'd lost his brother and turned into a lousy father and husband, something he'd always been halfway decent at.

His wife was talking. "All I know is I'm not letting Tommy's death ruin our lives."

Emotion threatened to overcome him. Sam ruthlessly pushed it back. "It won't, Terry, I promise."

She hesitated. "You get so mad."

An excuse, he needed an excuse. "I hated seeing you with that bitch Jeanine."

Reed, who'd been quiet since the kids left, raised his brows. "Who's Jeanine?"

"Tommy's wife."

"Tommy's fu—" He caught himself. "Tommy's freakin' *ex-wife*."

"That's right," Reed said thoughtfully. "I met her at the funeral."

"She didn't have no right to be there."

Again, Terry reached out for his arm. "Honey, that's un-Christian."

Sam wanted to hoot with laughter. Where the hell had God been when Tommy went down? "I don't give a shit, Terry. I don't want that woman in my house."

Straightening, Terry faced him, like she always did when she was gonna defy him. "It's my house, too."

"Yeah, you payin' the mortgage?"

Right before his eyes, his wife crumbled. "You've never said anything like that to me before," she told him tearfully. "We agreed I'd stay home with the kids."

Reed waited. When Sam said nothing, he made a comment. "We say hurtful things when we're in pain. Do you mean that, Sam? Are you resentful that Terry isn't working outside the home?"

Damn it! Sam sat back. Closed his eyes. He couldn't do anything right. He wished like hell for a cigarette. He wished like hell he was anywhere else but here. He wished he was...

"Sam?"

"I don't mean it about the work. I mean it about that whore."

"I think maybe we should talk about Jeanine." Macauley was playing the psychologist big-time today.

"No way!" Sam sat forward. "We talk about her, I'm outta here."

For a minute Reed just watched him. "All right, there's plenty of other stuff to discuss."

Sam checked the clock. God, wasn't this over yet?

CHAPTER SIX

"DR. SHAW, YOU GONNA PLAY Murder Marauders with me?" T. J. Leone looked like a typical adolescent, standing before her in sagging khaki shorts and a T-shirt with the rock band Phish on the front. For the first FAN social outing, all the firefighter families were enjoying the top floor of the teenage wonderland called Jillian's, a converted warehouse with exposed pipes and cement floors. The place had a sports video area and billiards downstairs, with bowling and a dance area. Upstairs—where they all were now—was a gargantuan room full of video and arcade games. Amid the rock music blaring from the speaker system and the pings and whirs of video games, Delaney could hardly hear herself think.

She nodded to the game across the way. "Get over there, kiddo, and get in line. I'm gonna blow you away."

The boy smiled and hustled to wait in line for Jillian's most popular video game. Delaney grinned, watching him behave like a normal kid.

"He's a dork, Dr. Shaw. All guys are."

Circling, Delaney found Marcy had come up to her. In a denim miniskirt and multicolored T-shirt, Marcy—at sixteen—already turned heads. Over the girl's shoulder, Delaney caught sight of Reed across the room on the roped-off fifteen-by-fifteen-foot putting green, a golf club in his hands. Dressed like all the firefighters who came today, in the navy RFD T-shirt and jeans, he looked heartbreakingly young. Ben pointed out something in Reed's stance, Jake concurred and they laughed at whatever Reed shot back. Chief Talbot was also with them, chuckling and keeping a watchful eye on his granddaughter. They were all good men, solid, strong and full of integrity. "*All* men are dorks?" Delaney asked her young friend.

"Well, not older men."

He's old enough to be your father...or is that why you're seeing him?

Ruthlessly Delaney quelled the memory, as she'd done with most thoughts of the good captain. Instead, she concentrated on Marcy. "You checking out somebody older, Marce?" she asked.

Marcy's gaze trailed to a table full of rookies. One of them, Trevor Tully—kept glancing in their direction, then looking away fast. Oh, Lord, Delaney was going to have to deal with this, too.

"Maybe," Marcy said. "Some of those new guys are way cool." Her light blue eyes sparkled when she turned to Delaney. "I love your overalls."

Delaney had thrown on lightweight denim overalls and a deep red tank top, along with navy canvas sneakers. "Got 'em at the Express."

"My favorite store!"

"Yeah? Maybe we can go there sometime together." Staring at the golfers, Delaney thought, *And I can talk to you about the dangers of falling for older men.*

She dragged her gaze from Reed and focused on Eric Scanlon, who'd come tonight, too, because she'd told him she'd be here. He was in front of the batting cage, waiting to slug away at machine-pitched balls. They'd had an interesting few weeks together. She had indeed gone to Toronto with him on his boat, but she'd made it clear she liked to slip into relationships gradually, not dive in headfirst.

Except with Reed.

Forget Reed.

Eric lifted his drink to his lips and scanned the room. He caught her eye and waved. She smiled back. She liked being with him, liked his sense of humor. Maybe the rest would come.

"Think Daddy's having a good time?" Marcy asked.

Delaney's gaze swung to Sam, who sat in the Daytona U.S.A. car and drove the simulated stock car with maniacal concentration. Carl Roncone and his new girlfriend and Terry Leone looked on. Sam's face was animated, yet there was something forced about it; at least he'd come today with his family and was trying to enjoy himself. Reed was making progress with him, even if it wasn't by leaps and bounds. In cases like Sam's, it was usually three steps forward, two back. "He seems to be having fun, honey."

Marcy bit her lip. "I hope so." A young girl joined the foursome. "Oh, there's Suzanne Roncone. Her dad's on my dad's shift. I'm gonna go talk to her."

Delaney smiled as she sat down on one of the hundreds of stools perched around the room at tall tables. FAN was working. Part of her goal was to get kids of firefighters together so they could share some common experiences—and fears. As she watched Marcy dart away, she resolved to ask Reed, in one of the cold, stiff planning sessions, which were the only times they saw each other these days, about starting a firefighters' children's group.

"Enjoying yourself, Delaney?"

Delaney looked up into the kind but hard-to-read face of Beth O' Roarke; without an invitation, the woman sat down on the adjacent stool. Delaney had bumped into Beth several times since beginning FAN, and had worked with her on the fitness schedule. The other woman had been friendly but seemed to be…searching for something in their brief discussions. If Chelsea hadn't loved Beth like another sister, Delaney would be worried about Beth's unusual behavior. She looked harmless enough today in a shiny green sleeveless shirt and matching shorts.

"I'm having a ball. I can't wait to get on the Marauder."

Glancing over at the game, Beth rolled her eyes.

"Dylan still champ?" Delaney asked.

She nodded and gazed across the room to where Dylan pinged and ponged with absolute glee. "Looks that way." Her grin was so loving, so unconditional, it made Delaney's heart twist in her chest. "He's a kid trapped in a man's body."

"Everybody loves Dylan."

"I know." Beth threw a purposeful glance to the other side of the room. "Everybody loves Reed, too."

Delaney's radar went up. She fiddled with her soda. "He's a great guy to work with," she said neutrally.

"He's a great guy *period.*"

Delaney waited.

Beth sipped her coffee, then lifted her eyes to Delaney. "Worth waiting for, I think."

Shocked, Delaney gripped her glass. "Are you trying to tell me something, Beth?"

Rumor had it that Beth was one of the most private people at the academy. Dylan O'Roarke had blown her world apart with his single-minded pursuit of her, but Chelsea said Beth still didn't open up easily to others. But now Beth said, "Reed and I are kindred spirits, Delaney. Nobody knows him well, but I know more, sense more, about him than most people."

"You spend a lot of time with him."

Beth shrugged. "I try. When he'll let me. Which isn't often."

Join the club.

"Why are you telling *me* this?" Delaney asked bluntly.

Beth stared hard at Delaney as if she was deciding whether to trust her. Her eyes were smoky green, like her outfit, and right now were tinged with resolve. "Because I think you'd be good for Reed."

Obviously the woman knew something. No sense in dissembling. "Yeah, well, so do I. But since Dr. Macauley doesn't agree, it's a moot point."

"Don't give up on him, Delaney."

She shook her head. "I appreciate your kindness and your concern for Reed, but you don't know what's gone on. He's frozen me out, Beth. It's over."

Scanning the room, Delaney caught sight of Eric about to enter the batting cage. He turned and motioned her over. Beating the hell out of a few balls sounded perfect to Delaney right now. "Excuse me. I'm going to play with Eric."

She'd taken only a step away when from behind her she heard Beth O'Roarke mumble, "It's not over till it's over, girl. Believe me, I know."

REED SANK DOWN ONTO a chair in the corner and surveyed the hottest spot for kids in Rockford. The place appealed to adults, too. O'Roarke's idea to have FAN's first social event here was fantastic. The man was a kid at heart, hobbling from machine to machine on his crutches, and playing with all the smoke-eaters' children.

Delaney was a kid at heart, too, he thought as he watched her through the wires of the batting cage smash the ball whipped at her by the machine. Dressed in those overalls and red top, she looked about eighteen. Scanlon adjusted her stance—her hips, actually—and Reed had to turn away.

What did he expect? He'd practically handed her over to the guy on a silver platter. Bereft at the thought, Reed swallowed hard, sipped his coffee and studied two guys from Engine Six play table hockey.

Ben plopped down next to him. "I can't keep up with my kids," he said, nodding to Francey.

Smiling, Reed tracked his gaze and saw Francey at the virtual skateboard machine. Watching was her brother Nicky. A huge screen magnified an aggressive downhill skater, while the player controlled the action on a real skateboard attached to the mechanism. "Francey feeling okay?"

"Are you kidding? Seven months pregnant and she's doing all those games like she was in competition. Nicky eggs her on. And she's still working out. It drives me crazy."

"She knows what she's doing."

Ben harrumphed and signaled the waitress to order a drink.

Reed scowled as he stared across the room.

"What?"

"Sam Leone just ducked outside."

"Probably to steal a smoke."

"Maybe."

"How's he doing?" Ben asked, lazing back in his chair.

"On the surface, good. I know I'm making some progress, but not as much as I'd like. I've got a feeling things aren't quite what they seem with him."

"Are they ever?" Ben asked. "Which reminds me. I need a favor."

Reed shifted his gaze to Ben, whose face was still flushed from competing with his daughter. "Sure, anything."

"I know you're busy with FAN and the Leones, but I wish you'd make some time to talk to Joe Santori. He's still smarting over Francey. Though he denies it till the cows come home and puts up a front, her pregnancy is tough for him."

"I'd be glad to see him, Ben." Reed's gaze strayed to the batting cage. "Do men ever win that battle?"

"What battle?"

"Getting over a woman they love. One they can't have."

Ben quieted. Reed glanced at him. Ben stared straight ahead at his wife, who was now playing a *Star Wars* game with her son and daughter. "No, you never do, Reed. And you can waste years thinking you will. Suddenly you end up alone wondering how your life got that way." Seeming to come out of a trance, Ben cocked his head. "What's going on with you these days? You look like you've lost your best friend."

I feel like I have. "Nope. But you know what? I need a date."

"A date?"

"Yeah. My social life sucks."

"Want Dee to fix you up? She's got a lot of single friends."

Reed stood abruptly and stared over at the far side of the room. Delaney must have beat Scanlon, as she jumped up and down and thrust a fist into the air. Taking advantage of the situation, Scanlon grabbed her and swung her around. Then he tugged her close, his hands in all that glorious hair of hers.

"No need to fix me up." Reed rarely dated anyone whom he hadn't known and liked for a long time. Since he knew he wasn't the settling-down type, he didn't want to mislead anyone. "I know just what to do."

Okay, Pandora, he thought. *Time to take back control.*

Heading across the room, Reed grew more determined. As he neared the batting cage, he felt his body tense. With a casual salute to Delaney and Scanlon, he bypassed them and found the alcove that housed the phones. In minutes, he was connected. A pretty feminine voice answered on the third ring.

"Ellen, this is Reed Macauley. I was wondering if you were busy tomorrow night."

When he'd arranged to see Ellen Marshall, the sociology professor from the college who understood he wasn't making promises, and who didn't seem to want to make any herself, he hung up the phone and started back to his table. Delaney was now ensconced in a simulated Harley-Davidson and running the track like a competitor. Scanlon stood behind her with his hands on her shoulders.

Reed swallowed hard and averted his gaze as he passed them by.

"THEY ARE ABSOLUTELY driving me crazy!" Francey said as she entered the back room of Chelsea's gym. Dressed in gray sweat shorts and an oversize T-shirt to cover her stomach, she dropped down onto the floor disgustedly.

FAN was in full swing, and just a week after its kickoff at Jillian's, participation was high. Tonight was the first family fitness outing, and a good crowd had shown up at The Weight Room, which Chelsea had reserved for firefighters and their families.

"Who's driving you crazy?" Beth asked, winking at Delaney and sitting down beside her friend.

Beth and Delaney had been preparing to lead an aerobics class and Delaney needed to warm up. Tucking back stray tendrils escaping the knot on top of her head, she crossed to the barre and kept her eye on the two women.

"My father. And my husband. You'd think no one on this planet ever had a baby." She clasped her arms around her rounded belly. "Dad practically blew a gasket when I tried to show T. J. Leone the proper way to lift a barbell."

Beth said dryly, "How dare they be concerned for their son and grandson." She extended her legs, clad in black tights, out in front of her, and bent over to stretch her calves.

"Do you know you're having a boy?" Delaney asked as she lifted her leg up to the barre and bent over it.

"I'd better have a boy. They'll smother a girl."

"Are we talking about the men in your life, dear?" From behind Francey, Diana Cordaro appeared in the doorway. Wearing a hot pink leotard and tights with a matching netting over it, she looked like she belonged on the cover of a fitness magazine.

Accompanying her was Theresa Leone, who smiled at the byplay. In plain blue gym shorts and white T-shirt, with her hair clipped away from her face, Theresa looked tired and a little drawn. But she'd sworn to Reed things were better at home with Sam. T.J. and Marcy had said the same thing to Delaney in the two additional counseling sessions they'd had.

Reed was still concerned about the family, though, and so was Delaney. Sammy seemed just a little bit too *adjusted*. Right now he was avidly lifting weights with the guys in the gym and pushing himself hard.

Francey grinned up at Diana. "Hi, Mom."

Diana smiled lovingly at her daughter. Delaney knew Francey had not grown up with Diana in the house, and things had been tense when Diana returned to Rockford. Now they seemed to have a relationship made in heaven. Delaney was jealous as hell of it.

Diana crossed to her daughter and gracefully dropped onto the floor. She kissed Francey's head and patted her tummy.

For a minute, Delaney was overcome by the tenderness of the gesture. She'd never had a mother who fussed over her that way, or a father like Ben Cordaro to worry about what she did. But she hoped someday she'd have a man to caress her pregnant belly with the same awe and joy Diana displayed.

As Theresa Leone joined them on the floor and cooed over the baby-to-be, touching Francey's stomach, too, Delaney had a flash of an image—Reed's big, masculine hand tenderly caressing her swollen stomach. The vision was so real, she closed her eyes and let it play out....

He'd tug up her shirt and put his ear on her bare skin. He'd say something sweet to his child, then kiss her exposed belly. When he raised his head, his eyes would be shining with love instead of their usual wariness....

"Laney, where are you?" She opened her eyes to find Chelsea standing before her. Sweaty, wiping her face with a towel, her sister frowned. "Lane?"

Delaney shrugged. "I was daydreaming." Without meaning to, she glanced to the group of women on the floor.

Following her gaze, Chelsea frowned. "About that?"

"Maybe."

"You have friends, honey."

"It's not that," Delaney confessed to her older sister, feeling vulnerable and raw. Removing her leg from the barre, she did a few *demi pliés*. "It's the...baby."

"Ohmigod, what happened to you? Did you get hit over the head or something?"

No, I got hit big-time by a stubborn-headed firefighter.

"Very funny." Angry at her weakness, Delaney straightened, turned from the barre and started to walk away. Class wouldn't start for ten minutes. Maybe she could get some air.

Chelsea caught up to her inside the larger gym area. "Delaney, wait."

She turned to her sister. "I never said I didn't want kids, Chels."

"Honey, I'm sorry. I was just teasing."

Delaney wilted. "I know you were. I didn't mean to snap." She refused to search the big gym for Reed, who'd been working out on the treadmill when Delaney had retreated to the back room a half hour ago. "My nerves are frayed lately."

"Isn't it going well with Eric?"

"Eric?"

"Yeah, the guy you've been seeing for the last few weeks. Reed says you're quite an item."

She went rigid. "You talk to Reed about me?"

Brows raised, Chelsea stared at her as if she'd just spit on the floor. "Well, no. He told Jake, as a matter of fact." Chelsea plopped her hands on her hips. "What's going on with you, kid?"

"Nothing." Delaney started to panic. She didn't

want to be questioned about what she was doing with Eric Scanlon, where it was headed. Or worse, about her depression over Reed. "Look, I left something in my car. I'll be right back."

Without another word, Delaney hurried out of the gym. Dusk was falling and the air was warm and heavy. Sweat beaded on her chest and shoulders, exposed by the white tank-top leotard she wore. Studying her ballet-slippered feet, she wasn't looking where she was going and bumped into somebody coming the other way. "Oh, sorry."

"Delaney?" Strong hands she'd recognize even blindfolded grasped her gently. His voice was all but a caress.

She looked up. "Reed! Sorry. I wasn't watching where I was going."

His hands still on her bare skin, he asked, "Are you leaving already?"

"No, I'm teaching the aerobics class with Beth at eight."

He frowned. "It's close to."

"I know. I…um…need something from my car." She noticed how he was dressed. A red-and-black checked shirt, sleeves rolled up, black jeans and Docksides on his feet. And he smelled wonderful. Male. Sexy. "*You're* leaving?"

"Yes." Dropping his hands, he stepped back, fished in his pocket and pulled out the keys.

She stared at him.

He stared at her.

"Where are you going?" God, she didn't want to know. Shouldn't have asked.

He angled his freshly shaven chin and held her gaze sharply. "I have a date."

Her stomach felt as if she'd fallen three stories in an elevator. "I see. Mind if I ask with whom?"

Staring beyond her shoulder, he expelled a heavy breath. "Ellen Marshall."

"Ah, the sociology professor."

"Yes."

"Well, you'd better get going, then."

"How's Eric?" His face was blank, but his eyes flared.

She stared him down. Damn if she'd be cowered. "Good. He's helping me get over you, Reed."

Reed's face paled, making Delaney sick inside. She didn't want to hurt him. But, hell, when he'd told her to sleep with Eric, it had broken her heart.

"It's what you wanted, isn't it?"

His mouth thinned and she saw his fist clench the keys. "It's exactly what I wanted. Now, if you'll excuse me. I don't want to keep Ellen waiting."

Delaney's eyes stung. "By all means, don't keep Ellen waiting." As she circled around him, she tried to call out "Goodbye," but she couldn't get the word past the lump in her throat.

REED TUGGED THE PRETTY WOMAN in his arms closer on the dance floor of the *Spirit of Rockford,* a dinner-dance boat the RFD had hired out for a social event at the end of July, two weeks after the excursion to Jillian's. Even with the short notice, forty couples had signed up. FAN was working well for most of the RFD families. Reed still had his doubts about the Leones, though. The counseling sessions had been…odd. He questioned whether he was really getting through to the guy. Sam seemed happy enough tonight, though, and Theresa was a knockout.

"Reed?"

He pushed away work thoughts. "You look very nice, Ellen," he whispered against her short brown hair. It smelled like the perfume his wife used to wear.

She shrugged her shoulders, the gold lamé of her long tunic rippling softly. She did look nice in the outfit, with her hair and makeup done to perfection.

Reed was furious that he couldn't make himself respond to her tonight. They'd had a nice low-key, sexually satisfying relationship off and on for years—neither wanting to take it further. But since his night with Delaney, he couldn't summon interest in sleeping with Ellen.

Ellen was giving it her best, though. She inched closer, aligning her body provocatively with his. "Thank you. Perhaps I can convince you to come into my house tonight."

He tightened his grasp on her. "Hmm." He was seriously considering giving it another try when he caught sight of the long black shiny skirt he'd tried to keep his eyes off all night. Looking up, he watched Delaney glide across the floor with Scanlon, who was dressed in a black tux—a little too fancy for Reed's taste. Most of the guys wore suits, like the lightweight gray pinstripe Reed had chosen.

With her pretty skirt, Delaney had worn a tight, strapless black top, over which she'd thrown a see-through net shawl. It kept slipping off her shoulders, and Scanlon kept tugging it back up. Any excuse to touch her bare skin.

Feeling the ice around his heart crack a bit more, Reed turned himself and his partner away from the other couple. Seeing Delaney with another man was really getting to him tonight. He shouldn't have had that last glass of wine after dinner; his defenses were down.

When the song ended, he escorted Ellen back to the table they were sharing with the O'Roarkes, the Cordaros and Chase Talbot and a pretty dark-haired woman named Nancy. As Reed and Ellen sat, the band struck up some oldies. Reed glanced over to see that Eric and Delaney had not left the floor. Instead, they fell into step together like Fred Astaire and Ginger Rogers.

First the twist…which tugged at the poor excuse for a top that she wore; she'd forsaken the shawl altogether, exposing her creamy shoulders and back.

Next came "Rock Around the Clock."

"Hey, they can swing," Dylan said, watching the couple.

Talbot chuckled. "In our day, it was called the jitterbug. Want to dance, Nancy?"

His date accepted.

Ben smiled at his wife. "What about you, babe?"

Diana rose, a vision in a beaded top and long black skirt. "Of course."

Dylan pouted and sipped an after-dinner drink. "I can't dance."

Beth said, "Poor baby. Want to go up on the deck and neck?"

"I can't climb the freakin' stairs."

During a break in the music, Delaney laughed at something Scanlon said and fell into his arms; Reed stood. "Well, I can climb the stairs. Let's go get some air, Ellen."

Recognizing the implication, Ellen's smile was all feminine. "I'd love to."

Reed vowed to enjoy the star-speckled sky and the soft breeze that swept off Lake Ontario. As he strolled along the deck with Ellen, he pulled her close, his arm tight around her. She was shorter than Delaney, a little curvier but...

Damn. He needed some distance from Delaney. He couldn't spend so much time with her. Counseling sessions during the week were one thing. But social activities on top of those were wreaking havoc with his self-control. He'd have to talk to her about it, work something else out. Maybe if she wasn't always around, within touching distance...

"Penny for your thoughts?"

They stopped at the railing and looked out over the calm water, lapping against the boat. He said, "The night's nice, isn't it."

"Hmm. July's been hot for Rockford."

"Are you having a good time?"

She lifted her face and smiled at him. "Did we come up here to neck, Reed?"

He smiled back and lowered his head. Her lips were soft and warm. Her body melted into his. She was all feminine curves against him so he drew her closer. Deepened the kiss.

And felt nothing.

He drew back. *Damn it.*

Not knowing what to say, he was precluded from commenting by a gruff male bark about ten feet away. "What do you mean, you don't want to?"

A soft female mumble.

Ellen buried her face in his chest. "This is private, Reed. We should move."

Reed set her away from him. "Ellen, go down below. I think this is one of my patients. I need to…check it out."

When she left, Reed walked down in the couple's direction.

"You been raggin' on me about bein' closer. I wanna be close."

"Not out here, Sammy. This isn't private."

"I want my wife."

Tears.

"Shit."

"Please, Sammy. You've had too much to drink."

"Haven't had enough…" Sam stumbled out of the shadows. Right into Reed.

"Hi, Sammy. I was just coming over to tell you guys you could be heard by anybody passing by here."

The man's suit was rumpled. His tie was off, his shirt was askew. And right before Reed's eyes, in the light from the full moon and few strategically placed lamps on deck, Sam's mask fell back into place. "Yeah? Sorry."

Theresa appeared at his side. "Hello, Dr. Macauley."

"Theresa. Everything okay here?"

"Yeah, yeah, it's fine." Answering for her, Sam

grasped his wife's hand. "We're goin' back down to find Carl and his new girlfriend."

Theresa wouldn't meet Reed's gaze.

Sam said, "Don't worry, Doc, everything's cool."

Reed nodded, stuck his hands in his pockets and watched the Leones walk away.

Nothing was cool with them.

CHAPTER SEVEN

"DAMN IT TO HELL!" Reed slammed his office door, threw his notebook on his desk and paced back and forth. "Son of a bitch." He let loose with every obscenity he could think of. When, *when* would he stop hurting this woman? He could barely stand what he was doing to her.

He'd *had* to tell her their contact needed limits. But he had no idea it would hurt her so much. She'd stared up at him with confusion in those blue eyes after he'd gotten the first bumbling statement out....

"Why?" she'd asked, swallowing hard, wrapping her arms around her slender waist. Today she'd worn a sundress the color of orange Popsicles.

Because he wanted to grab her to him so badly—tell her he cared, he needed her—he had no choice but to be honest. "It's too hard for me to see you this much."

She shook her head, the action sending that wild mane tumbling down her back. "What does that tell you, Reed?" Her voice had quivered on his name.

"Nothing. It tells me *nothing*. Look, I know I have no right to ask this of you. To ask anything of you. But I can't deal with seeing you so much. We have to work together here—" he indicated the academy conference room where they'd been discussing FAN

"—but I thought maybe we could alternate the outside activities we participate in. Tell me which ones you're going to and I'll choose the others."

She bit her lip. Her eyes moistened and she looked away.

"I'm sorry," he said starkly. "But I just don't know what else to do. How else to control this stuff inside me."

Still she'd said nothing more.

Desperate, he'd resorted to pleading. Gently, he grasped her upper arms. "If you care about me as much as you say, please do this for me, Laney."

He thought she'd argue. Push him. Deep down, he'd *wanted* her to do that.

"All right. You win. It's getting to me, too, seeing you so much." Without saying more, she walked out of his life. Again.

He was barely calm, seated at his desk an hour later, rereading the same rookie profile for the third time, when Ben skidded to a halt in the doorway.

"I thought you'd like to know," Ben said when Reed looked up from his desk. The usually calm battalion chief's demeanor was agitated. "There's a nasty two-alarm fire. A church near Dutch Towers."

"The senior citizens complex?"

Ben nodded.

"Do any residents go there?" Reed knew the Dutch Towers occupants were favorites of the fire department, especially Quint/Midi Twelve.

"Yeah, and today there was a Get Out and Gab meeting in the church hall." He drew in a deep breath. "Reed, Engine Seventeen was called."

Reed took off his wire-rimmed glasses and scowled.

"It's the first interior attack the group's had since Tommy went down."

Standing, Reed grabbed his cell phone and pager. "I'm coming." On the way out of the offices, he called to the staff secretary to cancel his last appointment of the day and followed Ben down the hall and out of the academy. Without discussing it, they jumped into Ben's chief's vehicle and spun out of the parking lot.

Ben said, "We have to get there fast. Talbot's at another fire on the other side of the city. The other BC on duty is at a bad car accident." In fires, it was customary for a battalion chief to run the operation. "Jimmy McCann's a good man, but he doesn't have enough experience for this."

Once on the road, Ben pressed two buttons; a siren began to blare and lights flashed overhead. They startled Reed. The car darted in and out of traffic, sending its occupants first to the left, then to the right. Reed held on to the panic strap and tried to salvage his sanity. His heart began to thump in his chest. The speed, the sound and the flashing lights transported him back eight years. To the last truck he'd ridden, the last fire he'd fought.

The day Crash Marx was killed.

Reaching down, he rubbed his leg. The scar was there, reminding him of his inadequacy. As the staticky report of the site came over the radio, Reed ordered himself to think about something else.

"I hope all the old people get out." He thought for a minute. "Joey Santori's grandparents live there, don't they?"

"Yep. And Joey's on duty. He's at the church."

"Firefighters are exiting the building...." Reed caught the end of the radio blurb.

"Damn!" Ben said.

"What? I wasn't listening carefully."

"The church is fully involved." Ben took a corner fast. "After the firefighters got inside to put out the fire, some kind of gas stove in the fellowship hall exploded and they were all ordered out. They're mounting an exterior attack now."

Reed wondered if Sam was safe. If Sam wanted to be safe. This last thought had been bothering Reed for a long time. He would have shared it with Ben, but they pulled up to the site in seconds and stopped on a dime.

As they bolted out of the car and hurried over to Incident Command, the smell hit him first—burning wood, gas, the cloying scent of thick, ugly smoke. It was charcoal gray and billowing out the side and the roof like giant thunderclouds.

Jimmy McCann stood at the makeshift command post with a radio at his ear. "I'm here, Jimmy." Ben took the radio the man offered to him. "Fill me in."

Reed noted the relief on the young lieutenant's face. "The church was smokin' when we got here, but it wasn't fully involved, so I didn't call for another alarm right away. We laid a three-incher, and a couple of hand lines, then Engine Six ventilated the roof."

"Sounds right to me," Ben said encouragingly.

"We got the occupants out." He nodded to the side. Reed saw a group of older people huddled near a truck. One was a small, frail woman he recognized as Adelaide Lowe, a resident Jake had come to know after he'd saved her cat in a fire. Next to Mrs. Lowe was a couple Reed had seen at the hospital the night of Tommy's death when Joey got hurt. "Ben," he said, "Those two are Santori's grandparents."

Ben nodded. "They seem okay." He faced Jimmy. "Go on."

"Just as the church was cleared, there was this big boom on the far side, where the church hall is." He pointed to a drawing spread out on the hood of a fire department vehicle. "Flames went up right away. I ordered the crews out. Called for other trucks. Quint/Midi Twelve just got here and is setting up the aerial on the west side of the building."

"Good work, Jimmy." Ben stared down at the drawing. Reed came around to the side and studied the sketchy floor plan somebody had made. "Everybody out?" he asked.

"Yeah, I think so."

Ben made contact with the Quint's officer by radio. Several firefighters trudged around the end of the building. One of them jogged toward Incident Command. Too grimy to be recognized from a distance, the guy was on top of them before Reed realized it was John Wanikya.

His dark features were set in a scowl. He looked worriedly at Ben, then Reed. "Um, Chief, I..." He sighed. Shook himself, as if he was making some kind of decision. "Oh, hell. Leone isn't out, sir."

"Isn't out?" Jim and Ben asked at once.

Reed stiffened. Somehow he knew what was coming.

"We had plenty of time. All the old people were evacuated. We were on the other side of the building when the explosion hit. The lieutenant ordered us over the radios to get the hell out of there, and we were following out the hose. I...I glanced behind me. Sammy didn't come. I ran back, grabbed his arm." Wanikya's black gaze darted worriedly from Ben to Reed. "He shook me off. Said he had to see something...he had to go to the sanctuary of the church...he knew what would be there...." The young rookie swallowed hard.

Reed and Ben exchanged worried looks.

"What did he say would be there, John?" Reed asked.

"Tommy. He said Tommy would be in the sanctuary."

SAM STUMBLED OVER a two-by-four, but righted himself by grasping the doorway to the narthex, the outer part of the sanctuary. Over the static of the radio he carried, he could hear another authoritative voice order him to evacuate immediately. It sounded like Chief Ben Cordaro.

He turned the radio off.

The smoke was gray in here. Other trucks had arrived—he'd heard the sirens. The Red Devil would be out soon—gone back to hell, waiting to spring up and devour somebody else at a moment's notice. Sammy knew he wasn't in any jeopardy, at least for today. Hell, he felt invincible. For the first time since Tommy...left... he felt good. In control.

He smiled into his SCBA mask. It was going to be

okay. Everything was going to be okay now. Tommy would be here. This time, he'd be able to get to his brother. He had another chance.

Pops. Snaps. Something fell behind him. He turned around. As if in slow motion, as if watching from somebody else's body, Sammy saw part of the narthex wall collapse. Quickening his pace, he hurried toward the sanctuary. Reached the doors. Opened them. Light poured in from the stained glass windows along each side of the pews, creating an eerie spectrum through the thin curtain of smoke. Squinting, he could see a figure up by the altar. He opened his mouth, yelled "Tommy," but the sound was muffled by the SCBA gear. An alarm beeped and his face mask vibrated, signaling he was out of air, anyway. What did it matter? What did anything matter anymore?

Determined, he dragged off his headgear. Now he could yell. Man, he'd whip the kid's butt for this one. "Tommy!" he barked, hurrying down the aisle. Scraps of charred wood crunched under his feet as he strode toward the altar. "Tommy, I'm here...."

"I'M GOING IN." Reed turned to the rookie on Ben's left. "Tully, get me some gear. Quick."

Ben glanced over at him, brow furrowed, jaw rigid. Sweat beaded his brow and face, just like Reed's. This close, the fire was an inferno. "You sure? You haven't been on the line in a while."

"It's like riding a bike." He refused to give in to the fear pummeling at his insides for release. "The fire's almost under control. I won't be in any danger."

"If the fire's gonna be out soon, you don't need to

go in." Ben shifted the radio and studied Reed. "You don't look so hot, Macauley."

Two firefighters jogged up to the command post. One was Peter Huff, a guy on Chelsea's crew. "Hey Chief, there's a guy walkin' around in there."

"Yeah, we just heard."

Joe Santori removed his headgear and wiped his brow. "Want me to go in?"

"No, go see how your grandparents are."

Joe's eyes widened. "My grandparents are here?"

"They're okay." Ben pointed to the truck. "You got your hard head from them."

Peter socked Joe in the arm. "Let's go see." He dragged Joe over with an arm slung around his shoulders. Brother to brother.

Tully returned. Reed kicked off his shoes, stepped into pants and bunker boots and whipped on a coat. The weight of the coat, once like a second skin, seemed ludicrously heavy. Each boot felt clunky, unnatural. Assembling the SCBA mask, his fingers fumbled. He finally said, "I should have seen this. I should have done more for Leone. I'm not letting somebody else die because I couldn't..." He stopped himself, met Ben's puzzled gaze.

"Reed, you couldn't have saved Tommy."

"Tommy?" What the hell was Cordaro talking about?

"You just said you're not letting anybody else die. Tommy was on his way to the hospital by the time you got to the Jay Street fire."

"Yeah. Sure. I know that." Reed struggled for a way to divert Ben. "Look, Ben, somebody's got to get Leone. You're the ranking officer at the site and need to stay at the command post. I'm next in line.'' He didn't give Ben more of a chance to object. Or to ask him to explain his earlier slip. Instead he jogged toward the building.

A blast of heat—he'd forgotten this particular detail—hit him in the face when he stepped inside. From the floor-plan drawing, he'd picked this entrance because the sanctuary was off to the right, then straight ahead. It was only about thirty feet to the inner core of the church. Surely Reed could make that without panicking.

Smoke curtailed his sight. He remembered how good he'd gotten at finding his way blindly in any kind of haze. With each step he took, his breathing sounded more labored in the air pack. He went through the doorway. It got hotter, so he dropped to the floor. It would take longer, but he knew the drill, knew how to keep himself safe. Sweat poured from him, soaking his uniform inside the turnout gear. Crawling now, he made his way to the sanctuary. Once there, he saw a figure at the front, looking upward, surrounded by swirls of light pooling in through the colorful windows. Reed tracked Sammy's gaze. He was staring up at a huge cross dangling oddly on the charred wall. Suddenly, the smoke and heat abated dramatically; the crew had ventilated again. That meant the fire was probably out. Reed stood and approached the altar, his feet crunching on fallen debris.

Fists clenched, head up—without his face mask on—Sammy stared at the battered body of Jesus. He coughed intermittently.

"Sammy," Reed called out from behind so as not to spook him.

Sam didn't turn. He continued to gaze upward. Then Reed heard him yell, *"Answer me."* He coughed again.

"Sam?"

"I said *answer me.* Damn you, God. Where is he?"

Behind them, Reed heard the pounding of feet. In his peripheral vision, he could see that other firefighters had entered the building. They were looking for their brother.

Up close, Reed touched Sam's arm. He said gently, "Sammy, Tom's not here. He's gone."

Sam looked over at him. Without the headgear, Reed could see him clearly—the glazed eyes, the puzzled expression on his face. "Gone?" More sputtering from the smoke.

"Tommy's dead, Sam."

"I saw him." His head whipped from side to side. "Up here. Standing."

"No, Sam, you didn't," Reed said gently.

"I—" he broke off coughing "—didn't?"

"No. Let's go outside and talk about it."

"Macauley, you need any help?" a voice asked from behind. He thought it was Roncone.

"Sam, your crew's with me. You're spooking them. You need to come out of the church with them. With me."

"Without Tommy?"

"Yeah, buddy. I'm sorry. Without Tommy."

And then, Reed saw tears leak from Sammy's eyes. His shoulders sagged and he seemed to crumple into himself as he collapsed like a rag doll to the floor.

MUCH LIKE HE HAD the night Tommy died, Sam looked around the ER cubicle; the smells of antiseptic and lemon wax on the floor and the sounds of a hospital—phone ringing, PA system crackling—brought him back to that nightmare almost two months ago. And once again, like a little kid, he wished he could crawl under the covers of the narrow, starched bed where he lay and never come out. What the hell had happened to him tonight?

He thought he'd seen Tommy. But Tommy was dead. He *knew* that. Sam closed his eyes, trying to make sense of it all.

A light knock sounded on the door.

"Yeah, it's open. I ain't goin' nowhere."

Reed Macauley walked in; his face was composed, but behind his wire-rimmed glasses, his eyes were troubled. "At least you haven't lost your sense of humor."

"Nope," Sam said lightly. "I just lost my mind."

Reed smiled. Took a seat on the chair.

"You look like hell," he told the shrink. The guy did—his face was lined with weariness and something else Sam recognized but couldn't name.

"Yeah, well, I'm not used to traipsing into burning buildings to rescue the likes of you, Leone. I'm too old for this."

Sam didn't react to the jibe. "Am I, Reed?"

"What? Losing your mind?"

"Uh-huh."

The psychologist sat forward, clasping his hands between his legs. "I don't think so, Sammy. But you've got a problem that goes deeper than the delusion you had tonight."

"Okay, I'm ready to admit that. But..." He clenched his fists. It went against everything he was inside, had taught himself to be to stay alive, to say this out loud. "Can we talk about what happened tonight for a minute?"

"Music to my ears, buddy. Shoot."

"I thought I saw Tommy in there."

"I know you did."

"Why?"

"Extreme stress, I'd guess. Intolerable grief." Reed sighed and looked him straight in the eye. "There are several clinical terms for it, but you get the gist."

Lying back on the pillow, he closed his eyes. "I *am* nuts."

"No, you need help with your grief." Reed hesitated. "And your survivor guilt, if my guess is right."

"What do you mean? I've heard of that but don't know exactly what it is."

"You didn't care if you came out of that fire, Sammy. Because Tommy's dead."

Bingo!

"You endangered your crew."

No response.

"And what about your family? What would they have done if you didn't make it through the fire?"

Reed was right about everything. Frantic at hearing his soul bared by somebody else, Sammy scanned the room. "I know all that." He drew in a deep breath. "I need help."

"Good. That's the first step. Admit it."

Sam thought hard, tried to get his hands around this thing. "I need to tell the chief about this."

"Cordaro already knows. He'll report it to Talbot."

Sam asked, "You tell him?"

"I didn't have to. But I would have. The guys on your group all saw it, Sammy."

"You know what? I don't even give a shit."

"Well, buddy, when you hit bottom that often happens."

He felt his gut twist. "But I gotta tell Terry myself."

"Good idea."

His whole body sagged. "God, I've been rotten to her."

Reed got a faraway look in his eyes. "We often take out our problems on the people we love, the women especially." Reed pulled a cell phone out of his shirt pocket. "Here, call her. Tell her to come and get you. You got a clean bill of health from that pretty little doctor."

Sam took the cell phone. "Okay." He started to punch in his number, then hesitated. "What'll happen to me, Reed?"

"You won't be on the line for a while, Sam. But you'll get compensation. Your mind got hurt on the job, and the RFD's gonna give you time to fix it."

"Thanks." Sam smiled. "Now, leave me be while I call my woman."

Reed left, and Sam sank back into the pillows.

It was one of the hardest things he ever had to do, but he punched out his home number.

It was time to let his wife in.

DEPRESSION HUNG LIKE a heavy weight on Reed's shoulders as he opened the door to his house and entered the foyer. He knew he could have another flash-back, but right now—like Sammy, he thought, ironi-cally—he didn't much care. Had he hit bottom, too? The grandfather clock he'd bought at an estate sale chimed nine times as he closed the door, and his stom-ach growled. He hadn't eaten since breakfast. For a minute he just stood in the stillness of the house that had become both his haven and his jail. Except for the clock and the hum of the refrigerator, it was quiet. Too quiet. He headed for the kitchen to order a pizza. As he reached the window seat, he stopped.

Images swam before him. Delaney—even when she was upset and vulnerable she was so strong, straight-ening her shoulders to take the newest rejection from him. Sammy—at the church, looking for his brother. Later, in the hospital, admitting he needed help.

Had Reed done anything right in the last few months?

He said out loud, "Feeling sorry for yourself isn't gonna help."

Neither would opening the window seat and taking out Pandora's box. But he did it, anyway. He needed Delaney tonight, so much he was afraid he'd end up calling her. He'd probably confess all, then drag her down into the morass of grief and guilt he felt every time he allowed himself to think about that night eight years ago. In a couple weeks it would be the anniver-sary of that horrible night.

To avoid thoughts of the date—he knew only too well what happened to PTSD sufferers on anniversa-ries—he took the box and went to sit in the living room. Comfortably ensconced on a chair, he ran his hand over the silk cover and let himself think about Delaney—how pretty her eyes got when she laughed, how cute she looked in that dance gear he'd seen her in a few times, how husky her voice got during sex. He removed the lid.

He'd added a few more items since the last time he'd wallowed in this ritual. God, maybe *he* was losing his mind. Smiling despite his negative thoughts, he picked up the small music box he'd found at an antique sale the weekend he realized he'd be working with her. A delicately carved figurine—a ballerina—perched on top, with long black hair like hers and vivid blue eyes. As he lifted the top, the strains of Debussy tinkled in the quiet of his house. Right at that moment he'd give his life savings to see Delaney dance.

Over the music, around the pleasant memories, thoughts intruded.

I gotta tell Terry myself.... Now, get out of here while I call my woman.

Physician heal thyself.

Weary, he lay his head back on the tapestry chair he'd spent way too much money on. He'd spent way too much money on this whole house.

Because he had nothing else to spend it on.

He looked down. Except for a few paltry gifts she'd never see. He shook his head. *God, you're pathetic, Macauley.*

The doorbell rang, interrupting his self-flagellation, and startling him so the top of the box fell to the floor. Could it be her? Could he have conjured her with his thoughts? It was possible she'd found out about today and come to see how he was doing. He remembered her response to his latest dictum....

All right, Reed, You win. I'm done with you.

But still, she'd said it before—and come, anyway. Carefully setting the box on the floor next to his chair, he crossed to the foyer and whipped open the door.

It wasn't Delaney.

It was Ben Cordaro.

Reed couldn't remember the last time he'd been more disappointed.

What does that tell you, Reed? she'd said to him today.

The night was chilly, though stars punctuated the sky; Ben wore a light canvas jacket and had changed into jeans and a T-shirt. In his hands he carried a huge carton of what smelled like Chinese food. Reed's stomach growled again.

"You got some beer, I got some chow."

Reed stared at Ben. "What are you doing here?"

Ben shrugged.

He nodded to the carton. "Why don't you take that home to your bride?"

"My bride's having a baby shower for my daughter at our place." Ben took in a deep breath and Reed noticed his dark eyes were troubled. "I'd be here, anyway. I wanna talk to you, Macauley, but I'm starved." Shouldering his way inside, he stopped dead in the foyer and looked around. "You know, I've never been in your house."

"Haven't you?"

"Nope. You do a pretty good imitation of a hermit, Doc."

"I'll throw a gala next month," Reed said dryly, causing Ben to tell him to do something anatomically impossible.

Reed laughed. The camaraderie felt good.

It felt even better over beer and moo goo gai pan as they sat in the carved oak booth area of his kitchen with the food spread out before them, eating from cartons. They talked about little things—the house and how Reed had worked on it, Ben's own carpentry endeavors, Ben's obsession with keeping Francey safe. Anything but Sam Leone and, Reed suspected, Ben's concern over Reed's behavior tonight. He ditched his misgivings, though, and savored the soya sauce flavor and ice-cold beer. The hell with everything else.

When they'd finished their meal and Reed had gotten them two more Michelobs, Ben sat back and stretched his legs out in front of him. "All right. I gotta say a coupla things."

Reed leaned back in his side of the booth, too, and mirrored Ben's position. "I thought you might."

"First, I talked to Talbot about Leone before I came over. We're suspending him indefinitely, with pay, until he gets some things straightened out. After a few weeks, we'll reassess the situation. In an official capacity, I have to ask you this. Do you think you can help him?"

The heavy weight of responsibility invaded Reed's calm mood. "I'm not sure." He stared out the window. It was dark and he couldn't see the new wooden lawn furniture he'd ordered. "I haven't done such a great job so far."

"Reed, his baby brother died in a fire. It's only been

a couple of months. You're not a miracle worker. I strongly suspect he'd be a lot worse off if he hadn't been working with you."

A voice from the past intruded. The first shrink he'd seen. *How could you have saved them? You're not a miracle worker.*

"Has he made any progress at all?" Ben asked.

Automatically, Reed started to say no. Then he remembered Sammy's face earlier in the hospital. He was ready to heal. And Reed had been partly responsible for that. "He seems to want to get better. He realizes he has a problem." Reed shook his head. "Seeing dead people in a church, in front of your whole crew, will wake you up, I guess."

Ben chuckled. "Okay. Think about it. If you don't believe you can help him anymore, we'll get somebody else. But for the record, my money's on you."

Old habits surfaced. Reed didn't want anybody counting on him. Not this time. "I'm not a good bet, Ben."

Cordaro stared at him intently. In the little ways he'd let himself know the man, Reed had picked up that Ben Cordaro was astute in reading people. Right now his black eyes were knowing. "Why do you think that, Reed?"

"What?"

"So little of yourself?"

His heart started to pound.

"And before you answer, maybe this'll make you tell me the truth. Something else was goin' on with you at that fire tonight. I'd stake my life on it. I'm not leaving here tonight without finding out what it is."

Reed stared at him blankly.

"What's been doggin' you for the whole time you been at the academy?"

"You asking me in an official capacity, Chief?"

Real fury came over Ben's face. "No, jerk, as your friend." Then, as suddenly as it came, the anger drained away. Ben sat forward. "That's it, isn't it? You don't want any friends. You don't let anybody close. Beth and I have talked about it." He leaned forward. "Why do you keep yourself off limits to people who care about you?"

Reed opened his mouth to deny the allegation. To weasel his way out of any disclosure. But he saw Sam's tortured face. *I need help...I need to talk to somebody...* and then Delaney's *Let me in, Reed, I can help...*

Suddenly Reed was very tired. Of being alone. Of slamming the door on his emotions and using most of his energy to keep it shut. Maybe if he took his cue from Sam, let a little out, he'd be better. He said starkly, "Eight years ago, in the last fire I fought, I lost...like Sammy, only..."

Ben's swarthy complexion paled. "You lost a brother?"

"No."

"Another smoke-eater?"

"Yes. My best friend." Reed saw the scene before him and began to sweat. His stomach began to churn. Abruptly, he stood and crossed to the window. Opened it. Took in some air. "I can't talk about it, Ben. It brings back...too much."

Ben was silent for a long time. Then he asked, "It's

what you meant tonight when you said you wouldn't lose anybody else.''

His back still to his friend, Reed nodded. The air, the distance, and Ben's calm voice held back the demons. He stood at the window, silently, for a long time, letting the night soothe him.

Then he felt a hand on his shoulder. At first he started. Other than a few macho bear hugs initiated by O'Roarke, he couldn't remember the last time he'd let some other guy touch him. But he allowed Ben's hand remain where it was.

''Do you think losing your buddy was your fault?'' Ben asked softly.

''In my head, no. I can't shake the idea outta my heart, though.''

Ben said nothing. Just stared out at the lawn with him.

Finally Reed said, ''Like you guessed, I've purposely closed others out since then.'' He smiled sadly. ''Or I've tried to. You and Beth O'Roarke... you both got a stubborn streak a mile wide. You snuck in a few times.''

''Good,'' Ben said.

Reed glanced over at him, but then looked away. ''No, it's not good, Ben.'' The dimly lit kitchen allowed him to go further. ''I suffer from post traumatic stress disorder. I've had some episodes because of you two.''

''No shit?''

''No shit.'' He sighed. ''Not as intense like with...''

''With?''

Reed shook his head. ''I can't. I can't get into *that*

now.'' Again the waiting. "I don't know how much you know about it...PTSD comes in degrees. Cranky, grouchy episodes and anxiety attacks are milder symptoms of it.''

"You sayin' Beth and I are responsible for your bad moods, Macauley? 'Cause if you are, I'm not buying it.''

Reed welcomed the levity. "Now, why doesn't that surprise me?''

Ben walked back to the table. Returned with their beers and handed one to Reed. They sipped silently. "Anything I can do?''

Was there? Reed shook his head.

"You ever get help with this?''

"Some. Not enough.''

"Is there somebody...you know...a woman, maybe...you could talk to about this?''

Reed's radar went up. "What are you getting at?''

Ben ducked his head. "Look, I'd be lost without Dee to talk to.'' He harrumphed. "Oh, hell, it's pretty obvious a certain little psychologist is interested in you, Macauley. Maybe you could let her in.''

Reed shook his head at the irony. It was exactly what his weak side wanted. To talk to Delaney. To lean on her. "I...she's...I can't drag her into this.''

"She's strong, I think. Like Dee.''

Was she? "Maybe.''

Ben sighed. And then, like the smart leader he was, he didn't preach, he didn't push. He just put his hand back on Reed's shoulder and said, "Well, *I'm* here for you, buddy, if you ever need me.''

"Thanks,'' Reed said simply.

He wasn't sorry he'd opened up to his friend. If the nightmares came later as a result of this lapse, he'd deal with them. Right now, the comfort he was feeling seemed worth it.

CHAPTER EIGHT

REED FOUND HIMSELF immobilized—at least where Delaney was concerned—the following week. He hadn't seen her since he'd told her they couldn't spend time together, though they'd communicated twice early in the week through e-mail about which FAN functions she planned to attend. They'd also had one stilted conversation on the phone, where he'd informed her how Sam had behaved at the fire. He did know she'd missed an appointment with the Leones because she wasn't feeling well. By Friday, he sat staring at the phone, calling himself a coward and thinking about Ben's words—*Is there somebody…you know…a woman, maybe…you could tell about this?*

Unable to take that step, he got up from his desk and left the office. He stopped at the bulletin board in the hall just outside to read Jake's firefighter questions posted there.

And froze. He was sure Jake had picked the topic out of thin air, but the questions were more meaningful for Reed than Jake could ever know. The top of the sheet read All About Arson and the questions were multiple choice. Reed knew he'd score a hundred on this, after all the research he'd done.

First asked was, Which of the five reasons for arson—pyromania, revenge, vanity, juvenile and fraud—is the most common? The correct answer—revenge.

The typical arsonist is all but which of the following? Male. Young. Below average intelligence. Black. Has a criminal history. The typical arsonist, Reed knew, was Caucasian.

Question three. What percentage of fire injuries are caused by arson? It was fourteen percent and the second-leading cause of fire deaths. What percentage of arsonists are arrested? Fifteen percent. And an odd statistic, How many church fires are arson-originated? Twenty-five percent. A final grim point that would intrigue Delaney. In 1998 what percentage of arson fires were set by juveniles? Reed was pretty sure it was half.

To escape the reminders, he turned around and bumped into Beth O'Roarke. This time, she chased away the nightmares.

"Are you all right? You look like you've seen a ghost."

"No, I'm fine."

Frowning with concern, she studied him. "Got a second, then?" she finally asked.

Apprehension nipped at his insides. "Of course. Come in." When they were seated he asked, "What's wrong?"

"I hope nothing. Have you seen Delaney this week?"

"No."

"She was supposed to work with the fitness classes Tuesday and Thursday nights; she called about the first one and said she didn't feel well, but she just didn't show up last night." Beth hesitated. "Reed, this is so unlike her."

"Yes, it is. She's reliable as hell." He frowned. "She missed an appointment yesterday, too."

Theresa Leone had called him in the afternoon. At the time he'd thought little of it....

"Dr. Macauley, it's Theresa Leone. I've been trying to reach Dr. Shaw. She left a message on our machine about rescheduling the kids' sessions yesterday, but we can't contact her."

"Did you call her office?" he'd asked.

"Yes, one of her partners said she had a mild case of the flu, but he was sure she'd get back to me. When she didn't, Marcy used her cell phone number, but no one answers." Theresa was obviously upset. "I wouldn't bother you, but everybody's nervous here...about Sammy's...incident at the fire, and about his not working..." Theresa didn't finish.

"I'm sure Dr. Shaw wouldn't cancel unless she had to. I'll get in touch with her and call you back. Meanwhile, I can see the kids today if they need to talk."

Despite her obvious concern, Theresa chuckled. "No offense, Dr. Macauley, but they think Dr. Shaw walks on water."

Reed smiled. "No offense taken. I'll get back to you..."

"Reed?" Beth's face had darkened. "What's going on?"

He returned to the present. "Delaney canceled the Leone kids yesterday. Her partner says she's not feeling well." He punched out her cell phone number and waited.

"This is Delaney Shaw. Please leave a message."

"Laney, it's Reed." He could hear the edge in his voice, struggled to quell his concern. "Call me as soon as you get this message." He clicked off.

"No answer?"

He shook his head. "What does Chelsea say?" he asked Beth.

"Chelsea and Jake took some furlough to go to the Adirondacks."

"That's right." He dialed Delaney's office. The secretary told him her partners were in session and one of them would return his call. "I'm going to find Scanlon. They've been pretty tight. Maybe he knows something."

Beth checked her watch. "I've got a meeting in five minutes. Let me know what you find out." She stood, too, and he followed her out. When they got just outside the door, she snagged his sleeve. Her expression held a hint of amusement. "Oh, and Macauley?"

"Yeah?"

"Don't try to tell me again there's nothing going on with you and Delaney." Beth left without giving him the chance to respond.

Too concerned to be embarrassed, Reed strode down the hallway and found Eric Scanlon working at his computer. The guy looked young, even though he was almost a decade older than Reed.

"Eric, have you seen Delaney this week?" he asked from the doorway.

Swiveling around his chair, Scanlon narrowed his eyes on Reed. "No. She wasn't feeling well, so she canceled our date tonight."

"Did you talk to her today?"

He shook his head. "She left a message on my machine yesterday." He crossed his arms over his chest. "Why?"

"No reason."

"Planning to trespass, Macauley?"

That spiked his temper. If Delaney belonged to anybody... "I didn't know she was your property."

"Leave her alone," Scanlon said knowingly. "You just upset her."

Reed bit back a retort. Now wasn't the time for territorial disputes. Deciding to deal with Scanlon's possessiveness later, Reed pivoted and headed back to his office.

He tried her cell phone twice more, and by noon, gave up and strode out of the academy. As he drove to her house, he had to fight back the trepidation gnawing at his insides. He couldn't afford to lose control now. Something was wrong here, he was certain.

There was no sign of life when he arrived at the small suburban house nestled in the trees. The bad feeling had escalated to real concern by the time he pulled up in front of the house. Hurrying out of the car, he peeked through the little window in front of the garage door. Her blue Miata was jauntily parked in the big space. He frowned. She was home.

The worry became foreboding; he crossed the porch and rang the doorbell. No answer. He waited. Rang again. Still no answer.

Something drove him to the side door of the garage. It was locked, of course. Still...should he? Damn it! He thought of the comments...she wasn't feeling well…she didn't show for a fitness session…she canceled the Leone kids. Picking up a decorative rock from the ground, he broke the window. The street was quiet and glass shattered the stillness. Carefully, he stuck his hand inside and unlocked the door. He was hoping that Delaney—like many people—had left the side door to the house unlocked, thinking the garage being secured kept her safe. It didn't, of course. If she was all right, just lounging in bed, he'd yell at her for being careless with her safety.

Please, God, let her be all right. Let her be just lounging in bed. But he didn't think she was, as he darted around her sports car and headed for the house. Canceling appointments, not returning phone calls, were too unlike the conscientious, responsible woman he knew. He breathed a sigh of relief when he found the house door unlocked. Opening it, he strode inside and called out to her.

No answer.

He took only brief notice of hardwood floors and gleaming appliances as he marched through the kitchen. "Delaney, are you here?"

No answer.

Next was the living room. A huge, airy space with windows at both back and front. A hall veered off to the right. Probably the bedrooms. His stomach in knots, he started down the corridor. A door was open at the end. He hurried to it, had just reached the room, when he heard a moan.

Oh, God.

What he found inside stopped his heart and clogged his throat. Delaney was in bed under a mound of sheets, blankets and a bedspread. It was eighty degrees out, no air-conditioning was on, and she was covered as if it were the dead of winter.

He crossed to the bed.

She lay on her back, her arms raised, her palms open and on the pillow; her head lolled from side to side. Her hair was soaking wet, her face sweaty and chalk white. As he watched, a shiver passed through her.

Sinking down on the side of the mattress, he raised his hand to her cheek. She was hotter than a room on fire.

Instinct kicked in. Suddenly Reed became very calm. "Laney, wake up."

She moaned again.

He grasped her shoulders, shook her gently. "Sweetheart, it's me, Reed. Wake up."

To the side on a night table, he saw water, an analgesic and an empty pan—for vomiting, he guessed. He went into the bathroom, found a washcloth and soaked it with tepid water.

Back at the bed he bathed her face. Fear skittered through him. "Baby, please, wake up."

She roused. Her eyes opened. They were glassy and unfocused. "Reed?" She tried to reach out, but her hand dropped to the mattress as if the exertion was too much. "What—"

"How long have you been sick, honey?"

"Mmm." She licked painfully cracked lips. "A little while." Her brow furrowed. "Since Monday."

"*Monday?* It's Friday."

Her eyes began to close. "Can't be..." she said, turning into the pillow.

"What are your symptoms?"

"Just have the flu…"

This was a lot more than the flu. His First Responder training told him she was seriously dehydrated. He contemplated calling Beth or Dylan, when she moved onto her side and her knees came up; she grabbed her stomach. "Oohh…"

"Where does it hurt, sweetheart?"

"Stomach." Her hand flew to her mouth. "Gonna get sick. The bowl."

Reed reached for the bowl. She had the dry heaves, which meant there was nothing left in her stomach.

Immediately he drew back the covers. She shivered again. "Nooo, cold."

Oh, God.

Wrapping her in the lightest blanket, he picked her up and cradled her to his chest. She was too weak to put her arms around his neck and just lay in his arms limply.

Suddenly Reed was very afraid. But he'd be damned if he'd let his fear interfere with helping Delaney. Continuing to hold her, he strode through the house and out the door and settled her in the back seat of the Blazer.

As he drove, he spoke to her. "It's okay, sweetheart, it'll be all right now."

He only wished he could convince himself of that as they sped to the hospital.

THE DREAM WAS SO REAL….

"Start the IV…give me that bag of saline…"

"Hook it up...let's get the first dose of antibiotic in her...."

Somebody soothed her face with a cool cloth.

She shivered.

"...get a blanket..."

Warmth.

All the while her hand was grasped tightly by a big, strong, safe one. It became her lifeline. If she could just hold on to it...

Struggling, she opened her eyes. Above her, the light was bright and painful. There were doctors or nurses—medical people—huddled around her iron-railed bed. She must be in the hospital.

"It's all right, honey, they're going to take care of you now." The voice belonged to Reed. He was here with her.

Suddenly her stomach lurched. "Please..." she whispered. "Give me something...for my...stomach... just make me stop throwing up..."

A pretty dark-haired woman looked to the side. "Get me a shot of..." Delaney didn't hear the rest. The woman smiled down at Delaney. "I'm Dr. Samantha Camp, your gastroenterologist. We'll take care of the nausea right away. How long have you been vomiting?"

"Since Tuesday."

Reed's hand on hers tightened.

"What other symptoms have you had, Ms. Shaw?"

"Diarrhea...fever."

The doctor murmured something to the others about taking samples.

Delaney's eyes focused in on Reed, then Dr. Camp. "What's wrong with me?"

Before anyone could answer, she was given a shot by a nurse who'd reentered the room.

"You've got all the symptoms of food poisoning, but we can't be sure that's it." She poked around Delaney's abdomen, causing her to cry out. "You have unusual tenderness here."

The woman looked at Reed. "We need to do some tests, Reed."

He nodded stiffly.

"What else could it be?" Delaney asked.

"We don't know yet. We're going to take some X rays of your liver, kidneys and gall bladder." She spoke to someone behind her. "Let's get her down there stat."

The doctor turned away to confer with the others, and somebody picked up the phone. Reed leaned over and smoothed back her hair. "It's all right now, Laney. They'll take care of you."

"What's happened, Reed? I don't understand. I thought I had the flu."

"No. It lasted too long. You're dehydrated." He nodded to the IVs. "Badly." He swept a thumb along her lips. "That's why you feel so awful. The IV will kick in soon." He placed a hand on her stomach. "You'll feel better here, too. The shot will work fast."

She closed her eyes. She'd been nauseated for so long…nothing would stay down. "I thought it was just the flu," she repeated.

He brushed his knuckles against her cheek. "I know, baby, it's okay."

The doctor came into view. "An orderly's going to take you down to X ray in a wheelchair. Can you stand?"

Delaney tried to cooperate; she lifted her head and shoulders…and fell immediately back into the pillows.

"No need." Reed whipped off the covers and scooped her out of the bed. She lay her head against his chest while the IV was positioned and the chair secured. If she could just stay close to him, she'd be all right. She wasn't afraid then. He settled her into the chair and got a blanket to tuck around her.

She said, "Don't leave," and grabbed his hand again.

The doctor smiled when Reed replied, "I won't, I promise."

He grasped Delaney's hand as the orderly took control of the chair. Lying back, she held on to him as they left the small ER cubicle.

Dusk had fallen. Reed sat by Delaney's bedside watching her sleep, once again holding her hand. He couldn't seem to let go. Seeing her so sick and scared made something inside of him shift. He'd never allowed himself to think anything could happen to her. He *couldn't* allow himself to think that.

"Reed?" Sleepily she opened her eyes.

"I'm right here, honey."

"Can I have some water?"

Thankfully her nausea had abated, and she could keep down some liquid, though Dr. Camp had ordered a constant IV drip of saline and antibiotics. It had been running for the eight hours they'd been here. Holding the glass, he raised her head, letting her sip from the straw.

"It was good news, wasn't it?" Her voice was uncharacteristically raw.

"The X rays?"

"Uh-huh."

"Yes, of course. No liver or kidney damage is the best news we could get."

She bit her lip and glanced out the window. The sun had set, leaving Rockford in a summer night haze. "What could it be, do you think?"

"Samantha said your tummy tenderness is probably from the excessive vomiting and diarrhea. Her guess is the tests will show food poisoning."

Wearily she closed her eyes. "I can't believe I just thought it was flu."

"Well, the two ailments have the same symptoms." His thumb made circles on her still-dry skin. "Don't go ragging on yourself because you didn't know you could be sicker than you thought. Samantha says the symptoms can sneak up on you and worsen quickly."

She raised mischievous eyes to him. "Yes, sir." It was good to hear the sass.

He leaned over and tucked her hair behind her ear. Unable to stop himself, he kissed her forehead. "You gave me quite a scare, lady."

"I was terrified, Reed. I'm still worried."

"You're getting better every hour. The IVs are working."

She lifted her hand. "They itch." She looked down at her body. "And I'm a mess."

"You were pretty sweaty." His smile was intentionally male. "Want me to give you a sponge bath?"

"Mmm, yeah." Her eyes twinkled.

He stood. "On second thought, I'll call the nurse."

Fear flashed back into her eyes for a minute. "Don't leave."

He smiled reassuringly.

"Please."

"I won't leave, honey. I promise." He cupped her cheek. "I'll go check my voice mail. And I want to call Beth. She was worried about you."

"Nobody's to call Chelsea and Jake. I don't want their vacation ruined."

"All right."

"And get something to eat, too."

"Yes, ma'am."

When he got to the door, she called out, "Reed?"

"Hmm?"

"Thanks…"

He just smiled. She looked like a little kid, small and fragile in that hospital bed. Had he really thought she was strong enough to take on his demons? "You're welcome."

After his calls, he stopped in the cafeteria. Grabbing a sandwich and coffee, he sat at a table in the near-deserted cafeteria.

Only one other time could he remember being so scared. Biting into tasteless tuna on stale rye, he chewed, experiencing again the stark terror he'd felt when he'd found her ill. Life was so tenuous.

You should live it to the fullest, then.

You should avoid involvement. What if something had happened to her?

You should make use of the time you have.

You can't handle another loss. And she can't handle your pain.

His mind bounced from one thought to the other.

Then the symptoms struck. Sweatiness. Nausea. Dizziness. He let them come, sat there for a few minutes until they abated. Thankfully, there was no flashback.

When it was over, he rose to go back upstairs. He'd stay until she fell asleep—then get away from her. Again.

God, he was tired of this seesaw.

THOUGH SHE WAS EXHAUSTED and feeling the effects of her illness, Delaney was pleased to see Reed stride back into her room.

"You look better," he said. Then his eyes sparked with humor, and for a minute, she wondered what a younger, less-beleaguered Reed had been like. "Great fashion."

She plucked at the hospital gown. "My pajamas were dirty." She shifted in the bed. "I wish I had some clean boxers."

"I'll bring you some of your own things tomorrow."

"It's a deal." She watched him. "Did you eat?"

He rolled his eyes. "So to speak. God, I hate hospital food."

"You've been in the hospital before, haven't you?"

Very subtly, he stiffened. "How do you know that?"

"New Year's Eve, I saw the scar on your leg."

When his expression turned grim, she smiled and added, "'Course, I saw a lot more than that."

He crossed to her and sank onto the bed. "Honey, you're sick. Let's not get into any of that tonight."

On cue, she yawned. Exhaustion prickled at her. "All right. I'll drop it if you promise me something."

"What?"

"You won't leave."

"I won't leave until you're asleep."

She shook her head. "I don't want you to go at all."

"What?"

"I'm scared, Reed. I need you." It was true, she didn't want to be left alone with only the shadows and the unknown to keep her company. Ordinarily she would die before she asked for help. Depending too much on a man—like her mother had—was abhorrent to Delaney. But her defenses were down. They still didn't know what was wrong with her, and would have to wait the weekend for the food poisoning tests to incubate.

"I could stay here…"

"All night?"

"Yes."

"You aren't worried about your reputation, Doc?"

"I think bringing you in wrapped up in a blanket and in night clothes took care of that."

She smiled. "Thank you."

He was so attractive, even now with the ravages of fatigue and worry on his brow, wearing his glasses, which he wore when his eyes were tired. She wanted to drown in him.

"You scared the life out of me, you know." He

brushed her cheek with calloused fingertips. "I was so worried."

Scooting to the side of the bed where the IV post hung, she patted the mattress. "Here. I want to sleep in your arms."

Shaking his head, he said, "Don't think I don't know this is the worst kind of manipulation." Still, he kicked off his shoes and came around to the vacant side of the bed; he stretched out on the mattress and encircled her with his arms. She snuggled into him, as naturally as a wife to her husband—or a longtime lover.

Her hands dropped to his belt.

"What are you *doing?*" he asked.

She loved the feel of his hard chest against her face. "Making you comfortable."

Before he could object, she'd whipped off his belt. Had his dress shirt half undone. "I think T-shirts are sexy. Take off your captain's garb."

Chuckling, he shook his head at her; resignedly he whipped off his shirt and settled back down. She cuddled into him then, burrowing her cheek into his shoulder, wrapping her arms around his waist.

And yawned. "They gave me a sleeping pill."

He kissed her head. "Good. You need rest."

Sleepily, she mumbled, "I need *you.*"

Reed held her as night came, as she drifted in and out of sleep.

And never once did he turn away from her.

"WHY THE *HELL* DIDN'T YOU call me sooner?"

Delaney glanced up as her sister rushed into the room. "And ruin your vacation?"

Chelsea grabbed Delaney's hand, studied her face and relaxed a bit. "You look okay."

"I'm fine now. Especially since they took out that damn IV. I gave it a name, started calling it Ernest, we were attached so long."

"Hi, kiddo." Jake meandered into the room, leaned over and kissed Delaney's cheek. "You sure you're okay?" He curled his hand around Chelsea's neck in a gesture that reminded Delaney of how Reed often touched her.

"I'm fine now." She glanced longingly out at the warm early-August sunshine. "I'm going home to-day."

"All you said on the phone was that you contracted food poisoning." Delaney had called her sister early this Monday morning. The Scarlattas had returned from the Adirondacks late last night.

"Yes, the report came in today. It's called campy-lobacter."

Chelsea shivered. "That's a nasty one. I've seen cases before." Her sister was an EMT. She was also the biggest mother hen in the universe.

"I've no idea where I picked it up."

Reed strode through the door, staring down into a big tote bag he carried and tugging something out of it. "All right, I picked out the most outrageous T-shirt you had. And this underwear—" Three feet into the room, he stopped short, a red lace thong in his big, masculine hands. After a telling pause, he nodded. "Chelsea, Jake."

Chelsea's jaw dropped.

Jake smiled knowingly. "Macauley, fancy meeting you here."

Reed stuffed her underwear back into the bag; his gaze whipped from Jake to Chelsea to Delaney. She smiled an I'm-not-gonna-get-you-outta-this-one smile.

"I was...um...because we work together, I knew she was..." The hesitation made things worse. As did the blush.

Delaney bet he was grateful when the doctor walked in behind him. From the doorway, she caught Delaney's eye and gave her an us-girls wink. "Moving in, Doc?" She nodded to the tote he carried. "I told you last night that bed's only big enough for one. Though you two managed—" Coming fully into the room, Samantha Camp noticed Chelsea and Jake, who'd been blocked by the door. "Oh, sorry. I didn't know you had company."

Smooth as honey, Delaney introduced her sister and brother-in-law to the young doctor who'd taken care of her.

Obviously trying for a professional demeanor, Dr. Camp quelled a grin and crossed to the bed. "Everything's fine. All the tests check out." She handed Delaney some slips. "You need to take this antibiotic for ten days. Drink plenty of fluids. Get a lot of rest."

"When can I go back to work?" Delaney asked.

"When you feel up to it."

"Don't tell her that," Reed snapped. "She'll be at her desk tomorrow."

Chelsea's eyes widened. Jake chuckled again.

Dr. Camp smiled. "Protective guy, isn't he?" She faced Delaney. "Wait till next week. You won't have your strength back until then. And take it easy. You had the worst case of food poisoning I've seen in a long time." She stepped away. "I'll do the discharge papers right now." She spoke to Reed on the way out. "Take care of her, Doc." And Delaney heard her stage-whisper, "Hope you enjoyed your stay in the hospital."

When Samantha left, the room was church-quiet. Reed stood stock still, staring at Delaney. Chelsea looked as shell-shocked as if she'd found the two of them making love. Finally her sister asked, "What's going on, Laney?"

"I got sick, sis. I've been cooped up here for four days."

Chelsea glanced meaningfully across the room. "Not alone, apparently."

Raking a hand through his hair, Reed said, "She wouldn't let me call you." He looked so uncomfortable Delaney wanted to rescue him. But she wanted to hear what he was going to say even more. "I stayed with her because she shouldn't have had to go through it alone."

Jake touched Chelsea's arm. "Honey, I'm not sure this is any of our business."

Reed threw Jake a grateful look.

Paying no attention to her husband, Chelsea asked, "What's going on with you two? I thought you hated each other."

Reed crossed to the nightstand, set the bag on it and faced them. "Nothing's going on, Chelsea. Now that you're here, you can take over." He barely met Delaney's eyes. "I'll be going."

"Okay." Delaney's light tone belied her determination. If he thought she was letting him go now, after this…she hadn't forgotten how tenderly he'd held her all night, how solicitous he'd been. "Hey, thanks for all this." She waved her hand around the room. She wanted him to come to the bed, kiss her, say goodbye properly. Instead he nodded to the Scarlattas.

"Goodbye." He took one last look at her. "I'm glad this is over for you, Delaney."

Delaney watched his retreating back. Beth's words came to her. *It's not over till it's over, girl.*

From her chair, Chelsea showed elder-sibling exasperation. "La-ney?"

Delaney faced her sister. She said simply, "I'm in love with Reed Macauley, Chels."

CHAPTER NINE

REED HAD BEEN IN A black mood before, felt its ugly oppression on many occasions, but the angry cloud around him had never been as smothering as it had been this week. In the foyer of his house, he picked up a paintbrush and dipped it in a can of stain, thinking about Ben coming to check on him twice this week, and Beth's solicitous concern. He'd spurned both his friends—again.

Just as he'd done to Delaney. She'd been home from the hospital four days, and though he'd talked to her daily, he hadn't seen her. She was still recuperating, and sleeping off and on for hours. He hadn't visited her, but knew she was recovering.

Reed watched as the expensive oak turned a golden brown under his brush. The color brought out the grain, accentuating the small knots and grooves. So far, he'd finished five jobs around his house this week in an effort to keep himself from seeking Delaney out. As he'd built a closet in the basement, he'd reminded himself how fragile she really was, how he couldn't batter her with his nightmares. By the time he'd put up half the shelves in a new pantry, he'd admitted that it was fear that kept him from going to her. She could have died in the hospital, and he doubted he could survive that kind of loss again.

"It's what emotional numbing is all about, idiot," he berated himself aloud. "It's what you've done all these years."

His gaze strayed to the stairs, where Pandora's box perched on the last step. He'd taken it out of the window seat when he'd finally gotten round to staining the wood. Tonight he was going to throw the collection out. No more seeking comfort in the contents of that godforsaken thing. He'd make a clean break. It would hurt initially, but he'd heal better in the long run.

His rumination was interrupted by the doorbell. Swearing—damn it, he never *invited* anybody here, but they kept coming—he put down the brush and wiped his hands on his stained and holey sweatpants. Jeez, he didn't even have a shirt on. *The hell with it.* He ordered himself to be civil to Ben or Dylan or Beth or whoever it was; he had his psychologist's mask in place when he opened the door.

And there she stood.

Dressed in loose gym shorts and a T-shirt that read Don't Annoy the Crazy Person, she was thinner than before her illness and her eyes were tired. "Well," she said archly. "If the mountain won't come to Mohammed..."

Ignoring the hopscotch his heart was playing, he said sternly, "Coming here isn't a good idea, Delaney. You should be in bed."

The corners of her mouth curved up. "Is that an invitation?"

"*Home* in bed."

"Join me and I'll crawl right under the covers."

His shoulders ached with the unique kind of fatigue insomnia induced; he'd had two horrendous flashbacks since he'd been at the hospital with this woman.

She shivered as a sudden early-evening August breeze swept around her.

"Damn it, come on in."

Inside the house, she literally gawked. "Wow, Reed, this place is gorgeous. I thought so from the outside, but the interior is breathtaking."

He scanned the huge foyer of oak and stucco, with its window seat, ceiling fan and carved oak staircase leading upstairs. "Thanks. It was a mess when I bought it."

She peeked into the living room. Again he viewed it from her perspective. Huge front picture windows. High ceilings with beams that had been a bitch to stain. More stucco there. Big comfortable couches and chairs.

"Oh, look at that fireplace."

Ah, his favorite feature. Made of old fieldstone, the fireplace had been cleaned professionally, which had taken days. But the restoration had left it smooth and gleaming.

"I had no idea you liked things like this." She waved her arm to encompass the room.

"I know." He tried to inject coldness in his tone, but it was hard when his heart rejoiced in seeing her. He ushered her into the living room. "Sit down on the couch. Better yet, stretch out."

She smiled as she sat, then lay back on one of the brown chenille pillows that accented the taupe leather; gracefully, she extended a long length of leg out on the cushions. Jeez, she wore white canvas sneakers and little lacy socks. It underscored her youth and innocence.

Towering over her, he placed his fists on his hips. "What do you want?"

"You have stain on your cheek. And on your chest. Nice, pecs, Doc." She gave him a saucy wink. "Though I've seen them before."

Till then he'd forgotten he was dirty and half dressed. "I need to get cleaned up."

"Go ahead, I'll wait."

His hands fisted. "What do you *want?*" he repeated.

Her eyes sparkled like twin blue flames. "You."

"You can't have me."

"Wanna bet?"

"We've been through this."

"Yeah, but after last weekend, I've decided to fight for you."

Shit! "I haven't changed my mind."

"You will."

"No, I won't."

She yawned and lifted her arms over her head, stretching out farther. "Well, then, you have a problem on your hands. I had a lot of time to think in the hospital. I was scared I was really sick. Could die. It made me realize we have to live life to the fullest. And my life could never be full without you."

"Your life would be full of nightmares with me."

"Yeah, there'd be some. But I'm trained to deal with problems like yours. I can handle them."

He'd begun to think so but had changed his mind during her illness. Had he been wrong to back away again? Goddamn it, he was weakening. "I'm going to shower. We'll talk more about this after." He wagged a finger at her. "Don't get off that couch, young lady."

"Yes, sir!"

Preoccupied, Reed bounded upstairs and took his time in the shower. He was afraid. Truly afraid that she was going to win this bout. He summoned all the horrors of what he'd done to his ex-wife Patrice in the past—the nightmares that kept her from sleeping, the times he'd bruised her in anger or in the middle of a dream or flashback, the emotional withdrawal, the sexual dysfunction...

No! he told himself, opening the glass door and stepping onto ceramic tile he'd grouted at 2:00 a.m. one morning when he couldn't sleep. *No, I won't do that to Delaney,* he reaffirmed as he dried off, ran a towel over his hair and left the bathroom to dress.

"Damn it, Delaney, have you no shame?" He was acutely aware of his nakedness.

She stared at him from the bed, looking so right on top of the brown-and-white-striped masculine covers it took his breath away. At least *she'd* left her clothes on. Mischief incarnate, she let out a wolf whistle.

Stalking to the dresser, he drew out gym shorts and quickly pulled them on. Then he faced her. "I won't be seduced into this."

"Wanna bet?"

"Delaney, don't do this."

"Why?"

God, he *was* going to give in. How could he not? And yet, it was wrong. An idea came to him. One cruel, last-ditch effort to save her from him. "Look, I thought you'd take the hints. But I guess I have to tell you outright.''

Beautiful sculpted brows formed a vee at his grave tone. ''What?''

''My relationship with Ellen. It's gotten more serious.''

''Ellen?'' Her voice quivered. ''The professor?''

''Yes.'' His heart hammering in his chest, he glanced at the clock. ''She's been coming over every night since you were in the hospital. At about nine.'' He hesitated. ''She stays.''

''I don't believe it.''

''Check the closet. Some of her clothes are there.'' He prayed Delaney didn't call his bluff.

Her face crumpled. She sat up and drew her knees to her chest, circled them with slender arms. ''Are you...are you in love with her?''

Only visions of Patrice sobbing that she couldn't live with the man he'd become, made him able to say, ''We've been seeing each other a long time.''

''But this weekend...you stayed with me.''

''Like a father would, Delaney. I thought you understood that.''

The phrase, the concept, the kick into her past, worked. She bounded off the bed. She rushed to the door, but not before he saw the tears in her eyes.

It was the hardest thing he'd ever had to do in his life, but he let her go. He waited frozen like a statue where he stood, ignoring the pain in his heart that rivaled cardiac arrest. *Please God, make me let her go. Please!*

And then he heard the crash.

BLINDED BY HER TEARS, Delaney took the stairs fast and didn't see the object on the last step until she kicked it with her foot and sent it flying.

Tough! Whatever was in the pretty box, he could clean it up himself. Stopping abruptly, she wiped her eyes to assess how much damage had been done. The floor at the bottom of the staircase was littered with...items. Hell, who cared? But her eye caught on something that had slid across the oak floor. A wood carving of her name.

Her name? What the hell?

Kneeling down, she picked up the gorgeous teak artifact. Ran her fingers over the delicately crafted letters. She didn't understand. What was Reed doing with this? Then she saw the T-shirt. Read the saying. She reached for the box. It was beautiful, covered with silk. When she grasped the end, it tipped the rest of the way and out fell a small ceramic box. She picked it up. On top perched a ballerina. One of its arms had broken off, but the figure gleamed with long black hair and blue eyes.

Her name.

A blasphemous T-shirt.

The ballerina that resembled her.

Oh, my God.

Opening the music box, a melody by Debussy tinkled out. *Claire de Lune.* It was her favorite song.

Her eyes clouding, she lovingly traced the ceramic figure as she tried to make sense of what this meant.

She became aware of footsteps. A shadow loomed over her. She looked up. He stood there, on the third from the bottom step, naked emotion on his face. It was as if she was seeing his soul.

She sank back on her heels, hugged the music box to her heart, and said only, "Oh, Reed."

HE COULD LIE. Or least he could try to. Instead, he dropped down onto step and buried his face in his hands. In that brief instant, he knew, deep in his heart, his entire existence was never going to be the same.

It scared him to death.

"Reed." She breathed the word softly.

Lowering his hands, he met her gaze.

"When...why...?"

He nodded to the peach-silk-covered box. "I call it Pandora's box."

She laughed a little. "When did you...?" She glanced down, saw the book, the scroll, other things. "How long have you been doing this?"

"Since New Year's Eve."

"Oh, Reed," she whispered again.

He raised disgusted eyes to the ceiling. "I know, it makes me seem unbalanced. Like a stalker, maybe."

"How about a man in love?"

"No! No! Don't say that."

"Reed, I—"

"Honey, please, no. Don't say any more."

Her eyes narrowed. "If you're going to try to convince me you don't care about me, that Professor Ellen has her clothes in your closet, you're freakin' nuts, buddy. I'm not buying any of it." She picked up the T-shirt. "You collected all this for me over the last few months because you care about me as much as I care about you."

"Yes, I did." He coughed. "I do."

Her face softened. "Then why have you done everything in your power to push me away?"

"Because I can't drag you down with me."

"With the PTSD?"

"Yes. You just don't know…"

"Then tell me. Everything, this time. Right now."

Is there somebody…a woman maybe. Reed, it should be her choice….

More afraid now than he'd ever been since that one night eight years ago, he said, "All right, honey. I'll tell you about it."

"EIGHT YEARS AGO…I'd been…God, this is hard…." He gripped her hand so tightly it hurt, but she didn't stop him. Next to him, half sitting, half kneeling on the couch, she watched the man she loved break out in a sweat, his dark complexion turning ashen.

"Take your time, Reed."

He cleared his throat. "I…I've never told anybody the whole story. I could never get the words out."

"Tell me," she said simply. She raised her other hand to his shoulder and squeezed.

"I was a firefighter for the FDNY." The biggest, most dangerous department in the state because of all the traffic and the high-rise buildings. She had no idea he was from New York City, though he'd said the PTSD came from an incident when he was a firefighter.

"I loved it. The camaraderie, the risks, the high I got every time I walked in the station." He stared straight ahead, wouldn't look at her. "I worked there for ten years. I went to college first, thought I wanted to be a teacher, but my buddy..." His throat worked convulsively. "I had this buddy, Marx. His first name was Hank, but we called him Crash because of all the car accidents he got into in high school. The Cap wouldn't let him drive the fire truck, either." Reed drew in a deep breath. "He joined the FDNY right out of high school. I ended up in the fire service after college."

She squeezed his hand. "I wish I had known you then."

He snorted. "No, you don't. I was a cocky son of a bitch." He paused. "A lot like Dylan O'Roarke, only more of a hell-raiser."

She couldn't picture this deliberate, cautious man taking risks like O'Roarke. "Go on, Reed."

"Because I was smart, had a higher education, I got to be a lieutenant by the time I was twenty-six. I didn't work with Crash until the last few years. Finally, we finagled it. It was one of the happiest days of my life when we got assigned to the same house."

"Were you married then?"

"Yeah, I got married when I was twenty-five. Patrice was a waitress in a restaurant the smoke-eaters frequented." He shrugged. "I fell for her, married her. We were trying to have kids."

Delaney smiled weakly.

The grip tightened. "Crash used to tease me about it, *tough job but somebody's got to do it* kind of thing. He and I were both only children, and he had three kids already. It was time for me to catch up." Reed ran a hand through his hair. "It was a normal shift...we were working...nothing much was going on, except that there'd been a rash of unexplained fires. There was a suspicion that they were incendiary."

"Arson?"

"Yes. Arson. Turned out, the brass was right."

She waited, sensing he needed time.

Letting go of her hand, he stood and started to pace. "We'd been warned about arson. Given the profile of a typical torch." He shook his head. "Funny, Jake's firefighter trivia game was about arson this week."

"Was it?"

"Mmm. Do you know what a vanity fire is?"

"No."

"Somebody sets a fire, then calls the fire department, and might even aid in the rescue. He does it to get credit, attention for his heroism."

She nodded.

"We were called to a car fire at a high-rise garage. Just our crew—four guys, on an engine—because the blaze was small." He smiled. "An engine carries water and we had the Hurst equipment in case anybody was trapped."

"The Jaws of Life."

"Right. We got there quickly, and put out the fire. Crash... he was joking with Castleman and Johnson, the other two men on our group, about the sissy fire, when somebody approached the scene. I was fiddling with the rig's water system, and noticed the guy first."

At his tone, Delaney's skin prickled.

"I walked over to him, was about five feet away, when I saw it."

"Saw what?"

"The gun."

"Oh, my God."

"He had a revolver, a nine millimeter that—it turned out—had six rounds in it." Reed stopped pacing by the front window. Looked out. Took a deep breath. Shook his head. "I handled it badly."

"What do you mean?"

"I tried to talk to him. Asked him what was wrong. Played down the gun."

"What did he say?"

"That he was a smoke-eater, and he was supposed to help us put out the fire, that we should have waited for him to help." Reed swallowed hard. "I said that was okay, we had it under control."

For a minute there was absolute silence.

"He started waving the gun around. Saying crazy things like nobody needed him anymore. Not his wife, who I found out later had divorced him; not his fire company, which was a volunteer group in a rural section outside of New York, and had recently been closed down." Reed stared outside as if he were seeing the whole event. "I caught on then. My men were behind me near the car, the truck was off to the left."

"Go on."

"I kept talking...then Crash...goddamn it, why couldn't he just leave it alone? Crash called out to me to get back with them. Get out of the way."

Now Delaney saw the whole thing. Reed had put himself between the shooter and his crew.

"I told Crash to shut up, but he didn't. I was trying to talk to this guy. And then he...and then he..."

Delaney rose and crossed to the window. Slowly, she touched his shoulder. He startled. She moved in front of him. Stood close. "What happened?"

"The guy...Cummings was his name...he shot me."

She glanced down, remembering the nasty scar. "In the leg."

Reed nodded.

"I went down. Before I hit the ground, I heard the other shots."

Delaney bit her lip. His face was stricken. His eyes teared. "He shot them all, Laney."

"Oh, no."

"They died. All of them. All my men died." Tears streamed down his cheeks. "Crash, in my arms. I crawled over to him. He got hit in the chest. He told me to take care of his kids for him." Reed grabbed on to her. "I'm their godfather."

"I'm so sorry."

He drew in a deep breath. "As Crash bled to death on the stupid concrete garage floor, the shooter turned the gun on himself."

"Oh, no." Could this get any worse?

"He put the gun to his mouth and pulled the trigger. I saw the back of his head get blown apart." She wound her arms around him and drew him close. "Everybody died but me that night. Everybody..." Total breakdown came then, the wrenching, racking sobs.

Delaney cried, too. Sobbed for the young lieutenant Reed had been and the tortured man he'd become.

When he finally drew away, she forced back her own emotion.

He gulped in a ragged breath, but raised his hands

to her cheeks and wiped away the wetness. "Now you know."

"Now I know." She knew a lot. The obscene event. The trauma of getting shot. The guilt he felt for surviving. "Come sit down."

His whole body radiated fatigue. She led him to the couch as if he were a child. He sank down on the cushions and laid his head back, closed his eyes, put his feet up on the coffee table. She didn't say anything, just stroked his bare arm with still-shaky fingers.

It was minutes before he said, "I never went back to the line."

"No?"

"I was on medical leave for six months. Then I quit the job."

"Just like that?"

"Uh-huh. Patrice had a fit."

"She did?"

"Yeah. She'd stuck by me through the whole thing, but the PTSD kept getting worse."

"After something like that, it's not a surprise."

"The first year, I had symptoms all the time. Moodiness. Anger. Flashbacks. Nightmares."

"Didn't you get some therapy?"

"Yeah, but it didn't help much so I quit going. The symptoms abated after I left the job, and New York. When I went to grad school to become a psychologist, the university recommended I undergo some more therapy. All I could do was get it under control—*managed*, they call it. I had only isolated episodes until I came to the RFD." He squeezed her hand.

She had a million questions but let him tell it his way.

"Ben Cordaro. The O'Roarkes. They got too damn close."

She smiled.

"And of course, being back in the fire department triggered some attacks. Still I had it under control." His laugh was self-effacing. "Until I met you."

Her heart bumped in her chest. Paradoxically, it hurt that she caused him pain. But then, it meant he cared, and she couldn't regret that. "I make it worse?"

"Yes. I've read all the literature. Diagnosed myself. It's called emotional overload."

She chuckled. "Wow! I send you into emotional overload? What a compliment."

He leaned over and kissed her nose. "This is serious."

"I know. I'm sorry. It's just that you've been so stingy with your feelings about me. I've lived for crumbs. This is like a banquet to a starving woman."

He ran his knuckles down her cheek. "I haven't been able to shut down with you."

"Emotional numbing."

"Right. And then Tommy's death…Sammy's situation…Ben and Beth battering at me to talk. Everything's come to a head."

She thought before she spoke. "Reed, as a psychologist, you know it's best to get all this out. To talk about it."

"I never could tell the story."

"What about the New York specialist?"

"I saw him but didn't tell him what happened."

Leaning closer, she kissed his hand, traced the scar on his knee. "I'm glad you told me."

He stared down at his bare legs propped up on the table. "I won't be glad. Later."

"Talking about the event brings on attacks."

"Yes. And intensifies them."

"Only initially. It'll get better now."

"You don't know that."

"Yes, I do."

"You can't be sure. In any case, I won't take the risk."

"What?"

"We can't be together. I can't subject you to a life like this, honey. Now that you know all the facts, know the whole story, you've got to agree."

"You're crazy, you know that?"

"That's what I've been telling you."

"No, I don't mean the PTSD. I mean if you think I'm going to back off now, you're nuts."

His body went rigid. He sat up straight and turned to her. "You don't know what it's like to live with a man with PTSD."

"Then tell me. And we'll deal with it together."

"It broke up my marriage, Delaney."

"It won't come between us."

Abruptly he pulled away. Stood again and crossed the room, to get away from her, she guessed. "Patrice thought so, too. She was a wonderful woman. She loved me. I was a monster to her."

"How?"

"What?"

"How were you a monster to her?"

He grew more frantic. Fisted his hands. "I don't want to talk about it."

She stood, too, and went to him. "Well, that's tough, Doc. You're going to tell me the rest." She breathed deeply to get her emotions under control. "I'm strong, Reed. What's more, I'm trained to deal with psychological disorders. I can handle this better than Patrice could, and I'm not letting you go." She folded her arms over her chest. "So you might as well tell me."

He swallowed hard.

"All of it."

"I was a horrible husband." She waited. "At first, I just cut her out. Isolated myself."

"A common response for a trauma survivor."

"Then there was the anger. I took it out on her."

"How?"

"I hit her. Once, when I was drunk. I drank a lot. Smoked grass every day."

"What happened?"

"A stupid fight about my wasting my life. I got so mad I slapped her across the face. I left her after that incident. But there were others times…the nightmares where I woke her up, grabbing her, bruising her. Physically it was bad."

"I'm not cowed by anything you're saying, Reed. Is there more?"

His eyes flared with temper. "Yeah, smart-ass, there's more."

"Like what?"

"Well, like sex with a PTSD sufferer, for starters."

"Sex?"

"Yeah, what it's like to make love with the Ice Man. That's the term applied to guys like me."

"There didn't seem to be any problem between us on New Year's Eve."

"Problems can still occur."

Delaney squared her shoulders, refusing to be intimidated. She knew she had to handle this right, and instinct told her sympathy wasn't going to cut it. "Like what?"

"Some men can't get it up."

"Well, that didn't happen with us."

"Or they can't finish."

"You're still striking out."

"They use sex as a sedative. To calm them down."

"Oh, gee, it would be tough being your sleeping pill."

"Or to feel alive."

"Hmm. Delaney Shaw, a mood-altering drug. I kinda like it."

Fire lit his face. He grabbed her arms. "Then they go for long periods of time with no sexual contact. Ignoring their wives."

She lifted her chin. "Okay, so I'll shop at Frederick's of Hollywood. Or I'll do myself up in plastic wrap and meet you at the door when you come home from work."

"Are you mocking this? Me?" He was horrified.

"No, I'm trying to tell you your objections are surmountable. Sure, I know there'll be problems. We'll handle them."

"No."

"Yes. Is that all?"

"No!" he shouted. "Many trauma survivors want sex on demand."

That made her laugh out loud. "And that's supposed to scare me? Jeez, Reed, what's the matter with you? Can't you see it? I crave your touch. I've fantasized about you constantly since New Year's Eve."

"Sometimes they want it three times a day."

"All the better."

"Don't joke about it."

"I'm making the best of it."

"You just don't know."

Soberly she said, "I realize that, Reed. I *don't* know. But I'm going to find out." He turned away from her, and she yanked him back around. "I'm in your life to stay. I'm not leaving you after this."

His eyes bleak, he said quietly, "What if you do?"

She stilled. "What?"

"What if you do leave me? Or if something happens to you… like the food poisoning…" His ragged words trailed off.

Ah, she got it now. The bottom line. The last and most frightening source of his objections. "You don't think you can handle another loss."

He nodded.

She thought about that one for a long time. "I'm sorry your feelings for me scare you. I can't promise that nothing will ever happen to me. And although I can't imagine ever letting you go, leaving you, I can't promise you that won't happen, either."

Silent, he watched her.

She lifted her hand to his face. "But I *can* promise you I'll be here to deal with your PTSD with you. I'll learn more about it, I'll help you cope. I'll help you manage it.''

He looked so torn.

Glancing to the foyer, she smiled. ''You know the story of Pandora's box?''

''She was the first woman of Greek mythology.'' He caressed her cheek. ''The epitome of womanhood, like you.''

Delaney smiled. ''Pandora's box contained the evils of the world. Until that time, the world was free of sickness, greed, envy, all sins. The gods warned Pandora not to ever open the box. But she was overcome by female curiosity and opened it.''

''I know that part, honey.''

''But the box didn't just contain evil, Reed.''

''No?''

''Uh-uh. One positive thing remained for the world.''

''What was it?''

''Hope.''

His eyes misted. ''I lost the capacity to hope on a concrete floor in a parking garage eight years ago, Laney.''

''Then let me help you find it again.'' She stepped back and reached out her hand.

He stared down at it a long time. Then, locking eyes with hers, he linked their fingers and turned toward the staircase.

Quietly, he led her upstairs.

IN THE DIM CONFINES of his bedroom, Reed had the crazy notion that some supreme deity had given permission and blessed the union that was about to take place. So he treated Delaney with tenderness as he turned her toward him and reached for the hem of her T-shirt. She was so pure, so untainted, he wanted to preserve and cherish that quality in her until the day he died.

Now that the dam had broken, he allowed the flood of feeling to burst forth. This lovely woman needed words, needed assurance, and he'd give them to her. He'd give her everything in his power. "You have no idea how much I want you." Burying his face in her neck, inhaling her flowery scent, he tunneled his hands in the mass of hair that fell down her back. "No idea how much I care."

"I care, too, Reed, so much."

"Good," he whispered against her cheek, unfastening the front closure of lacy scraps that passed for a bra. "I wouldn't want to be in this situation alone." He grazed her shoulder with his lips. Felt her arms rise up and wind around his neck.

"You'll never be alone again."

Vehemently he pushed down the fear. Inched away to cup her breasts. They were small, and firm, and fit his palms perfectly.

Her head fell back and she closed her eyes. "I can't believe this is happening," she whispered.

"Hmm." A little of the old Reed surfaced. He kissed the underside of her breast, ran the back of his hand over her nipples.

The provocative teasing worked. She squirmed. "Reed..." Her breath became ragged. He slid his hands to her hips, pushed down the shorts and knelt in front of her.

"Scandalous," he said about the purple lace that hardly covered her. "In the last eight months...every time I saw you, I wondered what underwear you had on." Burying his face in her stomach he reminded himself to give her the words, though his body was careering toward climax. "I missed you more than I can say." He kissed her flat tummy. "Sometimes, I ached so much I couldn't stand it."

When he had her undressed, he stood and shrugged off his shorts. Her hands roamed his chest, their feminine touch diminishing the raw ache of loneliness that had been there for eight long years. Desire kicked at his insides, but there was a wholesomeness about it, a decent clean need that freed him.

"I never knew," he said as he picked her up and placed her on the bed, then followed her down.

"Knew what, love?"

"That this—" he cupped her intimately "—could be so spiritual." His eyes met hers, which were shining with surrender. "Please, please believe I never meant to hurt you. I cared all along, sweetheart."

Her smile was bursting with unadulterated joy. "I believe."

So did he. And because of it, the bars around his heart collapsed. Long imprisoned needs escaped to claim the delights he'd forsaken years ago.

As if she knew, her smile turned totally carnal. And mischievous. "Let go," she whispered. "Let me have all of you."

When was the last time he'd given a woman free

rein over his body? Not in years; he lay back and let her touch him, rouse him in a way he couldn't control and didn't try to stop.

She wasn't passive. The hot brush of her hands was everywhere, stimulating his senses, rallying his emotions. "I want you," she breathed. "I'll always want you," she promised. "I'll always be here for you." Rolling on top of him, she kissed her way down his body, her lips grazing, her teeth taking tiny bites wherever she stopped. He feared he might ricochet off the bed when strong, supple hands closed around him.

He could take no more. It wasn't the celibacy of his body the last eight months that made him halt her ministrations. It was the end of the eight-year sentence he'd imposed on his emotions that had him ready to go off like an inexperienced teenager.

Roughly, he reversed their positions. He was inside her before he knew it, having taken a moment to reach into the nightstand for protection. Raw, aching need transformed quickly into acute, almost-painful pleasure at their connection. Somewhere in the dim recesses of his clouded mind, he knew that never in his life had anything felt so right.

Their fiery possession of each other consumed them both. He heard her scream, twice, before he climaxed. Her mouth clamped on his shoulder, her nails dug into his back as explosion after explosion hit him.

Then his mind blanked.

When he surfaced from sexual unconsciousness, he started again.

THE NIGHTMARE CAME, in the stark hour before dawn, and Reed fought the demons in his sleep once again. Only this time, Delaney was there to wake him and hold him through the terror.

CHAPTER TEN

THE MIDDAY SUN BEAT DOWN on Delaney's red baseball cap as she wiped the sweat from her brow and bent over to a half-squat position. "Watch out for this slugger," she shouted as Beth O'Roarke stepped up to the plate. Beth wore the dark green academy T-shirt while Delaney sported Quint/Midi Twelve's red one. She'd been playing shortstop on her sister's team for years.

Beth grinned at Delaney; Reed had confided in both her and Ben about his relationship with Delaney. That he'd share such personal information with his friends made Delaney's heart sing.

Yanking on the bill of her cap, Chelsea smiled over at her from the pitcher's mound. "Not to worry. I'm gonna burn the rubber right off this ball, sis. O'Roarke ain't goin' nowhere."

Waiting, Delaney fingered the chain around her neck. Tucked into her breasts was a necklace that had been in Pandora's box. The charm on the end read Firefighter's Lady. She'd cried when Reed had slid the delicate piece of jewelry over her head. It was tangible proof of how he felt about her.

Beth connected with the third of Chelsea's pitches. The ball arrowed straight at Delaney. Leaping into the air, she caught it but landed wrong, twisted her ankle and went down. From the corner of her eye, she saw Reed bolt off the bench.

What if...something happens to you...like the food poisoning...?

Quickly, Delaney scrambled to stand to let him know she was unhurt; with a flourish, she raised the ball and glove over her head and grinned proudly. Reed sat back down.

After three more at-bats, he strode to the mound, looking sexy as hell in the green academy team shirt and khaki shorts. Delaney cupped her hands. "Easy out," she yelled, bending over and sticking her fanny in the air. She punched her glove. "You're a klutz, Macauley."

He shook his head like he used to before they'd gotten close, yelled back for the hecklers to be quiet—and sent a line drive speeding right by her. Out in left field, Joey Santori stretched for it but missed. As Joey raced after the ball, Reed rounded the bases. Jogging by her, he taunted, "I'm gonna score, little girl," and kept going.

"You already did, Doc," she called out to his back.

He halted on third base and threw her a scolding look.

Delaney delighted in his good mood. For the past week—except for two nightmares and one episode of flashbacks—he'd been obviously happy.

As the academy's side retired, the Quint/Midi Twelve team hustled in from the field. Reed was just heading out. Delaney and Chelsea exchanged mocking quips with him, and Delaney plopped down on the bench, her shorts rising up. Reed had taken a few steps away when Chelsea barked, "Laney, what the hell happened to your leg?"

Delaney glanced down. A purplish bruise the size of a man's hand spanned her thigh. She froze when she realized Reed had stopped suddenly and turned around; his gaze dropped to her leg. Last night, in the middle of a dream, he'd grabbed her. She hadn't told him about the bruise, of course.

As he stared at the mark on her, his face got bleak. "I must have done it when I fell on the field," Delaney told Chelsea.

"You wouldn't bruise that fast."

"I've always bruised easily."

Reed's eyes narrowed on her. "Delaney—"

"Get the lead out, Macauley," Eric Scanlon called from the mound. Though Delaney had gently broken off with Eric, he hadn't been happy about losing her to Reed.

Reed said only, "We'll talk about this later," and took the field.

Chelsea dropped beside her on the bench, her ponytail bobbing with the action. Though Delaney had shared with her sister that she and Reed were seeing each other, she didn't tell Chelsea anything about Reed's PTSD. That was for him to share, if he ever chose to.

Studying the mark on Delaney's leg as if it were some kind of hieroglyphics, her sister said, "Laney, he didn't…" When she raised her head, there was fear in her eyes. "God, I can't believe this of Reed, or of you, but did he *do* this to you?"

Shocked, Delaney's jaw dropped. "Of course not. He's the gentlest man I've ever been with."

"What was that conversation all about, then?"

"Reed's protective is all." She pulled down the brim of her hat to hide her dissembling.

Chelsea rolled her eyes, a silent elder sibling's *Yeah, sure.*

"Okay, it's private stuff, Chels." She fingered the chain again. "I can't share his secrets."

"But if he—"

"Trust me, sis. I've never been happier in my life."

Delaney glanced out at first base where Reed stood punching his glove. Though his green cap partly blocked his face, she could tell he was scowling like Scrooge. *He* looked anything but happy.

IN THE TEMPLETON BACKYARD, next to a cedar shed that housed summer equipment, Reed peered across the grass and watched Delaney laugh with one of her teammates, Joe Santori. They were probably rehashing the play Joey had made in the outfield that had won the game for Quint/Midi Twelve. Reed drew in a deep breath and tried to stay calm, but it felt as if he were fighting brushfires. He'd just get one thing under control, and another would flare. His eyes kept straying to her leg, where he'd bruised her. He took a swig of Molson from the bottle in his hand; he willed himself to forget what he'd done and enjoy the late afternoon breeze that came off the lake and the August sun that still burned brightly in the sky.

But he couldn't forget. He'd been right in his dire warnings to her—revealing the secret he'd kept for years had caused nightmares and one flashback. Last night, he'd taken her down with him....

Wildly, he'd kicked at the covers on the bed. In the dream, he was trying to get the gun from Cummings. His leg was a mass of burning pain; he reached for it to stem the flow of blood...and in bed, he'd gotten Delaney instead. She'd awakened with a cry of pain— a hell of a way to come out of a deep sleep; he'd been horrified at what he'd done.

She'd been calm and sympathetic. Holding his head against her breasts—he could still feel the soothing comfort of her skin and smell the sweet scent of her— she'd crooned to him and told him a little pain was a fair trade-off for the hour of pleasure he'd given her before they fell asleep. He'd let her convince him, but now, in the brittle light of day, his shortcomings slapped him in the face. His worst fears were coming true about hurting her, and there wasn't a thing he could do about it.

Because he was lost in thought, Reed didn't see Delaney approach until she was practically on top of him. Since they were partially obscured from the group by the shed and a table with a big umbrella, she kissed him briefly on the cheek. They'd told their close friends about their feelings for each other, but Reed didn't want to broadcast it to the whole department.

"What's the scowl for?" she asked, looking like a kid in the baseball cap, shirt and matching red socks.

"I was thinking about your leg."

"You got a one-track mind, Doc."

He shook his head at her. "Are you always this irreverent about serious things?"

"It seems to work best with you." She lifted the beer she held and took a swig. "Otherwise you start playing the role of Arthur Dimmesdale."

"Who?"

"The guy from *The Scarlet Letter.*"

"Ah, I vaguely remember that. What about the guy?"

"He spends the whole book bemoaning how badly he's treating Hester, but he can't stop it. Even as a high-schooler, I thought he was a wimp, and she was a jerk to put up with it." She faced Reed fully. "I think men who constantly beat on themselves probably have little, tiny..."

He laughed out loud. God, she could tease him out of a black mood.

She turned to peer out over the Templetons' backyard. Sloping to the lake, it had three levels, with pretty lawn chairs, tables and umbrellas. On the deck was a hot tub, which several smoke-eaters were using after the exertion of the day. Though Francey was benched due to her pregnancy, the Templetons had cheered from the sidelines and thrown this post-game get-together.

Reed moved close behind Delaney so his bare knees grazed the back of hers. Knowing they were partly hidden, he slid his free hand under her team shirt and lightly rubbed her waist. "What kind of guy *do* you like?"

She closed her eyes and just about purred at his touch. "Hmm. Older men."

"Like Scanlon?"

"Nope, ten years is about right."

"And?" He scraped her skin with rough knuckles.

"Men who spoil me."

He thought about the romantic dinners he'd fixed for her, the yellow roses he'd sent to her office, a leopard-print thong he'd tucked under her pillow. "Did I spoil you enough this week?"

"Oh, yeah."

"What else?" He leaned into her, pressing his chest against her.

She leaned back. "Men who give me good sex."

"It's been good, Laney," he whispered against her ear. "Real good."

She turned. Lifted her face up to the sun. "Everything's been good. It's been the best week of my life."

His hand dropped to her thigh. "Not every—"

Covering his mouth with her fingers, she shushed him. "Shh. Please, don't ruin this. You didn't know what you were doing. And the bruise is a little thing."

He swallowed hard.

"You can kiss and make it better," she offered, her blue eyes giving the summer sky some competition.

He tried to let go of his worry. For her. "Yeah, how soon?"

"We could sneak out now."

Smiling he said, "Ah, a woman after my own heart."

"I am, Reed," she said soberly.

"What?"

"After your heart."

He bit the inside of his mouth to keep himself from telling her she had it all tied up in ribbons right now. He'd hurt her physically already. It was only a matter of time before he hurt her emotionally. Next week was the anniversary of the shooting, always the worst time of the year for him. God knew what he'd do then.

So he couldn't speak the words of commitment. The words he knew she needed to hear. But he couldn't send her away, either. He squeezed her shoulder and whispered one of her kid-phrases in her ear. "Let's blow this pop stand, sweetheart. I want you now."

"I knew this sex on demand wouldn't be so bad," she drawled, taking his hand and turning toward the lawn.

IT WAS WEIRD AS HELL, but Sam had discovered, on his third counseling session with Reed, that he could talk easier, talk more, if they *did* something together. When he asked Reed, the shrink had agreed eagerly, as if being active was good for him, too. So far they'd jogged around the park adjacent to the academy, worked out with the weights and played a few easy games of HORSE in the gym. Today they were playing racquetball.

"Your serve," Sam said. Sweat covered his face and dampened his shirt.

"We aren't talking much, buddy," Reed commented, bouncing the ball a couple of times on the academy's newly installed court and gripping his racket.

"Finish servin' and we'll take a break." The therapy had been as painful as third-degree burns for Sam. But things seemed to be better at home, so he kept coming back. Not that he had much choice—if he wanted to return to work. Although he still shuddered thinking about seeing Tommy in the fire, Sam had to admit Reed *was* helping him, to a degree, anyway.

Reed tossed the ball up and swung down hard. The ball slammed into the corner. It bounced back and Sam got a piece of it. But his shot wimped out before it hit the front wall.

"My game." Reed grinned.

Swearing colorfully, Sam headed to his bag and fished out a bottle of water. "You know, you look better lately."

Reed found his own water and drank. "Yeah? You getting used to seeing my ugly mug this much?"

Gulping the drink, Sam leaned against the wall. "Maybe. But it's more than that. Somethin' with you. You gettin' laid regularly, Doc?"

Jokingly, Reed told him what he could do with his crude question, and slid down to sit against the wall. Sam dropped beside him. Reed sipped his water, waited as if he was going to say something big. "I got a woman in my life, Leone. And I have to tell you, it's made me a happy man."

"No shit?"

"I wouldn't lie to you." He waited. "Speaking of women, how's it going with Theresa?"

Sam sighed. "Better. We…ya know…we been close lately."

"Close as in *physical* close?"

Sam studied the room. "Uh-huh."

"Is it good?"

"Jeez, Macauley."

The psychologist laughed and said, "I'm not playing

Peeping Tom. I just want to know if it's been easier to
let Theresa physically close?''

"Whatdaya mean?''

"Guys who're grieving, guys who've been through
a trauma—like seeing Tommy die—sometimes they
withdraw and don't let anybody close, not even women
they love.''

"Why?''

"So they can't get hurt again.''

Sam pounded his racket on the hardwood floor, the
sound echoing throughout the cavernous gym. "I feel
that way sometimes. But it kills Terry. She says sex
makes us closer, and when I wouldn't do it, she felt
rejected.'' His eyes narrowed on the floor, and his heart
started to hammer in his chest. "Not like that bitch
Jeanine. Tommy and me, we used to talk about...stuff.
He said she froze him out sometimes. It used to tear
him apart.''

When Reed didn't say anything, Sammy looked
over. "What?''

"We gotta talk about your ex-sister-in-law.''

"No.''

"I don't get it. You tell me about sex, but not this
woman? Why?''

"She hurt Tommy.''

"And?''

"He shoulda had the best. Always. I'll never forgive
the cu—'' He stopped. Glared at Reed. "Hey, pretty
clever. I'm talkin' about her.''

"Keep going.''

Sam jumped to his feet. "Nope. I'll tell ya about me

and Terry, and the kids. I want like hell to be a good husband and father. But that bitch is off-limits.''

Reed stood, too, and as he got up, Sam looked at the doctor's leg. Sam had noticed the scar before, but hadn't asked. ''What happened to you, Reed?''

Reed didn't even look down. His face paled.

Sam said, ''This have anything to do with losin' that buddy you told me about?''

Swallowing hard, Reed nodded. ''Yep.''

''Sorry, man. Musta hurt like a bitch.''

''It hurt more inside.'' Reed clapped Sam on the back. ''I told you I knew how you felt. But you gotta get it out to get better.''

Halfway back to the court, Sam stopped short. ''*Am* I gettin' better, Reed?''

''Yeah, I think you're making progress. It's slow, and there'll be some setbacks, but it's happening.''

''Will I be able to go back to work soon?''

''Not for a while, Sammy. You gotta talk about it all before I can okay your return.''

''All but…her.''

Reed sighed. ''For now. Let's play another game then get some coffee. I'm gonna ask you to dredge up some painful stuff today.''

''I know, that's why I'm beatin' the pants off you.''

''In your dreams, buddy. We're tied.''

''The hell we are….'' They argued through the next game. For Sam, it was better than blubbering like a baby.

But he knew that would come later.

DELANEY HAD CARTED SIX beanbag chairs to the academy's conference room, which was connected to

Reed's office, gotten two bulldozer-type firefighters to move the big oak table, and had arranged her space for today in a small circle on the thick rug. Two boys and three girls now occupied the crayon-colored sacks, in various positions of adolescent slouch. She sat on the big yellow one, as demurely as she could given the suit and heels she wore.

"I'd like to thank you all for coming," she said dryly.

Two kids nodded nervously. One snorted. One wouldn't meet her eyes. And T. J. Leone studied his sneakers.

"I know, I know, your parents made you come. It's okay, I understand."

"What do we call you?" Suzy Roncone, a pretty dark-haired girl, asked.

Marcy Leone smiled. "We call her Dr. Delaney. Or Dr. D."

"That okay with everybody?" Delaney asked.

Most of them nodded.

"T.J.?"

At the sound of his name the boy's head whipped up. His hair was shaggy around his dark eyes—his dark, *troubled* eyes. Delaney hadn't gotten through to him yet. He was proving to be as tough to reach as his dad.

"What are you thinking, T.J.?"

The boy shrugged.

"You gotta talk about it."

He cleared his throat. At fourteen, his voice had changed but was unpredictable. "Can somebody else go first?"

She scanned the group. No volunteers. "I've got an idea." Out of her bag, she drew a small tennis ball. "We'll start like this. Somebody shares, then gives the ball to another person who goes next."

"Can we pass?" a girl dressed in Goth—gothic was the latest fad—asked. Her name tag read Kassie Talbot. Ah, Chief Talbot's granddaughter. The all-black ensemble, as well as lipstick and nail polish the color of the night, probably flipped out her granddad.

"You can, but it won't get us far. I wish you wouldn't ask to do that, Kassie."

The girl shrugged. "What the hell."

Thoughtfully Delaney squeezed the ball. "I'd like everybody in the group to share something about his or her father." No one had a mother as a firefighter. "Say anything. Good stuff. Bad stuff. Anything."

She lifted her arm to toss the ball.

Kassie held up her hand, stopping the throw. "You a member of this group?"

"Of course."

"Then tell us something about your father."

Delaney had had patients corner her like this before. With kids, she'd had to give in more. Besides, sharing some of her past helped them open up, even if it did hurt to dredge up the memories. She thought back to the handsome dark-haired poet of a man who had given her life, and her heart squeezed tightly with regret. "My dad was a singer."

"No kidding?" Suzy said. "I wanna be a rock star."

"Well, think long and hard about it. Not only was he gone a lot, but we had to move when he got restless

or bored in one town. And sometimes he and my
mother would leave us alone for days at a time.''

"How old were you?'' This from the young boy who
looked like Ben Affleck. Delaney knew he was Kyle,
the son of a popular line firefighter.

"It started when I was about seven and my sister
was thirteen.'' Delaney tossed Marcy the ball. "Okay,
kiddo, your turn.''

Catching the ball, Marcy raised her eyes to the
group. "My dad's depressed since Uncle Tommy
died.''

From the corner of her eye, Delaney saw T.J. stiffen
and stare back down at his Nikes. He toyed with the
laces.

"Losing someone you love is hard, Marce. Think
about how you'd feel without T.J.''

"At least there wouldn't be his scuzzy towels all
over the bathroom floor.''

"Oh, yeah, and your makeup crap in every drawer
and shelf doesn't count as a mess?''

"I need my beauty aids,'' she said haughtily.

"You can say that again.''

Delaney let them quibble because T.J. was talking.
She'd seen this before. It was their way of communi-
cating.

Marcy tossed the ball to Suzy Roncone, but she
stayed quiet. Delaney nudged her. "Suzy, your dad
works with Marcy's father, doesn't he?''

Suddenly T.J. stood. "My dad isn't workin'. Haven't
you heard, he's off the line. He wigged out in a fire.''

Surprised at the outburst, Delaney stood, too. She

crossed to the boy. Grasped his arm and pulled him aside. He was trembling all over so she held on tight. "T.J., I'm sorry if your father's situation embarrasses you."

"I'm not embarrassed. I just want outta here. Can I go?"

She thought for a minute. "You can go sit in Dr. Macauley's office for a bit. Settle down. If you promise to think about sharing stuff with us." Sadly, she smiled at him. "I really think I can help you if you'd give me a chance."

In his eyes she saw a need so great it silenced her for a minute. "Please," she finally said.

"Maybe, but not today."

"All right. Go through that door." She pointed to Reed's office. "Dr. Macauley isn't there. He's with your dad."

T.J. bolted away as if he was being chased by bullies in a dark alley.

Delaney sat back down. "Sharing's hard, guys. Not everybody does it easily."

Marcy bit her lip. "It's about more than Dad, Dr. D."

"Is it? Maybe we can talk about that later. I don't think—"

"He misses Aunt Jeanine. They were pretty tight...."

Delaney filed away the information, but turned the conversation back to the group.

She tried not to show how worried she was about the young boy who was so much like his father.

DELANEY SHAW, Reed's own personal obsession these days, was quietly talking with T. J. Leone when Reed and Sam came through his office door. Dressed in a navy linen suit with a slinky red top underneath, and sporting red strappy sandals on her feet, she wore her psychologist's face as she sat on the couch with the young boy. Reed's heart battered his rib cage at just the sight of her.

"Hi, you two." Reed dropped his bag onto the floor by his desk. "Have a good session?"

Delaney shot him a quick look. It told him no. "It was a good start."

T.J. asked, "How 'bout you, Dad? Have a good session?" There was an edge to his voice.

Sammy Leone swallowed hard. "It was a bitch, kid."

That made T.J. smile, albeit weakly.

"Talking about your feelings is tough." Reed crossed to his desk, trying to appear nonchalant.

"Ready to go, son?" Sam asked, rubbing his shoulder. "I'm whipped."

T.J. stood. "Yeah, sure."

Sam watched his son for a minute. Reed knew the father in Leone was worried about the boy. "You wanna stop someplace on the way home?"

"We gotta take Marcy?"

"No, she's going over to Suzy Roncone's."

"Just you and me?" Reed caught the yearning in the kid's voice.

Sam smiled at T.J. "Tell you what. Let's go to the locker room first. I'll shower off some of this sweat. Then you and me'll do somethin'."

"What?"

"What do you like to do these days, T.J.?"

The boy shrugged. "Movies, mostly."

As they headed to the door, Sam rested his hand on T.J.'s back. "Hmm. Guess I can handle that. What you wanna see?"

"How about the new Bruce Willis flick?"

"Sounds good to me."

After the Leone men left, Delaney rose and went to the window. She stared out with her arms wrapped around her waist. He crossed to her and lightly clasped his hands on her shoulders. "I'm always surprised how slight you are, when I haven't touched you for a while."

"Why?" Her voice was smoky and she didn't look at him.

"Because you're such a pit bull, I forget your size."

"I feel like a puppy right now."

"Now, that's an interesting turn of phrase." He drew her back to his chest, folded his arms over the front of her. "What did you talk about with the kids?"

"Dads." Her hands came up to grasp his arms.

Ah, he got it. He thought for a minute. Then he whispered, "Tell me. About your father."

"Not much more to tell than you already know. He was gone all the time. When he was home, he wasn't really *with* us. He barely had time for my mother. Let alone me." She expelled a heavy breath. "Chelsea's father was almost as bad, but at least he'd come and take her some weekends. I always wished I could go with them."

"I'm sorry." With stunning force, Reed realized

something and could have kicked himself for missing it before. "It must be hard for you to trust men."

She nodded. Her hair tumbled softly down her back. He buried his face in it. Smelled its jasmine scent. Lifted his hand to touch the velvety softness. "Turn around, honey."

At first she didn't. Gently he nudged her to face him and saw the moisture in her eyes. Her distress twisted something inside him.

"All that rejection I dished out. It kicked into this thing with your father, didn't it?"

She nodded.

"And it hurt."

Straightening, she lifted her chin. "It's no big—"

His fingers on her mouth stopped the lie. "Shh, it's a huge deal. I'm sorry I never realized what I was triggering."

"Well, I never knew what I was triggering with you, either. So we're even."

Slowly, he ran his knuckles down her cheek. "Ah, sweetheart, we're nowhere near even. You've given me so much." He battled back the fear. Every time the connection with her deepened, every time he slipped more and more under her spell, he started to panic. "Let me give back to you. Talk to me about this."

"All right." She met his gaze. "Can I trust you, Reed?"

"What do you mean?"

"I'm afraid you're just going to bolt out of my life. That I'll wake up one day and you'll be gone."

"Did he do that?"

"Eventually."

When Reed didn't answer right away, she bit her lip. "Never mind, you don't have to answer that." Her hand went to the chain he'd given her. She pulled out the charm and fingered it as if it was a talisman. "I promised I wouldn't push you. It's only been a week. I'm just feeling a little vulnerable right now and—"

"Delaney."

"What?"

"Shut up."

"*What?*"

"Give me a chance to answer."

She stared at him so solemnly it almost broke his heart.

"I promise I won't ever just leave you. I wish I could promise we'll be together forever, but I can't." Not yet, anyway. "But I won't just leave."

Big fat tears swam in those beautiful blue eyes.

"Oh, honey."

Smelling of sweat, damp from the game, he pulled her to his chest. She clung to him and he was swamped by his feelings for her.

"Thanks," she mumbled against his shirt.

Reed's world shifted again. This lovely woman asked for so little. He hadn't given her nearly enough. And for the first time since he'd met her, he realized his responsibility to her.

She'd given him her heart. He couldn't break it. He just couldn't. And in the dim afternoon shadows that came in through his windows, he promised himself he *wouldn't*.

He'd work harder at getting better. Even next week, on the day of the anniversary.

CHAPTER ELEVEN

A FEW DAYS BEFORE the anniversary of the shooting, Reed almost broke the vow he'd made to himself about not hurting Delaney. The incident itself was a little thing. Like most *straws that break the camel's back.* FAN had an outing at Sea Breeze Amusement Park near the lake and the day had been enjoyable. Delaney had shamed him onto the Ferris wheel, where she'd shaken the car when they got to the top. It made him sweat worse than when he'd worn turnout gear in the summer. She'd wheedled him into a carousel ride, which had turned his stomach queasy. But when she'd challenged him to go with her on the Viper—the kids called it the *bitchinest* roller coaster in the world—he'd refused, claiming those things were for teens with strong hearts.

So, she'd gone over with Marcy Leone and Kassie Talbot, looking like a teenager herself. Today she wore a short denim skirt and a cropped top that showed some belly when she raised her arms; her dark curly hair was clipped back off her face.

"She's a daredevil, isn't she?" Ben Cordaro was standing beside Reed. Diana Cordaro had also chanced the Viper with Jake. Alex had to practically hogtie Francey to keep her off it. A promise of cotton candy had distracted his very pregnant wife, and Chelsea had gone with them to keep her entertained.

Chelsea, who'd been glaring at Reed as if he were Jack the Ripper these days—ever since she'd seen the bruise he'd given Delaney. Reed didn't blame Chelsea a bit.

"Reed?" Ben was calling his name.

"Sorry, what did you say?"

"I said Delaney has no fear."

"I know." He nodded to the roller coaster, which dipped and climbed and ground metal against metal, making his teeth hurt. "Jeez, I hate those things."

"Me, too."

Dragging his eyes away as the cars swayed dangerously to the left, Reed glanced around. "Where are the O'Roarkes?"

"Over in the kiddie rides. Timmy's fascinated with the baby race cars."

"Oh, no, another little Dylan in the making."

"'Fraid so." Ben munched on an ice cream bar. "So, things going pretty well for you?"

"They're okay." Embarrassed, he ducked his head. "She keeps me hopping." He watched the roller coaster. Someone in the front car had let go of the safety bar and was waving her hands in the air.

"Welcome to the club, buddy."

"What club?"

"The club where—"

Reed gasped. "What the hell?" The car holding Delaney circled around by them. All occupants had let go of the bar and raised their hands over their heads. Including her. A common maneuver, but it bothered him.

His heart began to thrum in his chest as he watched the *girls* giggle and toss their heads back into the wind; Delaney's hair trailed behind her and she laughed lustily. The car passed him and careered out of sight. He practically held his breath until it came around again.

And couldn't believe his eyes. It happened almost in slow motion. One of the girls slithered back away from the bar. She managed to get to her knees on the seat, her intention, Reed guessed, then she leaned precariously to the side. Delaney slid back, too, to drag the first girl down. Just then the car rounded a hairpin bend. Both of them took a dip to the side before Delaney managed to get them both settled again on the padded seat.

Spots swam before Reed's eyes. The coaster blurred. Loud noises, sounds, created fireworks in his brain. He saw only explosions, heard only the pop and crackle of...

"Reed."

There was red-hot fire in his brain.

"Reed!"

He came out of it to find Ben shaking his arm.

Still having trouble focusing, Reed noted that Francey and Alex had returned and stood next to Ben; they were sharing cotton candy with Chelsea. The O'Roarkes trailed up behind them with Timmy asleep in the stroller.

Only Ben seemed to have noticed Reed's reaction.

Reed's gaze whipped back to the Viper. It had come to a halt. Delaney exited the car with the girls and drew them aside.

Anger pooled inside him. It gave way to blind, irrational fury.

Diana and Jake were smiling as they approached the group. Delaney, finished with the girls, also headed toward them. Her step was jaunty and her whole demeanor animated. And she was laughing.

Laughing.

When she reached him, she said, "God, that was fun, except—"

And Reed snapped.

"Fun?" he roared, grabbing her roughly by the arms. "That was *fun?*" He shook her. Hard.

Wide-eyed, she stared at him and the laughter died on her face.

"Do you have any idea how much danger you were in? Anything could have happened to you. *Anything.*"

She managed to say, "Reed..."

He felt strong fingers on his arm. "Get your hands off her."

He didn't.

A hard punch landed on his shoulder. "I said get your hands off my sister. *Now.*"

The *my sister* penetrated. He eased his grip on Delaney and turned to Chelsea.

"Don't you ever touch her again. First her leg, then this." She ran her hand over Delaney's arm where red marks the size of his fingertips were beginning to form. "You bastard."

Delaney said, "Chels, it's not what you think. Let it go."

Chelsea did not back off. Somewhere in the dim recesses of his cluttered mind, Reed admired her for it. "No way, not again."

Ben stepped up to Chelsea. "Honey, come on over here. You don't understand."

Flinging off Ben's hand, she faced the group. "*What* is wrong with all of you?" She scanned the O'Roarkes, the Cordaros, who were watching with sympathetic eyes. Her gaze landed on her husband, who hadn't moved. "Jake, are you just going to stand there and let him abuse my sister like this?"

"Chels," Delaney pleaded, "it's not what you think."

"No?" She lifted her chin. "Then what is it?"

The blood pumped mercilessly through Reed's brain. Paradoxically, he froze, like a rookie panicking at his first fire.

Delaney moved in close to him, caressed his face. "Reed, it's okay. I'm sorry. I wasn't thinking. I won't ever do anything like this again."

"Oh, for God's sake." Chelsea was practically climbing out of her skin. "Laney, are you crazy?"

Reed came around then. Sounds and scents filtered in—the muted screams of more roller coaster riders, the screech of tires on the NASCAR ride, the smell of hot dogs and popcorn and fried dough.

Turning to Chelsea, he faced the firing squad in her eyes and said, "No, Chelsea, Delaney isn't crazy. I am."

"IT WAS AN ORDINARY SHIFT." Reed had settled onto a hard picnic table bench, his hands clasped in front of him, his eyes averted from the group that had gathered around him. They'd sought out an isolated pavilion for privacy when Reed had insisted he wanted to talk to all his friends.

Chelsea sat across from him, her face serious, as Reed told his gruesome tale. Jake flanked her, Beth perched on the end of the table with Dylan behind her. The Cordaro and Templeton women were on the bench across from him, too, their men close by.

And as the birds chirped in the bright sunlight, and kids played on the rides and with the games, Reed haltingly blurted out the entire story of the worst nightmare of his life.

"A gun...I couldn't believe it."

Diana gasped. Chelsea leaned into Jake.

From where she stood behind him, Delaney placed her hands on his shoulders, lightly rubbing through the checked sport shirt he wore. He was as rigid as granite. She was trying not to listen, but just the raw cadence of his voice cut her insides to slivers. She bit her lip to tolerate his pain.

Chelsea began weeping when Reed said, "They all died."

Reed glanced at Ben. "Imagine—" at Jake, then Dylan "—if it was your men..."

All three firefighters shook their heads.

Delaney noticed Reed was avoiding Beth's eyes. When Delaney looked at her, she saw rivulets running down the stoic woman's cheeks. Dylan had slid his arm around her and held her tightly.

More details... "Crash died in my arms...take care of his kids...I quit the line...went to grad school..."

As he neared the end of this part, when he said he

got his degree in psychology to help other smoke-eaters, Diana and Francey turned tear-streaked faces into their respective husbands' shoulders. Ben and Alex were grim; a muscle leaped in the battalion chief's jaw.

And Delaney continued to gently rub Reed's back, searching for some way to comfort him. The catharsis was good, but excruciating.

"A bad case of PTSD that I managed till I came here…"

"Back to firefighting," Ben said.

"Yeah." He nodded to Ben and Beth. "And you guys didn't help." Reed chuckled, Ben did, too, but Beth continued to cry. As Reed elaborated on the horror of his condition, the group was riveted. Except for Beth, who slipped off the table and strode to the other side of the pavilion. Dylan followed her.

Reed's face became even more stricken, but he focused on Chelsea as he ended his story. "I told Delaney I'm not a good catch. I can't control this syndrome." He grinned weakly. "But you know your sister. She wouldn't…*won't* listen." He cleared his throat. "I'm really trying to manage this, Chelsea. Still, I've hurt her…I'll probably hurt her again."

Her hands still on him, Delaney finally spoke. "Hush, we've talked about this."

Swallowing hard, scrubbing her hands over her face, Chelsea climbed off the bench and circled the picnic table. She looked small and unusually frail in a white camisole and jeans. She sat down, facing out, and Reed angled toward her.

"You're right, Chels. I don't blame you for wanting me away from Delaney."

"I've never been more *wrong* in my life, Reed." Quietly, she reached out and hugged him. Arms around him, she closed her eyes to keep back the tears. Female firefighters had to be tough, but the three women RFD members had melted into puddles during Reed's story. "And I'm sorry. For what I said and for all you've been through."

The hug lingered. Finally she drew back but stayed where she was. Ben, who knew part of the story, straightened. He commented on all that Reed had done to help the RFD.

Delaney noticed Reed listened but kept glancing toward Beth. "I've done some good here." He grinned self-effacingly. "I wanted to help other firefighters deal with their trauma, even though I couldn't deal with mine. Even though I couldn't stop..."

"Oh, Reed." Delaney wouldn't listen to him berate himself. "You couldn't have stopped Jack Cummings. Nobody could."

"We'll never know," he said, squeezing her hand. "But I didn't mean that." He shrugged. "Fire departments need programs like FAN to help guys like me and Sam."

Ben nodded in the direction of the amusement park. "Sammy Leone seems to be doing better." Delaney was warmed by how this firefighter family, now that they knew the truth, rallied around him.

"He is."

"And me," Alex said. "You've helped me in that significant others group."

"Thanks."

Chelsea grabbed Reed's hand and held it. "I'm so sorry, Reed."

"You ever been back to New York?" Ben asked.

Delaney had been wondering about that, too, but was trying to let him tell her things in stages.

"No. I talk to Tina Marx, Crash's wife, at least once a week. The boys e-mail me occasionally, though. The oldest just started college, and I've..."

Paid his tuition, Delaney would bet. *Crash told me to take care of his kids.*

"How old are they?" Diana asked.

"Eighteen, seventeen and sixteen." Again, he reached up and squeezed Delaney's hand. "Just the age you like."

Delaney smiled. "How are they doing?"

"Great. The kids are smart, funny, caring. Just like their dad was."

Timmy O'Roarke started to cry, effectively breaking the mood. Which was good, because Reed had had enough. Jake bolted off the picnic table and rescued the kid before Beth and Dylan heard him. He cuddled the baby to his chest and walked away.

The rest of the group began to move. Chelsea joined Jake, and the Cordaros and Templetons eased off the bench, too. Beth and Dylan approached them. Reed stood and Delaney stepped back.

Without a second thought, Reed took Beth in his arms. "This resurrects too much for you," he said simply.

Dylan's eyes moistened again as Beth buried her face in Reed's shoulder. "No, I'm okay with that. I just kept thinking how you helped me through my loss when yours was…'' She broke off, crying hard.

''Shh.'' Reed's hand went to her hair and stroked it. But his shoulders slackened and his stance relaxed.

When he drew back, she looked up into his face with watery eyes. ''You're quite a guy.'' Over his shoulder, she smiled at Delaney. ''I told you.''

Reed circled around. ''Told you what?''

''Girl stuff,'' Delaney said, winking at Beth.

Very good girl stuff.

DELANEY WATCHED THE SNAZZY red Eclipse pull up to the front of her office building. She was hurrying inside because she had an after-school meeting with T. J. Leone. Alone—without Marcy or the group. Something, though, made her slow her step. When she got close, she saw the windows were down and a beautiful blonde was talking with the passenger—T.J. Her arm stretched across the seat, the woman affectionately rubbed the boy's shoulder.

Without preamble, Delaney approached the driver's side of the car. ''Hi, I'm Delaney Shaw.''

Startled, the woman turned toward her. Out of a heart-shaped face, blue eyes stared up at her, heavily mascaraed and lined. ''Oh, hello.''

Ducking her head, Delaney said, ''Hi, guy. Your mom told me you were taking the bus here today from school.''

''I…uh…''

When he didn't finish, Delaney looked at the woman. ''I don't believe we've met,'' she said.

''I'm Jeanine Leone.''

T.J. misses Aunt Jeanine. They were tight.

Calling on professional reserve, Delaney bit her tongue not to question Jeanine's right to be here. "Well, thanks for giving T.J. a ride." She made a show of checking her watch. "We need to get inside, T.J. I have another appointment at five."

The boy bolted out of the car as if it was on fire. Without even saying goodbye to Aunt Jeanine, he was at the front door in no time. Delaney nodded to the woman—she was probably a little younger than Delaney—and followed T.J. inside.

She waited until they were seated comfortably in her office before she said, "What gives?"

"Whaddaya mean?" T.J. gazed at the floor.

"Don't diss me, kid. Why were you with your aunt?"

For the first time, when he raised his face, Delaney saw defiance in T.J.'s eyes. "Why shouldn't I be? Tommy knew I saw her."

"He did?"

"Yeah. He said it was okay. Tommy was..." The boy's Adam's apple bobbed. His defiance faded.

"Tommy was what?"

Bleak brown eyes got bleaker.

"T.J., you gotta talk about it."

"Is Dad?"

"Is Dad what?"

"Talkin' about it?"

"Yes, with Dr. Macauley."

The teenager's shoulders relaxed. Did parents have any idea the cues their children took from them?

"Tommy hoped him and Aunt Jeanine would get back together."

"Were they discussing a reconciliation?"

"Yeah."

"Did your dad know?"

T.J. shook his head. "He hated her. Tommy was afraid to tell him."

"Tommy told you that?"

"No, Aunt Jeanine did." The boy swallowed back emotion. "She makes it better, Dr. D." T.J. dropped his gaze to the floor again. Surreptitiously he swiped at his eyes.

Delaney's heart went out to the boy. "She makes losing Tommy easier for you."

He nodded.

"That's okay, buddy. It's good."

T.J. stared at his shoes, then he glanced up at her. "You gonna tell Dad?"

"No, of course not. I told you this was private." She motioned to her office, indicating the therapy. "Except if I thought any of you in the group were in danger of harming yourselves. And, of course, I give your parents general updates on your mental health."

His obvious relief didn't sit well.

"But you should tell him."

"No way."

"Why?"

"Dad freaks when her name is mentioned."

"Can you tell your mom?"

"Mom knows."

"Really?" That could cause problems.

"Yeah, but she's afraid to tell Dad, too."

"I'm going to share this with Dr. Macauley, T.J. He needs to know. In order to help your parents."

"Okay, I guess."

"Shall we talk more about Jeanine now?" She waited. "And Tommy?"

He raised bruised eyes to her and nodded.

Delaney leaned back into her chair. She couldn't help worrying that she was sitting on a time bomb. What would happen when Sam Leone found out about this?

IN HIS CITY HALL OFFICE, Chief Chase Talbot raised his arm and, still sitting behind his huge mahogany desk, tossed a Nerf ball high into the air. It dropped, swishing into the net across the room. "Two points."

Reed watched him. The fire chief was known for putting others at ease. He was a taskmaster, but almost all of the guys liked him. Talbot addressed Ben. "Cordaro, you missed it."

"Huh?" Ben glanced up from the trivia game he was studying. "I'm trying to answer this week's questions. Nobody at the academy's won since Jake took over." He scowled. "This time they're all about inventions in the history of firefighting."

Talbot stood and stretched. He was a tall man, powerfully built. Reed had heard somewhere he'd grown up on the streets in the South. He still had an accent, even after living up north for years. "Read me some. I gave a presentation once on that at a conference. Did a hell of a lot of research." He hustled over to the hoop and retrieved the ball he'd thrown into the basket on the floor.

"Sure, but the money goes to the academy if we win."

Talbot chuckled. "You guys sure are competitive."

"Damn right! Okay, here they are: What contributions did the following make to the evolution of fire suppression? Benjamin Howe, Commissioner Robert Quinn, George Hale, John Nelson Gamewell, John Walter Christie and Squire Boone?" Disgusted, Ben looked up. "Who the hell is Squire Boone?"

Reed enjoyed the byplay and sat back against the thickly padded chair. He'd been getting increasingly anxious as the days went on and the anniversary of the shooting came closer; he needed distractions. "Daniel Boone's brother. I happen to know what he developed—fire extinguishers."

"One down," Ben said.

"I know a couple," Talbot added. "Howe was the manufacturer of horsepower engines. Gamewell developed fire alarms. And I think the commissioner invented the first aerial buckets, from seein' cherry pickers on the farm."

"No shit?" Ben grinned. I know Christie. Dylan mentioned this. He was a race car designer who helped design tractors to pull the first steam engines."

Talbot scowled. "I have no idea what Hale did."

"Me, either," Ben said.

"Well then, let's get down to business." Talbot braced his arms on his desk and leaned over. "Tell me about Leone, Macauley. You helpin' him?"

Exchanging a quick glance with Ben—his buddy's look said, *Now's not the time to put yourself down*—Reed nodded to the chief. "Yeah, he's making progress.'' Reed believed that, though he feared something could come along and trigger a setback.

"The mayor's on me about it.''

"What?'' This was news to Reed.

"She heard about the incident in the church. Some snoopy newspaper reporter friend of hers was there. Apparently Her Highness was able to stop anything from getting in print.''

Ben chuckled at the chief's tone. "Vanessa Jordan still busting your balls, Talbot?'' It was common knowledge that the new mayor and the fire chief butted heads frequently.

"Is the pope Catholic?''

The men chuckled.

"Anyway,'' Talbot said. "I'm tryin' to play both sides of the fence here. Our guy gonna make it?''

"Yeah. I think so.''

"How much longer?''

"Not too long. If nothing else happens, I can probably release him at the end of next month.''

"Good.'' Dark gray eyes focused on Reed. "How 'bout you, Doc?''

Reed's gaze snapped to Ben again. Ben shook his head.

Talbot chuckled. "Cordaro keeps secrets, Macauley. For everybody. I heard stuff from the guys at Engine Seventeen, is all.''

"What'd you hear?''

"You lost a brother.'' Reed remembered telling Tommy's crew this the day he'd spent with their group.

Reed cleared his throat. "Actually, I lost several. All at once.''

"Sorry, man." The fire chief straightened. "Must be that's why you're doin' such a good job with FAN."

"FAN was your idea."

"Yeah, easy to come up with the ideas. You gotta put it to work in the trenches. Sometimes I miss that."

"Hey, any time you want to help."

"I been at some FAN things. I'll be at more." His look darkened. "I got a personal interest in this fire-fighter children's camp that wants to open."

Reed knew that Talbot's son had been killed in the line of duty.

"Got some grandkids that just came to live with me." Talbot raised his hand to his lip. "Shaved my mustache 'cause Kassie said it was too gray and made me look old." He rolled his eyes. "I been meaning to ask you, Macauley. Is this Shaw broad good?"

Yeah, she's good, all right. "Good?"

"With kids. I'm thinkin' Kassie needs more help than that adolescent group." The look on Talbot's face said that was an understatement.

"She's a miracle worker with teenagers."

"Glad to hear that." Talbot stood. "Anyway, I just wanted to get an update on Leone, and tell you what a good job you're doin'."

"Do I get a raise?" Reed asked.

"Yeah, I'll ask Ms. Jordan the next time we have tea."

The phone rang. When the chief picked it up, he made a face. "Sure, Mary, I'll talk to Ms. Mayor."

Ben and Reed left Talbot scowling into the phone.

"He's a nice guy," Reed said.

"Yep."

The two men stopped at the elevator and pressed the button. "You doing okay, buddy?" Ben asked as they waited.

Reed nodded. "Uh-huh. Sorry about all that at the park."

"Reed, we're your friends. And we've all got our demons."

Nodding, Reed was grateful for the elevator's ping, and stepped on as soon as the doors opened. "I know. Thanks."

When he finally arrived at his office, Reed tried not to think about those demons. But his gaze strayed to his desk calendar. In just a few short days, it would be the anniversary of the shooting. Reed wondered if this year would be any different.

Sighing, he reached for the phone and punched out Delaney's number.

CHAPTER TWELVE

THE SQUEEGEE TOPPLED into the bucket of warm soapy water, splashing suds down Delaney's bare legs. She let loose several unladylike curses, then heard an embarrassed cough behind her. Whirling around, she saw Lawrence Stead, long time resident of Dutch Towers, stifle a smile. His white hair was still thick, and his face showed fewer lines than might be expected for a man in his seventies. "My dear, think of the children."

She grinned sheepishly at the older gentleman. "Sorry, Mr. Stead. Where *are* my kids?"

"Right now, they're scrubbing the floor in the common area with that young lieutenant." He crossed farther into the room, and pulled some dead leaves off a plant on the shelf.

"Dylan? Oh, no, the place will be a disaster before they're done."

"As a matter of fact, Mrs. O'Roarke is trying to contain them. She's rather annoyed." He drew up closer to Delaney, his kind brown eyes sparkling. "What has you upset?" he asked, nodding to the window she was washing. "Surely not a few streaks on my apartment window."

Delaney shook her head, dislodging the ponytail her hair had struggled to escape all morning. Finger-combing it off her face, she secured the elastic more tightly. "No, it isn't the window. Somebody I expected didn't show up today."

"Half the Rockford Fire Department is here."

Despite her disappointment at Reed's absence, she smiled. "Jake did a good job organizing this volunteer day for FAN."

"We're grateful for your help," he said with a far-away look in his eyes. She wondered what stories, what memories were stored in his brain. "And, of course, Adelaide is in her glory."

"Jake's like a son to her." Still smiling, she gathered up her things. "I'll be going now. I want to see what Dylan's up to."

Delaney left Mr. Stead's apartment and headed for the stairwell, opting not to use the elevator.

Inside the stairwell, she leaned against the wall, closed her eyes and breathed deeply. When that didn't help she sat down on the concrete step. She was trying to be patient with Reed, but he'd turned back into a hermit these last few days. He'd spent as little time with her as possible, and when they were together, he barely talked to her. The other night was the worst....

"What do you mean you're going home?" she'd asked after they'd made breathless love and Reed had slid out of bed and begun to dress.

"I've got a busy day tomorrow. I—"

"Is that why you insisted we come to my place tonight?" she asked. She pulled up the pink flowered sheet on her bed and lay back against the pillow. "You engineered it so we'd be here—" she patted the mattress "—and you could leave."

Stuffing legs into pants and feet into shoes, he didn't face her. "Don't get paranoid, Delaney. This isn't some plot." His voice was impatient.

"What's going on?"

"Nothing." He shrugged into his shirt. "We don't have to sleep together *every* night, you know."

"We have since I found Pandora's box."

He threw her a withering glance. "Yeah, and you've got the black-and-blue marks to prove it."

"I thought we were past all that." When he finished dressing, she said, "Please, Reed, talk to me."

He stilled. "Give me some space right now, will you? I'll try harder, but... Just do it, please?"

She'd agreed, and he'd left.

She'd racked her brain to figure out what had caused this newest round of distancing. Dragging out one of the books he'd let her borrow, she began to read and hit on the answer in a half hour.

The next day was the anniversary of the shooting. The book indicated that anniversaries brought back many symptoms the PTSD sufferer had already conquered.

She'd glanced at her computer. Hmm. She had the date. Knew the location...

It took only fifteen minutes to find an article in the *Times* archived on the Net.

Tears clouded her eyes as she read the stark account; she hadn't been prepared for the pictures. Castleman resembled Jake. Johnson was a small, stocky guy. Crash Marx was big and burly and looked like Santa Claus.

And then there was Reed. *The lone survivor. Hero*

of the tragedy. The articles emphasized how he'd tried to save his men, how critically he'd been wounded. Even the newspapers were clear that he'd put himself between the shooter and his crew.

But it was the picture of a young Reed Macauley in his lieutenant dress blues that got to her the most. She'd wept as she traced his unlined face, his cocky grin, the arrogant arch of his eyebrows. He did indeed remind her of Dylan O'Roarke....

The thought drew her from the memory. She'd better stop moping and find out what O'Roarke had suckered her kids into.

The huge common room was spotless, if a little damp; Delaney heard screeches and yelps from outside. She followed the sounds and found chaos.

Beth stood off to the side with Adelaide Lowe, out of the line of fire. In the grass were Dylan and Joey Santori and all the kids—having a grand old time.

"Who brought the balloons?" Delaney asked.

"Joey's grandparents had them in their apartment. Joey filled them with water." Beth shook her head at her husband. "He's a disgrace to the department," she said as he chased one of the boys around the yard and drenched the kid's jeans and T-shirt with a well-aimed balloon. Meanwhile, Joey attacked two girls.

Right now Delaney would give her right arm for Reed to be in the middle of the fray. He would have enjoyed this.

Adelaide said, "I'm going to get towels and see how Jake's doing with the drainpipe in my kitchen." She trundled off to find her favorite firefighter.

For a little while, Beth watched the action; the kids

had ganged up on Dylan and Joey and were bombarding them with water balloons. Then Beth turned to Delaney. "Where is he?" she asked without preamble.

"I don't know. He said he'd be here."

"He snapped at me yesterday."

"At you? He adores you, Beth."

"Told me to mind my own business when I asked him why he looked like a character out of *Scream Two*."

Delaney wrapped her arms around her waist and pretended to watch the play. "Well, he doesn't like to be pushed."

"He practically came to blows with Eric Scanlon."

That brought her around. "Oh, no."

"We were planning the physical fitness program for the recruit class starting in a few weeks. Eric was needling Reed about something and Reed exploded. Eric was not...understanding about it. I really thought he might take a swing at Reed. But Ben came in and stopped them."

"Oh, God." Delaney buried her face in her hands.

Drawing Delaney around the corner from the melee, Beth asked, "What's wrong, honey?"

Delaney leaned against the wall. "Tomorrow's the anniversary of the shooting."

For several seconds Beth stared at the unmoving trees. Finally she said, "I know all about anniversaries. My husband, Tim, and my daughter, Janey, died on Christmas Day. I didn't celebrate a holiday for twenty years."

Delaney's heart took another tumble in her chest.

She reached out and squeezed Beth's arm. "Oh, Beth, I'm sorry."

"Dylan made me stop spending every holiday licking my wounds."

"What do you mean?"

"I used to work on an ambulance on Thanksgiving and Christmas. He forced me to go to Cordaro's with him the first Thanksgiving, then to celebrate Christmas with him." She closed her eyes, remembering. "He said he wanted to replace the sad memories with good ones."

Delaney sighed. "I wish I could do that for Reed."

"Hmm. Maybe we can help."

"There you are." Francey waddled around the corner, with Chelsea in tow. Francey looked healthy in gray fleece shorts and tank top, and Chelsea, in cutoffs and an RFD shirt, was smiling.

"What can we help with?" Chelsea asked, scrutinizing Delaney's strained face.

Beth said succinctly, "Tomorrow's the anniversary of the shooting Reed was involved with. Anniversaries are…hard."

Chelsea shook her head. "I'm sorry. Maybe we can spend it with him."

"If he'll let us." Beth's eyes sparkled. "We could plan a get-together at my house and try to get him to come."

Delaney hesitated. "Are you sure, Beth? I don't want to make things worse."

"Believe me, Delaney, you can't make the anniversary of something like this worse."

"Maybe if we play it low-key," Chelsea said.

"Just invite him over," Francey said. "Men do better when they're not coerced."

"Let's go inside and talk about it." Beth led the way.

Following the three women into the common room, Delaney prayed her friends were right, and Reed would let them all help him. It would really show he was healing, and Delaney wanted that more than anything in the world.

AT NOON THE NEXT DAY, Reed said into the phone, "Macauley." His caller ID identified the number on the other end as O'Roarke's. He'd rather eat ground glass than talk to anyone, but he couldn't very well not answer a call from Beth.

Her usually strong alto was raspy on the phone. "Hi, Reed, it's Beth."

He closed his eyes and sighed. This woman, these people, were important to him. Still, when Beth had asked him yesterday to come over to her house this afternoon, he'd begged off. He glanced at his watch. He was just about to get dressed and go for a drive. Delaney had been calling all week; he held her off but she would probably show up at his house today. *Today,* when the ghosts of Crash and Castleman and Johnson would come out in full regalia. It was only noon, so they could still be asleep in his unconscious.

But Beth wasn't going to let him off that easily. "I wanted to ask you again to come over today and be with us." She sighed. "You promised me you'd think about it."

"Oh, Beth. Anniversaries are...hard."

"Yes, Reed, I know."

He couldn't argue with that.

"Look, give me some space. Maybe I'll stop over."
He hesitated. "Is Delaney there?"

"Yes, she wishes you'd come, too. We all do."

"I'll think about it."

After the call, he grabbed his keys and tried to quell
the fear that rose inside him. He never spent this date
with anybody, always wallowed in his grief alone. It
was the only way he knew to deal with the avalanche
of feelings. Delaney would have a lot to say about that.

*Don't think about that. Don't think about how badly
you've treated her this week.*

*Can I trust you, Reed? I'm afraid I'll wake up one
morning and you'll be gone just like...*

Intending to drive around, think some more, he
found himself at the O'Roarkes' twenty minutes later.
When he pulled up to their log cabin nestled in the
trees of Corbet's Glen, he saw Dylan's bike parked at
an angle, and Beth's Accord next to it. Delaney's Miata
and the Scarlatta's car nestled in between them.

All his friends were here.

Could they help him?

Beth answered the door, accompanied by their dal-
matian, Quint. Her face broke out in a smile that made
the sun seem dim. But she tried to play it cool. "Hey,
buddy, good to see you."

He swallowed hard.

She held the dog by his collar, stepped back and let
Reed in. "I know it's hard," she said in her typical
no-nonsense manner after she closed the door and
leaned against it.

"Yeah, it is."

What else could he say to a woman who'd faced down her own fears; he couldn't very well act like the coward of the century in front of her.

And then, in a gesture so uncharacteristic of Beth, she reached out and hugged him. "I love you like a brother, Reed, and I know what an anniversary is like. I don't want you to go through it today alone."

He felt himself start to sweat. "I always get through it."

"So did I." She drew back and angled her head to the basement. "But you've got people to help you this year. Just like I did."

"Can anyone really help, Beth?"

"I think so. Dylan helped me. Being with the Cordaros on that first holiday made it…better. Just give us a chance. If it gets too bad, we'll let you leave."

A burst of laughter came from downstairs. "Is everybody here?"

Beth's mouth quirked. "No, Ben and Diana couldn't make it until dinner."

His heart beat like a thunderclap in his chest. "Dinner? You don't expect me to…"

"We'll be here all day for you, Reed. We'll understand if you can't stay the whole time. There's no pressure. I promise."

He didn't respond.

"Please just try."

The thought of keeping up a front for twelve hours scared him to death. But when Delaney appeared behind Beth, dressed simply in a white sundress and sandals, her hair loose down her back, he knew he had to try this. He had to make a real effort to break free from the claws of his PTSD.

He *would* do this.

When Beth left, he stared at Delaney.

"Hi." Her smile was tremulous. "I'm glad you're here."

"Me, too. I'm sorry about how I behaved all week."

"Today is what's important." Slowly, she walked to him. Held out a hand. "Is it so bad, being here?"

He shook his head but took her hand. "I'm never sane today, honey. It's like a black hole."

"You've got seven people here to fill up that hole today, Reed. Please, let us try."

She laid her head on his shoulder. Just a small innocent gesture that yanked his heartstrings. Of its own accord, his hand came up to stroke her hair. "Delaney…"

Suddenly, somewhere, at the very bottom of the black hole, he glimpsed a tiny ray of light.

"WHERE'D YOU GET THESE?" Dylan asked as Beth handed out booklets. The eight of them were seated around a table in the O'Roarke dining room for lunch. In hopes that he'd come, and to lighten up the mood, Beth had purchased joke books to use throughout the day. Delaney prayed the humor, along with the companionship, would take Reed's mind off what had happened eight years ago.

"I got them at Funny Bones, the new novelty shop on Clarissa Street."

"What topic did you guys get?" Francey asked, dishing out a heaping plate of macaroni salad.

"Firefighter-EMS jokes." This from Dylan. "How about you?"

Alex glanced at Francey's stomach. "We got *Advice from a Father to His Daughter's Dates.*" He ran a hand over his face. "Oh, God! I can't even think about that."

Chelsea had gotten *Bumper Stickers for Women;* Jake, the other side of the coin, *Rules Guys Wish Women Knew.*

Delaney, who sat next to Reed, smiled broadly. "Mine's *How to Keep a Healthy Level of Insanity While Driving Others Insane.*"

Beth said, "I've got *Children's Book Titles that Never Made It.* Let's eat and we'll share some of these."

As they ate their food, Dylan began the first round of jokes. "Firefighter Blake, a macho stud from Engine Five, just got back from a nudist colony. 'How'd you like it?' the guys at the fire station asked." Dylan grinned boyishly at the punch line. The firefighter answered, 'The first three days were the hardest.'"

Boos around the table. Delaney noticed a reluctant smile from Reed. More stupid smoke-eater stories followed.

"God, why are firefighter jokes so dumb?" Delaney asked.

"Don't get me started," Beth answered.

"Here's an EMS one for you, smarty," Dylan responded to his wife. "A female paramedic was so arrogant that when she took a patient's pulse, she deducted five beats just for the effect of her presence."

After everybody threw their napkins at Dylan, and

Beth told him what to do with his jokes, lunch was over.

"Come on, let's go outside onto the deck for dessert," Beth suggested.

Delaney glanced at Reed. Catching her eye, he nodded.

The sun beat down brightly in the backyard. Trees dotted the perimeter. A big picnic table and some stuffed lounge chairs were arranged on the deck. Over ice cream sundaes—and a banana split for Francey— Alex whipped out his booklet.

"I'll go next," he said. "*Advice From a Father to His Daughter's Dates.*" In a deep, fatherly voice, full of affected sternness, he read, "If you pull into my driveway and honk, you'd better be delivering a package because you're sure as hell not picking anything up. I'm sure you've been told that in today's world, sex without utilizing a barrier method of some kind can kill you. Let me elaborate. When it comes to sex, I am the barrier and I will kill you."

Francey laughed so hard she almost fell off the chair. "Dad would love that one."

Alex continued until he had everyone guffawing.

Chelsea held up her hand as she sputtered ice cream all over herself. "Stop. I'm choking."

"One more," Alex said. "Be afraid. Be very afraid. When my Agent Orange acts up, it takes very little for me to mistake the sound of your car in the driveway for a chopper coming in over a rice paddy. The voice in my head frequently tells me to clean the guns as I wait for you to bring my daughter home."

A chuckle escaped Reed, and Delaney felt calm for

the first time today. Next to him on the picnic table, she leaned her head on his shoulder.

Then Dylan stood. "Let's play some volleyball." Delaney had noticed the net at the back of the property. Reed drew in a deep breath. Delaney grasped his hand under the table. Jake, who'd been holding Timmy, handed the little boy to Beth. "Come on, old man," he said to Reed. "Let's show them the over-forty crowd still has it."

Surprisingly, Reed winked at Delaney. "I've still got it, don't I, babe?"

Shocked at his levity, Delaney kissed him on the cheek. "You betcha."

She offered to watch Timmy while the others played. She took him from Beth. As Delaney stroked the baby's hair and cuddled him close, she watched Reed.

He played well. A spike to Alex. A tap to Dylan. As the game went on, he let go more and more. His features relaxed and he began to smile.

Francey came out of the house and over to her. "You okay?" she asked Delaney.

"Yeah." She nodded to the players. "He seems better."

"Beth's idea was good."

Delaney kissed Timmy's head. "I hope so."

"You're in love with him, aren't you?" Francey asked, leaning against the table.

Delaney held Francey's gaze. "Uh-huh."

"I hope it works out."

When Timmy began to fuss, Delaney walked him. Reed kept darting looks at her. Could he tell how much Delaney wanted a baby—his baby? She tried to mask her features so he wouldn't see the yearning there; still he scowled at her. *Take it slow,* she told herself. *And for God's sake, keep it light today.*

After the game and over lemonade, Chelsea picked up her joke pamphlet. "Okay, my turn. *Bumper Stickers for Women.*"

"I don't want to hear this," Reed said.

"Tough. Here goes."

Her jokes were funny, too. But Jake pretended to be insulted and ripped the pamphlet out of her hands. "Tit for tat, sweetheart."

Chelsea whispered something in his ear and he laughed throatily. "*Rules Guys Wish Women Knew,*" he said, opening his jokes. "One—Learn to work the toilet seat—up and down—it's not that hard. Two—Don't ask a question that you don't want to hear the *real* answer to. Three—Sometimes, we're *not* thinking about you. Four—No, I don't know what day it is. Why can't you just mark the calendar. Five—Columbus didn't need directions and neither do we."

The female bashing brought more laughs from everyone. Reed laughed, too. They kept him busy through the afternoon: setting up a baby pool for Timmy and filling it with water so he could "swim," playing a few games of cards, checking out the attic Dylan wanted converted into a playroom. Reed was given absolutely no time to brood.

In fact, when Ben and Diana showed up at five, Reed was surprised at how fast the time had flown by. He shook his head as he watched his two friends enter the backyard. Maybe Beth had been right. Today hadn't been so hard.

Ben crossed to Reed, who sat alone on a chair sipping a beer. "Hey, you came."

Reed nodded.

"I'm glad."

"Me, too." Reed nodded to the group. "They're playing 'keep Reed entertained.'"

"Did it help?"

Reed rolled his eyes. "Yeah." He cleared his throat. "This is the day, you know."

Nodding, Ben clapped him on the shoulder. "Yeah, I know."

"Beth was right about it."

Staring across the yard, Reed saw Beth hand Diana something. Ben said, "Well, she should know."

"Yeah, she should."

Diana giggled at what she was reading. Reed filled Ben in on the joke theme of the day.

"I know her," Ben said, smiling at his wife. "That's gotta be something about me."

Sure enough, Diana told the last—and funniest—of the firefighter jokes after dinner. "An ailing battalion chief's wife accompanied her husband to his doctor's appointment. After his checkup, the doctor called the wife into his office alone. He said, 'Chief Smith is suffering from a very severe form of stress. If you don't do the following, he will surely die. Each morning fix him a healthy breakfast, be pleasant and make sure he's in a good mood. Prepare a nutritious lunch, and for dinner, always use china and candlelight. Don't burden him with chores as he probably had a hard day. Don't discuss your problems with him, it will only make his stress worse. And most important, make love with your husband several times a week and satisfy his every fantasy. If you can do this for a year, the chief will regain his health completely.'

"On the way home the chief asked his wife what the doctor told her. She glanced over at him and said simply, 'You're going to die.'"

By that time, mellow with beer and good food, Reed was able to laugh at the black humor. He glanced at his watch. It was ten o'clock. The day was almost over, and he was...sane.

And truthfully, he felt proud of himself. Smug, even. Maybe he'd wrestled another demon to the ground.

Delaney approached the lounger where he lazed. "Did it go okay?" she asked, sitting down on the edge of the chaise.

He grasped her hand. "Yeah, it did."

She leaned over and snuggled into his chest. "I'm so glad."

He stroked her hair and felt her relax in his arms. For the first time he realized how hard today must have been for her, how tense she'd been throughout the afternoon and evening. Her generosity swamped him. He owed her so much. "I think I got over a big hump today, Laney."

"One of the last ones, maybe?"

Rubbing her back in lazy circles, he enjoyed her nearness, the smell of her hair filling his senses, the feel of her against him. "Maybe."

He glanced around him as she cuddled closer. At the picnic table, Beth and Dylan sat across from Francey and Alex. They were probably exchanging baby stories.

Reed glanced down at Delaney's stomach. He'd seen her with Timmy earlier.

Ben laughed from the shadows where he lounged on a double swing with his wife. Reed saw Diana bury her face in his chest.

Jake and Chelsea were hunched over Timmy's stroller, talking softly, watching the baby sleep.

Cradling the woman who meant more to him than anyone ever had, Reed felt a flicker of real hope kindle inside him.

He hugged Delaney tightly, and guessed he'd just hold her and cling to that tiny speck of hope.

CHAPTER THIRTEEN

SIGHING HEAVILY, Sam steered his red truck down the street. He reached for a cigarette, then stopped the motion. He'd quit, or at least he was trying to; Marcy and T.J. had gotten on him about the habit. They made him smile—his kids, whom he loved so much.

He wished he didn't have to go to the Fireman's Ball tonight. As always, he was whipped after a late afternoon session with Macauley. In some ways, he was making progress, and he shuddered to think where he'd be if it wasn't for the therapy. But sometimes he felt like a freakin' split personality—like that Jekyll guy who turned into Hyde. He was better when he was with Macauley, but often when the session was over, Sam got really depressed, or angry about Tommy and the world shifted out of focus. He couldn't think as clearly. Macauley, smart bastard that he was, had guessed and talked about Sam going through stages of grief; he believed Sam's moods would eventually even out. But it was hard to believe what he said when Sam felt so lousy most of the time.

Glancing to the passenger side of his truck, he shook his head at his tux. Just what he needed—to stuff himself in some monkey suit tonight. But Terry had wanted to go to the annual ball, and things were better with her, even if he did have to keep his depression—and his rage—hidden. It was worth it, though. Even the sex had been better. He smiled, thinking that T.J. and Marcy were both spending the night with friends, and he and Terry would have the whole house to themselves. Just like the good old days.

But those days would never be the same.

Not without Tommy.

Shit! The oppressive sadness began to choke him. Thankfully he was almost home.

As he neared his house, his eyes narrowed on the driveway. He blinked, and slowed down, then swerved over to the curb about a hundred feet away. There was a red Eclipse at the end of his driveway. What the hell was *she* doing here? He'd told her to stay away. Why had she come?

You're transferring your anger at Tommy's death onto Jeanine, Macauley had said. *Let it go.*

I'll try.

Wearily, he lay his head against the seat. Maybe he *was* blaming Jeanine for stuff. He hated what she'd done to Tommy and he was mad at her for hurting his brother, but somewhere in the back of his mind, he remembered that Tommy had taken some of the responsibility for their breakup.

In minutes, she came out of his house. Dressed in jeans and a sleeveless white shirt, her blond hair pulled up in a ponytail, she looked young and innocent. Oh, hell. He'd just wait until she left and avoid an argument. See if he could let go, like Macauley said. He let his car idle on the side of the road.

And almost swallowed his tongue as he saw his son

follow Jeanine out the door. She turned, said something to the boy that made him smile. T.J. looked older, dressed in nice black pants and a gray sports shirt. His hair was combed, and he was laughing in a way Sam hadn't seen for months. Linking arms with Jeanine, he accompanied her to the car; then like the courtliest of suitors, he opened the door for her. She slid inside. T.J. slammed the door, leaned over and kissed her on the cheek.

What the *hell*...? Sam's head began to throb.

The boy circled the hood and climbed in the passenger side. The little sports car backed out of the driveway.

Fatherly instinct overrode the psychologist's logic. No matter what Reed said, Sam wouldn't, *couldn't* let the bitch get her claws into his son, for God's sake. He put his car in gear and followed them, staying far enough back so as not to be noticed. His heart beat frantically in his chest. His palms were sweaty on the steering wheel. Where was she taking his boy? And why?

The trip was short, two blocks down, two over.

We're gonna live close to you guys, buddy. Within walking distance. As Jeanine pulled up to the curb, Sam thought about how Tommy had loved that little house he'd bought five years after he and Jeanine got married. Sam had helped Tommy paint every single white spindle on the porch, put up black shutters and install a new roof.

When they'd divorced, Jeanine had gotten the house, and Tommy had lived with Sam and Terry for six months. Just a few months before he died, he'd rented a grimy little apartment on Meigs Street. Sam had wanted to cry when he first saw the dingy surroundings where his brother was forced to live.

Jeanine and T.J. continued to sit in the car.

Would she try to take his son into her house? And do what?

At the thought, Sam saw red.

She'd get her claws into his son over his dead body. Or hers.

DELANEY TOOK REED'S BREATH away. When she entered Bright Oaks Country Club and stood in the doorway searching for him, all the air in his lungs evaporated. He was besotted. A lovesick sap. A fool. But he couldn't help it and even if he could, he wouldn't want to. He liked being involved with Delaney. As he threaded his way through the crowd toward her, he was overcome with thanks that this lovely woman was his.

She'd turned away to say something to a captain who'd seen her alone and pounced. Possessively, Reed grasped her shoulders, bared by the stunning dress, and drew her back against him. "Hey, gorgeous. You meeting anybody here tonight?" he asked.

She laughed throatily at his uncharacteristic whimsy. "This hunky captain. He's a psychologist. Have you seen him?"

"Move a little closer, baby, and you'll feel him."

Again the sexy giggle. She leaned closer, and he was enveloped by the scent of her perfume. Little sprinkles of glitter glowed subtly on her shoulders.

He spun her around and gave her a very deliberate once-over. He stared at the thin, sparkly knit dress that hugged every curve from breast to ankle and was secured by a tiny halter strap around her neck. It was black and made her look sultry and seductive. He wondered if she wore *anything* under it. "You're beautiful," he said softly. "You take my breath away."

The smile she gave him made his pulse skitter. "You look pretty spiffy in that black-tie outfit yourself, Doc."

Sliding his arm around her waist, he drew her close to his side. "I want to kiss you."

"Hold the thought," she said, nodding to Captain Talbot as he approached them.

"Macauley," Talbot greeted Reed, who smiled back. The chief turned to Delaney. "Dr. Shaw."

Delaney gave him a grin. "Hello Chief Talbot. Good to see you again. And please call me Delaney."

Talbot's expression turned intent. "Delaney, then. I was wondering if I might if I call you next week."

Reed stiffened.

Catching the gesture, Talbot laughed. "Back off, Doc. It's purely professional. Like I told you, I got me a teenage girl who needs some help." His eyes darkened to the color of thick gray smoke. "My older granddaughter, Kassie, isn't adjusting to the death of her father. You met her, I think."

"Yes, we hit it off. I'd be glad to see her privately."

"Good, I'll call you."

When Talbot sauntered off, Delaney said, "I feel bad for him."

"Me, too. But that doesn't mean want you around him too much."

"Ah, I like that jealousy."

"Well, I don't. But you make me feel all sorts of crazy things, lady." He grasped her hand. "Come on, let's dance."

They took the floor to the song "When a Man Loves a Woman." "Did you have a good day?" she asked somewhat tentatively.

"Yes. They've all been good this week."

Which was true. Reed had feared that the friendship shown him last weekend by the Cordaros, Templetons and O'Roarkes would stir up too many emotions and might bring on nightmares or flashbacks. But he hadn't had one single episode since before the anniversary. In fact, he felt better than he had in a long time. Much of it was due to the lovely lady in his arms.

He'd tried to show her how grateful he was for everything she'd done for him. He'd spoiled her rotten all week—*I like men who spoil me,* she'd said. It was fun, sending her her favorite ice cream in the middle of the day, kidnapping her on her lunch hour and taking her to the most expensive hotel in downtown Rockford for what was supposed to be a *nooner.* But they'd never made it back to work, or out of the room for that matter, until the following day.

"Reed, I asked how your session with Sam went?"

"Good. He's making progress, I think, although today he said sometimes he feels like a split personality. He's fine when he's with me, but when he's alone, the demons come out."

Her hand fluttered at his neck. "Well, my money's on you, doctor. You're pretty good at dealing with demons."

He tugged her closer. "Right now, I feel like I could defeat Satan himself, sweetheart."

"I wonder why."

He grew serious. "Because of you, Laney," he said into her hair.

"Oh, Reed."

The song ended and he held on to her. "Honey, I—" He scanned the crowded ballroom. "Come on, let's go outside for a minute."

They headed for the French doors to the patio and reached the edge of the dance floor when somebody bumped into them, spilling beer down the front of Reed's tux.

"Hey, watch what..." Reed glanced up to see Joey Santori wavering next to them.

Joey wore a nice suit, but his tie was askew and his hair messy. "Oh, sorry, Doc."

Reed took out a handkerchief and wiped his coat. At Ben's request, Reed had tried to talk to Joey a couple of times about how he was feeling about Francey's pregnancy, but Joey had sloughed it off. Now he nodded to Joey's uneven stance and the drink he held. "You ought to slow down there. It's only eight o'clock."

Joey held up his beer bottle. "Haven't had enough." His words were slurred and his glazed eyes stared over Reed's shoulder. "Not nearly enough."

Tracking his gaze, Reed saw a very pregnant Francey on the dance floor cuddling her husband. No one had ever looked happier than the two of them.

Reed said, "Let's get some air, Joe. Maybe talk a bit."

"Nah, you take care of your pretty date." He stepped away. "Besides, I need another beer."

When Joe was gone, Reed made a detour to find Ben and Diana and the O'Roarkes at a table near the back.

As the women complimented one anothers' ensembles, Reed drew Ben aside and confided his concerns about Joey to Francey's father.

Scowling, Ben said, "I'll get Jake. We'll handle it."

"Jake and Chelsea are going to be late." This from Dylan who'd come up to them. "Chelsea wasn't feeling well."

After Ben spoke with Dylan, the two left to search for Joey. Reed crossed to Delaney. Before he could speak, he heard someone call from behind. "Beth, Diana. Oh, God, somebody. Come out to the patio."

In unison, everybody turned. Alex stood behind them, white-faced and shaky. "It's Francey. We went for a walk in the garden. She's outside now…"

Diana clutched his arm. "Alex, is she all right?"

"Yeah. I guess. Oh, God, Diana, her water broke."

DELANEY STOOD BEFORE Rockford Memorial Hospital's nursery window and stared down at the beautiful child in the warming bed. Angela Diana Templeton was as gorgeous as her mother, with huge blue-violet eyes, round red cheeks and a mass of dark hair, hidden now under a gauzy pink cap. Tiny little hands had escaped the blanket and nestled by her head. Periodically, they opened and closed.

"Oh, there you are." Chelsea sidled up to her sister and peered through the glass. "Oh, Lord, I can't believe it. She's gorgeous.'' Chelsea's eyes teared as she stared at the baby. ''I missed the whole birth.''

''So did Ben and Dylan. It happened so fast. We barely got to the hospital on time.''

Chelsea scowled. ''Francey's okay, right?''

''Are you kidding? She popped this baby out as if there was nothing to it. Alex said he was a wreck, but Francey was as cool as a cucumber.''

Laughing, Chelsea turned back through the glass. Her face softened. ''How big is she?''

''Nine pounds even.''

Her sister's hand went to her stomach. ''That's huge.''

For a minute Delaney hesitated.

''Why's the baby in here?'' Chelsea asked, indicating the nursery.

''Francey breast-fed her and the nurses insisted she rest because of how quickly it happened and how big the baby is. Francey wouldn't sleep with Angel in the room, and so Alex had them take her out for a while. *That's* when Francey cursed a blue streak at him.''

Chelsea giggled and stared through the window, almost wistfully. Delaney watched her trace her finger against the glass. Chelsea was dressed in a Weight Room sweatsuit. Her hair was a mess, as if she'd been lying down. Her face was pale, despite her happiness for Francey. ''How come you weren't at the ball, Cinderella?'' she asked.

Taking in a deep breath, Chelsea faced her. ''I wasn't feeling well.''

''Yeah?''

With a huge grin, Chelsea threw herself into Delaney's arms. "I'm pregnant, sis. We just did the test a couple of hours ago. I've been sick for a few mornings and tonight Jake insisted I do an EPT."

Suddenly, Delaney felt her eyes tear. She held on tight to her sister. "Oh, sweetie, that's wonderful." It was. It *was*. It was just that Delaney couldn't help feeling a twinge of envy. She wanted what Chelsea had—to be married to the man she loved, to have his child—so badly for herself it surprised her with its forcefulness. But she wouldn't allow her longing to take away from her sister's joy. She drew back. "When?"

Chelsea's face was wet. She wiped away the moisture. "I'm just a few weeks along. Looks like you'll have a niece or nephew in the spring."

"It'll be wonderful, Chels." She grinned. "I'll be *Aunt* Delaney."

"Aunt Delaney?" The voice was Reed's from behind her.

Chelsea looked over Delaney's shoulder. "Me and Jake," she said simply.

Turning, Delaney saw delight etch itself on Reed's face. "Oh, Chelsea." Without censoring his response, he hugged her. "Congratulations."

"Thanks." She swayed. "Uh-oh. I guess confirmation gave me permission to feel rotten. I'd better go find Jake. He was parking the car."

"He and Dylan are outside Francey's room, trying to calm Ben. Grandpa's furious that he missed little Angel's entrance into the world."

"Where was he?"

"Escorting Joey home." He smiled. "It's a long

story. Come on, I'll take you to your husband and explain it on the way.''

"I can make it myself, Reed.''

He winked at Delaney. "Get used to it, kiddo. You're gonna be coddled for a long time now.'' He said to Delaney, "Coming?''

"No, I'll just stay here and stare at the baby awhile.''

Giving her a questioning look, Reed took her sister downstairs.

You're strong, Delaney, she told herself as she turned back to the window. *You don't have to let this throw you. It's too soon to make demands on him. Be satisfied with what you have.*

She didn't know how long she stood there before she heard, "You shouldn't scowl at newborns like that, it gives them gas.''

Delaney laughed. She glanced over at Reed. His cummerbund was off, his black tie draped around his neck. And he'd shed the jacket to his tux long ago. Still she found him unutterably handsome. "Is that a well-known psychological truism?''

"Yes. Just like this one.'' Wrapping his arms around her from behind, he whispered something naughty in her ear. He was happy. *Be grateful for that.*

"Looks like people having babies makes you frisky, Doc,'' she quipped at his remark.

"Hmm.'' He stared into the nursery, his chin resting on her head.

The quiet around them, the proximity of the man she loved, the idea of her, Reed…and the sweet baby sucker-punched Delaney. She felt tears threaten again.

He noticed. Kissed the top of her head. "Happy for your friends?" he asked. "And Chelsea?"

"Of course."

Her voice wavered. Reed stilled. He'd come to know her well in the last few months. She felt him turn to the side. Moving away from her, he grasped her hand. "Come with me a minute."

She took the time to swipe at her cheeks. "No hanky-panky in the hospital, Doc. After my food poisoning incident, your reputation is still in tatters."

He didn't return the jibe, just led her to a small waiting room down the hall. Once inside he closed the door and faced her. His look was dark and concerned.

Please, God, she prayed. *Don't let me tell him this. Please…*

"Tell me what you're thinking," he said in his best psychologist's voice. His knuckles grazed her cheek, a lover's inducement to confidences.

"I did. I'm happy for my sister. And for Francey."

"I know you are. But something else is making you cry."

"Don't be silly." She tried to turn away. He kept her facing him.

"Delaney. Tell me."

Her throat worked convulsively to keep back the confession. Staring hard at him, she tried to remember all that this man had only recently overcome. "Reed, please, leave it alone."

"Why?"

She lay her head on his shoulder. "You don't want to hear this," she whispered raggedly.

"I do." His mouth was against her hair. "Tell me."

She wilted, like a stupid spring flower not given enough water. "I want this, too. I want a baby." She looked up at him. "Your baby."

As she knew he would, he said absolutely nothing.

"I love you, Reed. I have for a long time. I know you don't want to hear that, but that doesn't change the fact."

His face didn't go blank. Instead, his eyes got so bleak, his expression so stricken, it made her cry again. She lowered her gaze so as not to have to face him.

He tilted her chin. "Oh, sweetheart. I'm better, but I'm still not like other men." He looked panicked. "If I could be...if I could do this, believe me, it would be with you."

She swallowed hard. Rejection from her past came crashing into her present like an unwanted guest at a banquet. Never before in her life had she felt more vulnerable.

But she *did* love this man. And his problems were bigger than hers. If she had only two choices—leave him because he couldn't commit, or stay with him and accept his terms—there was really no decision to be made. At least for now. She gave him a watery smile. "I think you sell yourself short, Reed. But I hear what you're saying. It's all right. It's just the emotion of the night." She drew back. "I'm fine."

Now his face was ravaged.

"It's okay, Reed. Really."

"Laney, I—" He looked down. "Goddamn it. It's my pager."

Saved by the bell, she thought, and turned away to compose herself.

He crossed to a phone on a side table. Punched out a number. "Talbot, this is Macauley. What's going on?"

He waited.

"Oh, my God."

She spun around.

More conversation on the other end.

"What?"

Silence.

"All right, give me directions to the cabin. I'll meet you there."

When he hung up, he stood perfectly still, staring at the wall.

Delaney went to him. "Reed, what is it?"

No movement. She circled around him.

His face was absolutely white. "Reed?"

He seemed to come out of the trance. "It's Sam. Apparently he's got Jeanine Leone, Tommy's ex-wife, at a cabin out in Rush."

"Got her? What does that mean?"

"He found her with T.J. The kid says he misinterpreted their relationship, went off the deep end. Sam forced T.J. out of their car and he got in with Jeanine. T.J. heard him say something about the hunting cabin."

"Oh, God."

"T.J. told Theresa. She waited, hoping Sam would come home. But when he didn't, she tried to reach me but I left the phone in the car so she finally called Talbot. He called the police."

"The police?"

Reed shook himself again. "There are guns at the cabin, Laney." His eyes widened. "They want me to come out. Talk to Sammy.'' Again he stared off into space. Whispered, *''Guns.''*

She grasped his arms firmly. ''Reed, it's not like the last time.''

''No? They want me there, to talk to him, to convince him to give it up.''

''Reed—''

''I couldn't do it before. What if I can't do it again?''

She shook him, hard. ''This is different, Reed. Sam knows you. In any case, what choice do you have?'' She tugged on his arm. ''Come on, I'm going with you.''

He didn't budge. ''I can't—''

She tugged harder. ''Yes, you can. You'll do whatever you have to here, and I'll help you.''

''But what if…what if it *is* like last time, and I can't talk him down?''

''Then we'll deal with that together. But my money's on you. You have to try, Reed. Do you hear me?'' She tapped him lightly several times on the cheek. ''Come on, Reed. You have to try.''

It seemed to sink in. He grabbed her hand. ''Of course I do. Of *course* I do,'' he said, and headed for the door.

CHAPTER FOURTEEN

CROUCHING IN ONE CORNER of the cabin, Sam wadded up newspaper that had been stockpiled for months and stuffed it underneath the logs he'd brought in from the back porch; he'd crisscrossed them on the floor like an outdoor campfire. He and Tommy had learned how to build fires as Boy Scouts. Smiling, and simultaneously wiping the tears from his eyes, he could just picture Tommy in the dark blue uniform that was always a little too big, proudly displaying his merit badges. T.J. had never been a Boy Scout.

Tommy...T.J. They blurred in his mind. But then his son came into focus and the image of him getting into that bitch's sports car made Sam's hands fist. What the hell was she planning to do with him?

He heard her weeping across the room. Too bad, he thought, blocking out the sound. Those crocodile tears might have worked on Tommy, maybe T.J., but not on him. Sammy knew her for the conniving bitch she was.

No, buddy, you got it wrong. Even after the divorce, Tommy had defended her. *She's not the only one at fault. I'd get back with her if we could work it out....*

Sam scowled. Even T.J. had stood up for her. *It's not like that, Dad,* his son had said when he'd grasped the reason behind Sam's anger. But Sam had been beyond listening. He'd yanked the boy out of her car and slid inside. T.J. had stayed close, in order to help. Jeanine had tried to get out, but Sam had been slick. He'd picked up a few tricks from Macauley. Grasping her arm, he said softly, *It's okay, Jeanine, I just want to talk. Don't you think it's time we talked?*

It had worked. It took more schmoozing to convince her to come up to the cabin. *Let's go there. Remember how we all used to go there when we were kids? It was the place where Terry and I first...where you and Tommy first... Come on, it'll be good for us both.*

The bitch had always been dumb—a dumb blonde— and she'd bought his reason hook, line and sinker. It took him a minute to calm his son, telling the kid they were just going for a ride to talk, and he should hoof it on home. Then the stupid broad had driven straight here.

Like a lamb to slaughter.

Once he'd gotten her inside the cabin, he'd pounced. He darted a look to the side of the room where she sat, trussed up like a Thanksgiving turkey. He laughed. In a few minutes, he'd start cookin'.

Behind her was the huge brick fireplace that had kept him and Tommy warm on the nights when they'd come out here to hunt. In it, a fire burned hotly. It was September and still warm outside. Since he'd left all the windows and shutters closed—except for the small side window he was using to ventilate—it felt like a furnace in here. Sweat rolled down his back, soaking his T-shirt. He wiped the perspiration from his eyes and let the sweet scent of smoke calm him. A firefighter to the end, being in the heat and smell of the Red Devil was where he felt the best.

What had Macauley called this kind of thing? Coming full circle. Tommy had died in a fire. Now she would. And then Sam would follow. How appropriate.

"Sammy, please," he heard her say.

Ignoring her, he stood and strode to another corner of the room. He figured four campfires would do it, and squatted down to build the last; there'd be one in each corner of the room.

"Sammy."

"Shut up."

"Why are you doing this?" Her voice was whiny. She used to be able to suck Tommy right in with the feminine wheedling and round blue eyes.

He laughed, an ugly sound. "Gotta keep you away from my boy, babe."

"Sammy, he's like a son to me. Like he was to Tommy."

Bolting up, he dropped the kindling and turned to her. "Don't say his name!" he roared. "You don't deserve to even say his name."

Hiccups. More crying. Some coughing from the smoke that was beginning to fill the room. Ludicrously, he thought that the chimney needed cleaning. He'd have to get Tommy to help. His own eyes watered as he turned to finish assembling the fourth campfire.

"What...why are you building those?" she finally asked.

"Dumb, Jeanine. You're really dumb." The task completed, he clutched to his chest the shotgun he'd kept by his side and carried it back to his chair across from her. He hadn't planned on using the weapon, had loaded it only to scare her, but somebody on the outside had found out he was here.

They'd come. Called to him through a bullhorn. He'd gone to the side window and yelled out that he'd kill her if they came close. He shot the gun off into the trees to show he meant business.

Several minutes later, he saw somebody creep by the window, scoping out the situation. He shot off the gun again, high, into the ceiling, and then pointed it at Jeanine. The snoop had gotten the message.

His eyes glazed for a minute. He wished Tommy was here. He always came to the cabin with his brother. Where was he?

Sam's mind cleared. The bitch came into focus. Tommy was dead.

He scanned the room, then got up to close the side window. Now they were completely isolated, and everything was ready.

He went to a low cupboard and drew out the can of gasoline they'd kept on hand for the generator. He shook it, to be sure there was enough. There was.

Sam could do what he had to do.

A DEADLY CALM CAME OVER Reed as he drove the twenty minutes from the hospital to Rush, a small township on the outskirts of Rockford. Fear, hot and potent, burned his insides initially, but Delaney's soothing voice, her assurances and her innate practicality had kept him sane.

What choice do you have, Reed?…You have to try, Reed.

So he faced the oncoming headlights and listened to updates from Talbot on his cell phone with staunch determination. Even so, the faces of Marx and Castleman and Johnson swam before him as he reached the cabin and cut the engine.

The scene was right out of an action movie. Several police cars were parked at angles, some with their lights flashing like beacons. Men in uniform milled about. An officer, off to the side, was talking to Chief Talbot. A bullhorn dangled from the cop's hand. Some guns were drawn—all the weapons were trained on a small log cabin with shuttered windows and a closed door. When Reed looked at it, he could see flames through the cracks and smoke curling out from the chimney.

Exiting the car, Reed strode to Talbot, with Delaney right behind him. "Chief," he said simply.

Talbot turned. His normally down-home friendly face was strained. He'd shed his tux jacket and tie, and his shirt was open at the throat and smudged. "Macauley, thank God." Talbot introduced Reed to the police captain. "This is the doctor that's been treating Leone."

For support, Delaney grasped Reed's arm and squeezed gently.

Ignoring his self-recriminations, he asked, "What's the status?" Now that he was here, he *would* do something. *This time,* he would do something. He chanted the mantra in the back of his mind as he listened to the policeman.

"Leone's nuts," the officer told Reed bluntly. "He's got the girl tied up in a chair over by the back wall.

He's lit a fire in the big fireplace and when one of our SWAT team went to check—'' the cop nodded to four men, outfitted in black, all holding guns ''—he observed that Leone has also built what looks like campfires in each corner of the room. The crazy bastard's gonna burn the place down. With him and the woman inside.''

Delaney gasped.

''We called the Rush Fire Department,'' Talbot said. ''They're volunteer, and we're out in the middle of nowhere, so they won't be here for a few minutes.'' He glanced worriedly at the cabin. Now Reed could smell the smoke, mixing with the rich end-of-summer scents in the woods. ''I hope he doesn't do anything till they get here.''

Reed nodded to the SWAT team. ''You said something about guns on the phone. That why they didn't go inside?''

''Yep.'' The police captain's face was flushed and angry. Reed knew what it was like to care about your men's safety. ''He shot off a gun when an officer scouted out the situation. Yelled he'd kill her right away and anybody else who came close. Now he's boarded up that window, so we can't see inside anymore.'' The cop shook his head. ''He's loony. That's why I let Talbot call you.''

Reed said, ''Give me the bullhorn.''

The policeman handed it over gratefully.

''Sammy, it's me, Macauley.'' His voice came out tinny but loud. ''I want to talk to you.''

No answer.

Reed stepped closer to the cabin, vaguely hearing a

gasp behind him. "Sammy, it's me, Reed. Let me come in."

Still, no answer.

"Sammy, I'm coming to the door."

Suddenly shots rang out inside the cabin.

"Goddamn it." The officer scowled and turned to another man, probably trying to decide what to do next.

Reed faced Delaney. He grasped her shoulders. "I've got to do something," he said calmly. "You understand, I know you do. Somehow, I've got to stop this."

She trembled. Her eyes clouded with fear. But the strong, understanding woman she was surfaced. "Yes, you have to try. I understand."

He kissed her nose. "I have to try." He repeated it as much for himself as for her. "There's really no choice."

"You can do this, Reed," she whispered against his hand.

He turned away and headed toward the cabin, the whine of fire truck engines echoing in the distance.

METHODICALLY, SAMMY WENT from the first unlit campfire to the second, dousing each with gasoline. The pungent smell assaulted his nose and made his eyes water more. Tommy had always hated that smell, and Sam used to tease him about being a sissy. He'd razz his brother again when he got here.

Sam's head began to pound. Tommy wouldn't get here, would he? Wasn't Tommy dead?

As he passed by Jeanine, he stopped and stared down at her. She didn't look so pretty now. Her face was white and that gunk she put on her eyes was all smeared. Her clothes were a mess, and she was sweaty. It kept getting hotter and hotter in here.

"Tommy did a report once in junior high about the burial customs of ancient tribes," he told her.

"W-what about them?"

"I can't remember which ones, but in some civilizations, women threw themselves on the funeral pyres of their dead husbands." He stared off into a corner, hen strode to the third campfire. Doused it. Nodded to it. "This is fitting, don't you think, Jeanine?"

"I don't want to die, Sammy. Neither do you."

He laughed. "Now, that's where you're wrong, Goldilocks. I don't want to *live*. Not anymore. Not without Tommy."

But that wasn't true, was it? He'd told Macauley he *did* want to live, be a good husband and father. Confusion swamped him.

"Tommy wouldn't want you to do this."

Sam turned on her. "You talked to Tommy?"

Jeanine gave him a blank look.

"You've *seen* Tommy? I thought I saw him at the church." He shook himself. "But Macauley said no. He was—" Again the funny feeling in his head. The spots before his eyes.

There was a loud pounding on the door.

Sammy jumped and reached for the gun. Then he heard, "Sammy, don't shoot. It's me...Tommy."

REED SAT ACROSS FROM SAMMY, next to Jeanine, with his hands tied to the chair behind his back. Once again he stared down the barrel of a gun. Already he was sweating badly and his throat was raw from the smoke.

It was déjà vu, but he was calm. Thankfully, Sammy hadn't gagged him. Now his expertise—the expertise he'd gone to school to gain when he left the FDNY several years ago—was his only weapon.

You can do this, Delaney had whispered before he jogged to the door. *I know you can.* That thought would see him through it.

"You lied to me, you bastard." Sammy's face was mottled and he gripped the gun hard.

Reed nodded. "Yeah, buddy, I did. And I'd do it again." He smiled at Sammy. "I told you once I'd help you any way I could. I meant it."

Sam's eyes clouded. "I thought you were Tommy."

"Tommy's dead."

A venomous gaze swung to Jeanine. "Because of her."

Reed forced his voice to be casual, cocked his head as he sometimes did in a session. "No, Sammy, the Red Devil got Tommy. It's a chance we all take."

Restless, jittery, Sam bolted off the chair and, still holding the gun, picked up a can of gasoline. He went to the last campfire and doused it.

Reed knew one lit match near any of those campfires and this whole place would be cinders in minutes. He swallowed back the fear. It receded when he thought about the potential consequences of Sammy's actions.

Delaney would watch. Delaney—who loved him. And she'd never, ever be the same.

Not without a fight, he thought, determinedly. *This will* not *happen to her without a fight.*

"What brought this on, Sammy?" Reed asked as if they were sitting on couches in his office.

"T.J." His eyes were wild when he swung around to Jeanine. "She was puttin' the moves on my boy. Bewitchin' him, just like Tommy."

"No, no," Jeanine said, crying again. "I'd never do that. He was a connection to Tommy. I've always loved him like a son."

"Sam, you know your son. He wouldn't do something like that. As a matter of fact, I know about their relationship."

"What?"

"He talked to Dr. Shaw about Jeanine."

"He did?"

Reed pounced at the hope in Sam's voice. He guessed that somewhere inside himself, Sam didn't really want to do this horrible thing. "Yeah. T.J. told her he was seeing Jeanine. They were helping each other deal with Tommy's death."

"She divorced Tommy."

"She and your brother were talking about getting back together."

"That's a lie."

Jeanine jumped in. "No, it isn't, Sammy. We *were* talking about it." Her voice cracked. "We were seeing each other again."

Sam's face reddened and his eyes bulged. "How come I didn't know? Tommy always told me everything."

"Tommy was afraid to tell you," Jeanine said. "Because you hated me."

"I don't believe it."

"Theresa knew, Sam." Again Reed stayed calm. "You can ask her about it."

"Terry? She didn't tell me?"

"Terry loves you, Sam. She was afraid you couldn't handle it. She asked my advice in a session where we were alone. I told her to wait awhile."

"Then this is all *your* fault."

"Sammy, nothing's anybody's fault. Death happens to firefighters. Tommy's death just happened."

Suddenly, Sam started to cry. He sank down onto the floor on his knees. "Why?" He sobbed now. "Why did it have to happen to him? And not me?"

Ah, Reed knew that feeling, too. "There's no answer to that."

Lowering the gun, Sam looked up at Reed. "Then I don't want to live. And she doesn't deserve to."

Reed knew he was close. He sensed Sam only needed one little push. There had to be a way. Because in that instant—for the first time since his buddies died—Reed did *not* feel the way Sammy felt. Reed didn't want to lose all he'd gained—Delaney, of course, but Ben, too, and the O'Roarkes…and the new babies being born….

Babies…father…Sam… He considered it only for a split second. "What about Tommy's baby, Sam? Doesn't that little one deserve to live?" Reed prayed Jeanine was quick on the uptake.

Sam went still. His whole body froze. *"Baby?"*

"Jeanine's pregnant."

Sam glanced at her stomach as if he'd be able to tell. "I don't believe you."

"She and Tommy were sleeping together again. She

told Terry she was pregnant at the funeral. Terry told me.''

It only took Sam a few seconds to understand the import of Reed's words. And Reed knew intuitively he'd played the right card. Though Sam Leone might feel like a failure as a firefighter and even as a husband, he'd always tried to be a good father. "You wouldn't lie to me, would you, Doc?" he asked raggedly.

Right now Reed would have sold his soul to the devil to keep Sammy and Jeanine—and himself—alive. "Never, Sammy." He stared hard at the tortured man. "I'd never lie to you." He waited. "Put the gun down."

Slowly it dropped to the floor.

"Now, come on over and untie me. We can talk, then." When Sammy hesitated, Reed said, "Come on, buddy. I'm here for you. Just like I've always been."

CHAPTER FIFTEEN

"WELL, DOC, what do you think? Am I up for this little pilgrimage?"

"Yeah, *Doc,* I think you're up to it." Bill Connally nodded to Reed, who sat, relaxed and easy, on the PTSD specialist's couch. Then the psychiatrist smiled at Delaney, close by, holding Reed's hand. "Especially since you have the miracle worker here with you."

Brows arched, Reed shook his head. "Oh, no, don't tell her that. She'll be impossible to live with."

It was quite a different remark from the one Reed had made two months ago after the ordeal with Sam Leone at the cabin. "I couldn't have done it without you, babe." Or even in the weeks following. "Come with me to New York. I'm going to see that doctor again. I want this thing out of my life." And then again, this morning, on the day of the biggest hurdle he'd cross. "Be there for me, Laney," he'd said when he was still inside her. "I need you today."

"Always," she'd whispered.

As the final session wrapped up—Reed had seen the doctor a half dozen times—and they said their good-byes, Delaney marveled at how different things were this November from how they'd been last year. Then, she'd known Reed only as psychologist and all-around pain-in-the-butt; now he was her whole world. The thought often scared her to death, since she'd promised herself long ago she would never let a man mean this much to her. But she'd lost her heart on New Year's Eve and hadn't regained control of it in the months following.

She'd overridden common sense and moved into Reed's place right after Labor Day, even though he still hadn't made a commitment to her, never said he loved her. But he wanted her with him. In her saner moments, she figured that once he believed he had his PTSD under control he'd be ready to plan a future with her. When she was feeling crazy and insecure, she wondered if he'd ever ask her to be his wife. And if he didn't, would she have to leave him? But for now she tried to be content with what she had.

As they left the elevator of the swank Park Avenue practice, stepped out to the street and headed for a cab, the cold November wind blew around them and the smells of the city—not all good—assaulted them. "I don't know how I ever lived here," Reed commented as he faced her and drew her leather jacket closer around her neck. "It's so noisy, so busy."

"I like the bustle," she told him, returning the favor by zipping up his black leather jacket. They were dressed alike in jeans, sweaters and coats.

As a taxi stopped and they slid inside, she decided to tease him. "Don't forget we have shopping to do."

He rolled his eyes. "That's the worst in New York."

"Well, we've got to get T.J. a Yankee cap and Marcy a poster of *Riverdance*."

"Yeah, I know."

"Of course we'll have to hit FAO Schwarz for Angel, and for my two nephews-to-be." Chelsea had had an amniocentesis and discovered she would have twin boys in April. Delaney smiled at Reed's long-suffering look. "And I saw this underwear store in Times Square that I'm dying to check out."

Leaning over, Reed kissed her nose. "You'll wear me out yet, lady."

She laughed, noticing he'd grasped her hand and didn't let go. He touched her all the time now, openly and in private. And he talked. Sometimes, when the nightmares came—infrequently, now—he'd tell her everything he was feeling. His confidences were as priceless to her as pure gold.

Oh, they'd had their fights. He got angry when she insisted on paying half the bills at his place. And he wasn't happy when she went on a cruise with Francey, Chelsea, Beth and little Angel at the end of October. But mostly, things had been good since the cabin incident.

She'd practically fallen to her knees and thanked God when Reed had walked out into the dark night with one arm around Sam's shoulder, and another hand on Jeanine. Both Leones were crying and Reed had stood by to tend to them.

Sam had been taken into custody and charged with assault. In the intervening weeks, his lawyer had pleaded stress-induced insanity, and with Reed's testimony and Jeanine's cooperation, Sam was sent to a clinic in Pennsylvania to get the extensive psychiatric care he needed. When he began to recover, Sam even thanked Reed for tricking him out of lighting those fires.

Theresa had gone back to work as a secretary, and eventually, when Sam came home, he'd started doing some carpentry to earn a living. Though their life was in flux, they were handling it. Delaney knew Reed spent time with them, personally and professionally. And Delaney still saw T.J. and Marcy frequently. Jeanine had decided to move away from Rockford.

When the cab pulled up to a small clapboard-sided house in Queens, Reed stared out the taxi's side window and went still. His look was so poignant, Delaney wondered if this had been a good idea. Then he opened the door and got out. She paid the driver and followed him up to the tiny patch of yard. He'd stopped at its perimeter.

"The house is smaller than I remember." His voice was raspy.

"Things often are," she said, grasping his hand.

He sighed. "Come on, let's go." His face was sober as they walked up the brick sidewalk, climbed the stairs and rang the doorbell.

There was noise inside. Reed pressed the buzzer again. Finally, a tall, dark-haired boy opened the door. He cocked his head, then his face split into a huge grin. "Holy cow, I don't believe it. Ma will bust a gut." The boy gave Reed a bear hug that had Reed closing his eyes and hugging back. "Ma!" he yelled at typical teenage decibel level. "Come 'ere. Hurry."

A very pretty, petite redhead appeared next to the boy. He dwarfed her. "What are you...oh, God." The woman covered her mouth with her hands and tears sprang to her eyes.

Reed said, "Hi, Tina."

Sobbing, the woman reached for him. Latched on to him and wouldn't let go. Reed closed his eyes and held on to Crash Marx's widow. After long, emotional moments, Tina stepped back. She wiped her eyes and gave him a watery smile. Then she faced Delaney and held out her hand. "Hi, I'm Tina Marx."

Delaney took Tina's hand. "I know. I'm Delaney Shaw."

Tina angled her head to the boy behind her. "This is my oldest son, Reed."

Delaney's own eyes teared. "Hi, Reed."

"Well, come on in," Tina said, regaining some composure. "You'll stay for dinner, won't you? All the boys are here. My parents are coming tonight. And somebody else I'd like you to meet."

Grasping Delaney's hand, Reed said, "Yeah, we can stay."

As they followed Tina in, he mumbled, "I can do this. I can do anything."

IN THE COLD NOVEMBER morning, Reed stood on a narrow New York City street, stuffed his hands in his jacket pockets and stared grimly at the eight-story parking garage. His shoulders were stiff and there was a kick in his heart. "I thought it might not be here anymore."

"No such luck." Delaney stood by him, waiting for his cue, he guessed.

"I can do this, right?"

"You did pretty well at the Marx's house yesterday, and at the firehouse this morning."

He stayed where he was, stalling. "Crash's boys are big."

"Especially your namesake."

Reed scowled. "The second one wants to be a firefighter."

"You didn't discourage him."

"No, I didn't." He took another glance at the garage. "Tina's tough, isn't she?"

"Uh-huh. Though she got pretty exasperated when you gave her fiancé the third degree—all night long, I might add."

"I know." As a matter of fact, Tina had dragged him out to the kitchen after dinner and yelled at him. But then she'd hugged him and told him his blessing was important to her. He'd told her Crash would have wanted her to be happy.

You, too, she said back. Reed believed that now.

"The firehouse hasn't changed much," he said of the little red brick station they'd just visited. It was only two blocks from the garage.

"No?"

He shook his head. "I was surprised I still recognized some of the guys." In truth, the men acted like he was some superhero come back to earth.

Again, he glanced at the garage. "*This* hurts," he said, nodding to the structure that loomed against the sky. "To see it."

She took his hand. "We could come back some other time."

"No, I want to do it today." He drew her close,

stared at the place that had haunted his dreams for too long. "I want it done. I want to put it behind me."

They went inside. Reed remembered the smell right away. Oil. Gasoline. Exhaust. He hadn't been in a parking garage for eight years, had driven blocks out of his way to avoid them. He scanned the area. Several cars were parked at angles in most of the spaces. He breathed deeply as they headed for the elevator.

When they reached the fourth level and got out, he stared down the lane.

I want to see it, he'd told Bill Connally.

Why?

Because it's there, all the time in my mind. Bigger than life.

Follow your instincts, then, the psychiatrist had said.

Reed let go of Delaney's hand and walked by himself down three parking spaces. The spot where the car fire had been was empty. He stared at the small fifteen-by-ten area where Crash and Johnson and Castleman had died, then strode right into the middle of it.

It, too, looked small. He glanced to the side. The rig had been off to the left. He could hear the guys joking about getting back for the Jets game. He could see Crash drag out the one-inch hose and douse the fire, saying, "I could just piss on this and put it out."

Reed pivoted.

The arsonist had been right behind him. A small, wiry man with a heart full of hate.

But today, Reed didn't hear the shots go off, or smell the blood, or feel the fire in his leg, as he'd expected to. Instead, he saw the light of day peeking through the slatted windows.

Then he felt a hand on his shoulder. She didn't say anything, just stepped close.

"The ghosts are gone," he said simply.

"You've spent years exorcising them, Reed."

He turned toward her. "No, it's because of you." He tipped her chin. "You made me face them. You were right all along. About everything."

"I'll remember that the next time we have a fight."

Briefly he kissed her. Looked around again. Then took her hand. "Come on, sweetheart, let's blow this pop stand."

She laughed, the sound echoing through the levels.

And as they headed down the ramp, Reed vowed that *that* was the sound he'd remember next time he thought about the parking garage. Not the gunshots or the screams.

But the ring of Delaney's beautiful laughter.

"REED, I'M GOING TO GET sick riding in a cab like this."

She reached for the blindfold.

He stayed her hand. "You're fine. We're almost there."

"Honestly, I'm not feeling well. I'm going to barf all over you."

"Not in my cab, lady," the taxi driver barked.

Reed said, "We're here, anyway." Delaney could feel the cab swerve to the right and stop jarringly. Her stomach pitched. Reed had been playful a lot since the ordeal with Sammy, but giving the taxi driver directions for a side trip before they went to the airport, and then blindfolding her, for God's sake, was among the more unusual. But she'd been so worried about this visit to the Big Apple to lay his ghosts to rest, she didn't much care what last stop he wanted to make.

He paid the driver and helped her out of the cab. Cold air hit her in the face. She could hear people bustle around her, horns honking; and she could smell hot dogs. They were still in the city. His hands gentle, he untied the scarf around her eyes. It took her a minute to adjust to the 10:00 a.m. sunlight. She blinked, then the store came into focus. Discreet lettering. An unassuming front. Huge steel doors.

Tiffany's.

Her heart leapfrogged in her chest. She glanced at him, willing herself not to hope too much, but unable to quell that pesky little emotion Pandora had released. "What are we doing here?"

"You'll see," he told her, escorting her inside.

Delaney tried to suppress her excitement. She wanted to marry Reed more than anything in the world. But he hadn't said a word about commitment. And he still hadn't told her he loved her.

Confused, she looked around at the world-famous store.

"May I direct you, sir?" a uniformed employee at the entrance asked.

"Hmm. No thanks, I know what I want."

I know what I want. Delaney almost couldn't stand it.

As they threaded their way through the crowd, she fingered the chain around her neck.

"You know, you always do that when you're feeling insecure," he said, nodding to the chain.

"Ah, the joys of being with a psychologist."

Stopping, he kissed her hair. "Are you upset about something?"

"No, of course not. Why are we here, Reed?" she snapped.

"You'll see."

They started walking again, and she lagged behind as he approached a counter that sold gold jewelry. She'd just caught up with him when she heard the pretty clerk say, "Yes, Dr. Macauley, we were expecting you."

"Expecting you?" Delaney asked, edging to the counter. "Why?"

He shook his head. "Always so curious," he said, pulling her close. "My own little Pandora."

The woman returned with a long thin box. "Here you are, sir. Just what you ordered."

Reed reached down. His big fingers fumbled a bit, as if he was nervous. Odd for him. Finally he lifted the top.

Inside, nestled on a bed of maroon velvet was a chain, with a charm attached. But she didn't get a chance to read it because he picked it up quickly. "Oh, Reed, I hope you aren't thinking of replacing this." She pulled out the Firefighter's Lady charm around her neck. "I love this. It means a lot to me."

He detached the new chain from its velvet holder. "I think you'll like this one better."

She looked down at what he cradled in his palm. The charm was identical to the one from Pandora's box, except that it was obviously made of better quality gold.

And except for the fact that it didn't say *Firefighter's Lady*. Instead, it said, *Firefighter's Wife*.

The letters blurred. Delaney bent her head. His hand came around her neck and he cuddled her close. "You've been so good about waiting until I knew I could give you what you deserve in life. Thank you." He kissed her hair. She continued to look down.

"What about it, sweetheart?" he asked against her ear. "Think you want to be a firefighter's wife?"

Oh, God, she wanted that more than she wanted to take her next breath. But he still hadn't—

"Laney, look at me."

She managed to raise her head, though she was still crying.

"I love you." He smiled softly. "I haven't told you before because I knew if I said it, you'd never walk away from me, even if I never got better. But I'm okay. I'm fine. And I want to marry you. I want us to have a baby."

The tears came in buckets then. Gently, he slipped the chain over her head, bent down and kissed the charm. He whispered, "Say yes."

She nodded.

"Can't talk?"

She shook her head.

He drew her to him. "Well, this is a first. Delaney Shaw is speechless." Laughter rumbled in his chest next to her ear.

He lifted her chin again. "I've got an appointment with the ring guy, but if you're too overcome with emotion, I guess we'll have to go back to Rockford without ordering wedding rings."

"Not on your life, Doc," she said to him.

His face sobered. "You've given me *back* my life, Delaney. And I'm gonna spend the rest of it making you happy."

She smiled.

And in the middle of Tiffany's, in front of the embarrassed clerk and several jaded New Yorkers, he lowered his head and sealed that promise with the tenderest of kisses.

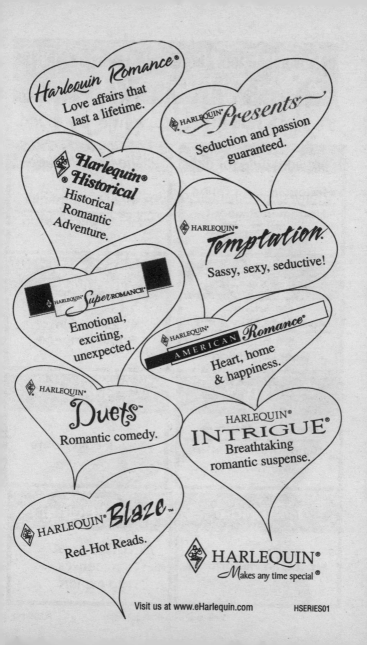

WITH HARLEQUIN AND SILHOUETTE

There's a romance to fit your every mood.

Passion

Harlequin Temptation

Harlequin Presents

Silhouette Desire

Pure Romance

Harlequin Romance

Silhouette Romance

Home & Family

Harlequin
American Romance

Silhouette
Special Edition

A Longer Story With More

Harlequin
Superromance

Suspense & Adventure

Harlequin Intrigue

Silhouette Intimate
Moments

Humor

Harlequin Duets

Historical

Harlequin Historicals

Special Releases

Other great
romances
to explore

*H*ugh Blake, soon to become stepfather to the Maitland clan, has produced three high-performing offspring of his own. But at the rate they're going, they're never going to make him a grandpa!

There's *Suzanne*, a work-obsessed CEO whose Christmas spirit could use a little topping up....

And *Thomas*, a lawyer whose ability to hold on to the woman he loves is evaporating by the minute....

And *Diane*, a teacher so dedicated to her teenage students she hasn't noticed she's put her own life on hold.

But there's a Christmas wake-up call in store for the Blake siblings. Love *and* Christmas miracles are in store for all three!

Maitland Maternity Christmas

A collection from three of Harlequin's favorite authors

Muriel Jensen
Judy Christenberry
&Tina Leonard

Look for it in November 2001.

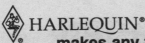

TRUEBLOOD, TEXAS

In October 2001 look for

A FATHER'S VOW

by Tina Leonard

Lost

One twin. Ben Mulholland
desperately needs a bone marrow
donor to save his little girl, Lucy.
The brother Ben never knew he
had is her best, maybe only, chance.
If he can just track him down…

Found

The miracle of hope. Caroline St. Clair
has loved Ben forever and she'll do
whatever it takes to ensure he doesn't lose his precious
daughter. In the process, old wounds are healed and flames
of passion reignited. But the future is far from secure.

Finders Keepers: bringing families together

HARLEQUIN®

Makes any time special ®